Lions
The Kind Ghosts

She sleeps on soft, last breaths; but no ghost looms
Out of the stillness of her palace wall,
Her wall of boys on boys and dooms on dooms.

She dreams of golden gardens and sweet glooms,
Not marvelling why her roses never fall
Nor what red mouths were torn to make their blooms.

The shades keep down which well might roam her
hall.
Quiet their blood lies in her crimson rooms
And she is not afraid of their footfall.

They move not from her tapestries, their pall,
Nor pace her terraces, their hecatombs,
Lest aught she be disturbed, or grieved at all.

Wilfred Owen

Other titles by Linda Newbery

Run With the Hare
Hard and Fast
Some Other War

The
Kind Ghosts

Linda Newbery

Lions
An Imprint of HarperCollins*Publishers*

The Kind Ghosts was first published in Lions in 1991

Lions is an imprint of the Children's Division,
part of HarperCollins Publishers Ltd,
77–85 Fulham Palace Road, Hammersmith, London W6 8JB

ISBN 0–00–694117–6

Printed and bound in Great Britain
by HarperCollins Manufacturing Glasgow

To My Parents

Contents

Part One: 1917 – 1918

Breaking the Rules	11
The Menin Road	27
A Second Death	41
Working Party	56
Philip Morland	72
No. 13 General Hospital	88
Stephen	96
In the Front Line	109
Spring Tide	125
Home	142
November 11th	157

Part Two: 1919

A Return to the Battlefields	179
Harriet and Sarah	199
Persuasion	219
Wounds	229
Jack and Alice	241
The Opening Meet	249
A Letter from Harriet	262
Remembrance	270

Part One

1917 – 1918

Breaking The Rules

The young officer on the stretcher wasn't Edward. Alice knew it couldn't have been, but the knowledge wasn't enough to stop her from catching her breath in a surge of stupid hope. The young man had dark curly hair, like Edward's, and a thin pale face like his, with eyes closed in pain or exhaustion.

"There's a spare bed here, behind the screens," the staff nurse told the medical orderlies. "Smallwood, take charge, would you?"

Alice hurried over and looked down at the new patient as the orderlies manoeuvred the stretcher into position. The young man's eyelids flickered open to reveal dark brown eyes, and the likeness to Edward vanished abruptly. Alice's disappointment was like a thud in the stomach, irrational as it was. This man was a German soldier, and Edward had died of wounds four months ago.

The staff nurse gave her a sharp look. "Fetch the dressing tray, nurse. That wound must be seen to straight away."

Alice did so, grateful for the familiar anaesthetizing effect of purposeful activity. Edward had ways of sneaking up on her, appearing fleetingly in a stranger's build and colouring or familiar gesture, disturbing her veneer of calm. But she mustn't think of him now.

"Badby, give Nurse Smallwood a hand. I'll start to find spaces for the rest," Sister Newsome said briskly, waving a second pair of orderlies towards the only other unoccupied bed in the ward.

The German soldier was still wearing his begrimed grey uniform, stiff with mud and dried blood. The torn tunic gaped open, revealing a field dressing which had been applied to his shoulder some while ago, judging by the blood which had seeped through it and then caked dry. He looked too exhausted to care much about his wound, closing his eyes and sighing occasionally as Alice removed the remains of the tunic and the dressing, and began to dab carefully at the exposed lacerated flesh with a Lysol-soaked pad. Connie Badby, one of the newer VAD nurses, stood beside her, holding the dressing tray and passing tweezers and lint, anticipating Alice's requirements. She caught her bottom lip between her teeth and winced perceptibly each time Alice applied the pad.

"Is it bad?" she whispered.

"It's a large wound, but not deep, and it doesn't look infected, at any rate. It should heal up cleanly. I think he's more worn out than anything else."

Badby nodded solemnly. She was only just out from England and looked far younger than twenty-three, the minimum age for overseas service. But many of the girls had lied about their age. Alice herself was still under age, but she felt quite old and cynical compared to Badby, who reminded her of her early days in nursing when she had taken a personal interest in every wounded soldier who passed before her. She could remember thinking of the older nurses as callous, and wondered whether Badby saw her in the same light. But it was inevitable, as Badby would soon find out. You had to stay sane.

She finished cleaning and dressing the wound. The German's eyes flicked open briefly, and he murmured, "*Danke, Schwester.*"

"*Bitte,*" Alice replied. She knew little German apart from the few words she had picked up since being moved to this ward. The wounded German officers were invariably polite, grateful for the treatment they received, flattering the VADs by calling them *Schwester* as if they were proper nurses. It was ridiculous, really, Alice thought, to be nursing and comforting men who could have been in the line opposite Edward a few months ago, aiming the shell that had killed him; even yesterday, this young officer could have been fighting against Jack, Alice's twin brother, who was with the Epping Foresters up in the Salient. But she simply couldn't reconcile the procession of wearied, pain-racked patients with the murderous Hun or Boche of newspaper caricatures. They were just injured men. Shrapnel, bullets and high explosives treated their victims with impartiality, heedless of nationality.

"He should be more comfortable now," Alice told Badby. "Could you finish washing him, and get him clean pyjamas? I'd better start seeing to the next one. Come and help me when you're ready."

Only when she came off duty two hours later did she remember that it was her twenty-first birthday – hers and Jack's.

The road to Étaples was busy with ambulances, staff cars and lorries. Later in the day, the routes back to the camps would be jammed with columns of troops returning from the Bull Ring – below the road, between the sand dunes and the sea, lines of distant figures could be seen parading, marching and forming fours to the bellowed command of instructors. It had rained earlier, so that the air smelled of sandy earth, horse-dung and dampened greenery, laced with a faint tang of salt.

Alice breathed deeply. "It's good to get away from the hospital. You forget what it's like, outside."

"That's what I've been trying to tell you," Lorna said sternly as they waited for a convoy of ambulances to pass before crossing the road. "You really don't go out enough, even when you get the chance."

"Well, I wouldn't have come today if you'd told me what you'd planned," Alice replied, only half-joking.

"Oh, you don't really mind, do you? I do want you to meet Charles, and I'm sure you'll find Captain Leary interesting. And I wanted to arrange something special for your birthday – otherwise you'd have spent all afternoon rolling bandages and scrubbing mackintosh squares."

"Thank you – it was kind of you to think of it. I suppose I'm a bit nervous, that's all, at the thought of meeting new people."

"Don't be so silly!" Lorna admonished. "I just want you to relax and enjoy yourself. Promise me you will."

"I promise, then." Alice gave her friend an affectionate glance. Lorna was Edward's older sister – disconcertingly like him, at times, with the same dark hair and blue eyes – and now Alice's closest friend. Without Lorna working close at hand in the same hospital, Alice didn't know how she would have got

14

through the last few months, and she hoped she had provided Lorna with at least some trace of similar comfort. If Edward hadn't been killed, he and Alice would have been married by now: a wild, provocative idea it seemed now, tempting fate, or God, or whatever you called it – Alice didn't know, any more.

Ahead, a hospital train clattered over the railway bridge, going up the coast towards Boulogne with its load of patients fit enough to be shipped on to England by boat. The little station at Étaples was constantly receiving and despatching troops. Units newly arrived from England underwent the compulsory training at the base, while departing battalions were bound southwards to Amiens and the Somme, or, more particularly at the moment, northwards to St. Omer, Hazebrouck and the Salient. And men came back that way, on the ominously silent hospital trains which brought wounded by the hundred, day and night, part of the wastage of war, like spent bullets or used shells. The tree-lined valley along which the railway ran towards Montreuil was misleading in its pastoral tranquility. Alice could never look in that direction without thinking of Edward and Jack, both of whom had travelled that way to Béthune and their first experiences of the front.

She and Lorna turned left into the town, with its typically French market square from which narrow streets and alleyways straggled in haphazard fashion. Estaminets and shops lined the square, supplemented by the wares of local farmers who had laid out their fruit, poultry and cheeses in baskets and barrows to tempt passing officers. Jack had been in Étaples at the base, but had never seen the market square; officers and

15

nurses were allowed to spend their free time here, but other ranks had to stay on the other side of the railway, in the camps which sprawled up the hill behind the town.

"I wonder where Jack's spending his birthday," Alice remarked.

"Mm. Has he managed to let you know where he is?"

"Still up near Ypres when he wrote a few days ago, but behind the lines, thank goodness. When I saw him at home last we worked out a way to beat the censor. He underlines two or three words in his letter and hides a place-name in them, you see, like *fallen shell* for Lens or *lovely present* for Ypres."

Lorna laughed. "Very clever! Let's hope he doesn't find himself in Vlamertinghe, then. That would be enough to strain anyone's ingenuity. We're a bit early – shall we go and have a look at the river?"

They took the side street beside the town hall and walked across to the middle of the road bridge which spanned the River Canche. Seawards, the dune-fringed estuary opened out into stretches of gleaming beach, where white-topped waves rushed in over the level sand. Small fishing smacks were moored on the town side, and black-headed gulls hovered overhead, balancing on the breeze, heads swaying in search of scraps thrown by the fisherwomen who sat gutting fish from the latest catch. The light was clear after the recent heavy shower; the woods and dunes and beaches on the opposite bank were sharply defined to the horizon. The raucous screaming of the gulls almost masked the distant trembling of the heavy guns to the north. Alice knew that the continued barrage of the

16

last days heralded a new offensive. Troops had been massing up at Ypres for nearly two months, following the successful attack on the Messines Ridge early in June; the wards at the base hospitals had been cleared of any patients who were fit enough to be moved on to London, and everyone knew what that meant. The nursing staff had been encouraged to take time off while they could – everyone would be needed when the convoys started to arrive in force.

To avoid dwelling on her fears for Jack, Alice turned her thoughts to the afternoon ahead. Really, she would have preferred going out with Lorna alone to the ordeal of meeting the two men. Captain Aldridge, an officer in the Royal Army Medical Corps, had been seeing Lorna whenever he could, and writing to her whenever he couldn't, since separating from his wife some while ago. Lorna had said that he was nearly forty; to Alice, it sounded very old for a boy-friend, although perhaps it didn't seem quite so elderly to Lorna, who was in her late twenties. The friend he was bringing, Captain Leary, was an adjutant in an artillery battery. Alice pictured someone stout and middle-aged, with medals on his uniform and a moustache like Field Marshall Haig's. She was sure she would be out of her depth, unable to contribute anything at all to the conversation.

"Where will we meet them?" she asked Lorna.

"In the restaurant. There's a screened-off section at the back where we won't be seen from the street. It's stupid, isn't it, to have to be so furtive over something entirely harmless? These ridiculous rules . . ."

In theory, nurses weren't allowed to consort with the opposite sex during off-duty horus. Lorna considered

17

this an affront, not because she was particularly anxious for male company but because she considered the intrusion into nurses' leisure hours to be insulting. Many of the officers, nurses and WAACs at Étaples got round this rule by going across the river to the resort of Paris Plage, where they were less likely to be seen by their superiors. And in practice, blind eyes were often turned to breaches of the rules, provided the nurses kept in pairs. The nurses performed the most intimate services for their patients on the ward, but were apparently thought to be in danger of corruption if they so much as spoke to a man outside the confines of the hospital.

"If what people say about deserters is anything to go by, you'd think the authorities would have more to worry about than nurses having tea with officers," Alice remarked, looking across towards the thick woodland on the south side of the river. These woods, according to rumour, harboured bands of Canadian and British deserters, in spite of spasmodic attempts by the Military Police to round them up. The undulating dunes and thick trees would certainly provide cover, but Alice remembered what Jack had told her about the fierce discipline at the Base and found it hard to believe that such flagrant rebelliousness would be tolerated for a moment.

Lorna looked at her watch. "Come on. We'll end up being late after all."

In the square, several restaurants vied for attention from off-duty staff; appetizing smells wafted out of doorways to tempt passers-by with alternatives to hospital or camp food, and groups of officers and nurses strolled from shop to café to market stall. The restaurant Lorna had chosen looked prosperous, with white linen tablecloths and little pots of geraniums in the shadowy interior.

"We'll go straight in. They might be here already." Lorna pushed the door open, and Alice, with renewed nervousness, followed her inside. The proprietor, who evidently knew Lorna, showed them to a discreet room at the back, where several other mixed groups defied the segregation rules. Two men sitting at a corner table got to their feet, and Lorna performed introductions.

"How do you do. I'm glad to meet you." Captain Charles Aldridge was less formidable in appearance than Alice had imagined, quietly spoken, with a high forehead, pale grey eyes and sandy hair, receding slightly. Shaking his hand across the table, Alice found it hard at a first impression to see him as a match for the strong–willed, vivacious Lorna, who had campaigned for votes for women before the war, and intended to campaign as a pacifist when – or if – the war ended.

". . . and this is Captain Leary."

Alice shook hands, registering thick dark hair, and brown eyes beneath strongly marked brows. Captain Leary couldn't have been more than twenty-three or four, far from being the crusty army veteran of Alice's imaginings. But why was she surprised, she wondered? Edward had been promoted to Captain at twenty-two.

"I'm pleased to meet you, Miss Smallwood. And many happy returns of the day," Captain Leary said, in a deep voice with a trace of a Southern Irish accent.

"Oh – thank you," Alice said, somewhat embarrassed.

19

Chairs were proffered, and a girl arrived to take their order for tea. She was looking at Captain Aldridge for instructions, but Lorna said, "No – this is my treat," and spoke to the waitress in rapid French. The girl, who was young and very pretty, wrote copious notes on her pad. Alice watched her, thinking not for the first time how much the war had changed her own circumstances. Three years ago, both she and Jack had been working at Greenstocks, the Morland family's Essex house; she would have been serving tea to guests like the two officers and Lorna, not sitting down at the table with them. But her lack of social ease still left her tongue-tied in unfamiliar situations; she was glad to sit back after the temporary diversion of placing the order, and to listen to the others.

Captain Aldridge and Lorna did most of the talking at first, comparing notes about their recent leaves in London. Captain Leary said nothing unless he was directly addressed, and then he took a long time to answer, apparently considering his reply carefully before speaking, so that several times Alice thought he hadn't heard the question. He was on a forty-eight hour leave from Bailleul, he said in answer to Lorna's enquiry. Alice looked at him with new interest: Bailleul was close to the Belgian border, not far from Ypres.

"It's a morass up there in the Salient," Captain Aldridge remarked. "Between you and me, I don't know why we've kept all our troops waiting up there for so long, through all the fine weather."

Captain Leary nodded. "We might as well have sent the German generals a full programme of what we're planning. They've got observation posts all round the

20

Salient – it's the worst part of the Front from that point of view. It must have been only too obvious what was coming, and now Jerry's had weeks to prepare for it."

"How long do you think it will go on for – the new offensive?" Alice asked.

Captain Aldridge gave an eloquent shrug. "Till we wear the Germans down, I suppose – or they wear us down."

At that moment the waitress brought the food – orange-scented tea, and elaborate pastries of various kinds, and there was a pause in the conversation while she unloaded the plates and cups and teapot on to the table.

"Alice's brother Jack is up in the Salient, with the Epping Foresters," Lorna said when the girl had gone.

Captain Leary gave Alice a regretful look. "Oh – I'm very sorry, Miss Smallwood, if I was tactless. I wouldn't have spoken as I did if I'd known."

"It's all right," Alice said. She looked down at the table, vaguely aware that the display of patisserie in front of her would have represented several weeks' sugar ration at home in England. Jack had been on active service for more than two years, and her fears for him were part of life – though that didn't make it any easier, especially since Edward had died, and she was acutely aware of how much Jack meant to her.

Lorna poured out the tea and passed plates and pastries, and launched determinedly into a more cheerful topic. "Did you see that show everyone's talking about while you were in London – *Maid of the Mountains*?" she asked Captain Aldridge.

"No, but a chap in my billet's got a gramophone and

he plays the songs from it incessantly – I know all the words by heart . . ." To Alice's surprise, he began to sing in an exaggeratedly sentimental baritone:

> *"At seventeen, he falls in love quite madly*
> *With eyes of tender blue,*
> *At twenty-four he gets it rather badly*
> *With eyes of a different hue . . ."*

He sang the song right through to the end, making cow eyes at Lorna and Alice across the table and making them laugh. A nearby group of officers and nurses turned round to listen, and applauded when he had finished. "Quite a comic turn, isn't he!" one of the nurses said to her friend. Alice, surprised by this extrovert behaviour, watched Captain Aldridge making a mock bow. She wondered whether Lorna's parents knew of her friendship with a married man, and how they would react if they did. Dr Sidgwick was fairly open-minded, but his wife was positively forbidding. Alice could well remember her own trepidation when Mrs Sidgwick had learned that she and Edward were fond of each other; a working-class girl was certainly not the wife she had had in mind for her son.

When the conversation moved on to other London shows and concerts, Alice realized that Captain Leary was staring rather gloomily at the tablecloth, saying nothing. "Are you expecting to have any longer spells of leave, long enough to go home?" she asked him.

He paused for a while before answering. He had a way of listening attentively with his head tilted, and it occurred to Alice that he might be slightly deaf; that would hardly be surprising, she supposed, in an artillery officer. "Well, when this current push is over, perhaps," he said. "I shall try to get across to Dublin."

"It must be difficult to get home for leaves when you live as far away as that."

"No, that's not my home. My fiancée lives there, and I sometimes stay with her family, or with my aunt and uncle. I had a long convalescent period there after I got wounded at Gallipoli. My father lives in Epping, in Essex."

"Oh – that's not far from us," Alice said. "We live in Littlehays. But your parents aren't Irish, then?"

"Oh yes – at least, my father is; my grandfather on my mother's side was English. It was through him my parents inherited their house in Essex. They left Ireland when I was still a boy, and I went to Bancroft's School in Woodford. That's where I met Edward."

Alice stared at him. "You knew *Edward*?"

Captain Leary nodded. "Yes. I think that's why Miss Sidgwick wanted me to come along this afternoon. She thought you might like to talk to someone who knew him. I was terribly sorry to hear he'd been killed, Miss Smallwood. I know you were due to be married quite soon, and he . . . he was a splendid fellow."

He spoke the last few words awkwardly, looking down at his clasped hands. Alice was surprised. He seemed upset, more than just a chance acquaintance of Edward's, obviously, but why had she never heard of him? She glanced at Lorna, who was talking earnestly about Winston Churchill's unpopularity with the women's suffrage campaigners, apparently unaware of the turn taken by the other half of the conversation.

23

"Did – did you know him well?" she asked.

"Yes, although obviously I didn't see him much after war broke out. We were at school together, and he came to stay with my family in Dublin once or twice. And we kept in touch after we'd both enlisted."

Alice nodded slowly, remembering fragments of conversation. "I knew Edward had been to stay with a friend in Ireland, long before I really got to know him. He once said he'd like to go back there. Your name's Patrick, isn't it?"

"Yes."

"When was the last time you saw him?" she asked, wondering whether Captain Leary had seen, as she had, how much Edward's army experiences had changed him. But could she expect him to have noticed? Edward wasn't the only young man to have been disillusioned.

"Well, he came to visit me in hospital when I got back from Gallipoli. He told me about you then. And the last time I saw him was when *he* was in hospital. That was fairly soon after the Easter Rising. I remember we had a long talk about it. Of course Edward was firmly in support of the Republicans."

"*Edward* was?" Alice echoed.

Patrick Leary looked at her in surprise. "Oh yes. He thought Ireland should have had Home Rule long ago."

Alice felt unsure how to continue the conversation, not knowing what his own stance was on the Troubles, or how far he may have been involved. "Were you in Dublin at the time of the Rising, then?" she ventured.

"Yes, I was," Patrick said rather shortly. After a

few moments he reached into his inside pocket for his wallet. "The only good thing about it was that I met my fiancée – Siobhan."

He handed Alice a small sepia photograph of a laughing, dark-haired girl with a delicate elfin face. "*To Patrick, with my love, Siobhan,*" was written across the top in brown ink.

"She's a lovely-looking girl," Alice said, studying it.

"Yes, isn't she," Patrick said with obvious pride. "She's working as an ambulance driver. We hope to be married as soon as the war's over."

At that moment Captain Aldridge turned to his friend to settle a dispute. "I'm sure I'm right, but Patrick will know. Didn't Churchill fall out with Asquith over Home Rule, just before war broke out?"

Patrick Leary put away his photograph and launched into a detailed explanation. Alice tried to pay attention, but was conscious of the strangeness of meeting a friend of Edward's who had materialized from nowhere. How odd to think that Edward hadn't mentioned his hospital meetings with his old friend, or mentioned his own interest in the Dublin Rising! She couldn't remember ever having exchanged a word with him on the subject. Although she felt she had shared so much with him – the best and most vital part of her life, it seemed now – theirs had been a wartime courtship, with regular enforced separation; the time they had spent together was really very limited. It jarred her to realize that other people had known him as well as or better than she had.

". . . so by then people were starting to blame

Churchill for deliberately stirring up violence in Ulster . . ."

Patrick was leaning forward, elbows on the table, talking with more animation than he had shown all afternoon. Alice looked across at him, illogically resentful.

The Menin Road

There was level ground ahead of them at last. Jack prised his boots out of the last stretch of clinging mud, and turned round to the others who were struggling behind him in the darkness.

"Here we are, lads - the Menin Road!" he shouted.

"Next stop, nice clean billets behind the line," Jimmy Taplin shouted back into Jack's ear.

They had a long way to go yet, and the danger was by no means over, with shells whistling overhead and explosions searing the dark sky with brilliant flashes. Jack waited while the rest of the platoon extricated themselves from the morass behind him. Sanctuary Wood, it was called. Whoever had named it must have had a grim sense of humour. It was neither sanctuary nor wood now – just a tangle of shattered tree trunks and sprawling roots, and a quagmire of clinging mud and water-filled shell-holes, so deep that a man could drown in them.

Jack counted the members of the platoon out on to the road.

"Good man, Trafford. You're nearly there, Woodall," he shouted. Wild-eyed white faces stared up at him in the flickering light of a star shell as the last two lurched across the final yards to the road. These two were only boys, in the line for the first time. Jack stepped off the road to give young Woodall a final heave out of the sludge.

27

"Well done, lad. It'll be easier from now on."

Jack didn't know whether he could be heard above the noise of the shelling, but the boy nodded and gulped, and stumbled after the others. The whole of C Company was on the road now, with Captain Snell somewhere ahead. A renewed burst of rain spattered into their faces. Jack took a last look back at the wood, where the Queen's Westminster Rifles had relieved the Epping Foresters and were waiting to renew the attack in the morning, God help them. Their objectives were exactly the same as the Foresters' had been; to capture Glencorse Wood and go on to Polygon. It had probably seemed a straightforward task to the Brigadier, looking at a couple of inches on a map. But when you got out anywhere in the Salient, it was almost impossible even to know where you were; villages and other landmarks had been smashed to unrecognizable heaps of rubble, and the front line was marked not by neat trenches but by linked shell-holes with men crouching miserably in them, sheltering behind the oozing heaps of sludge which passed for parapets. The Foresters, under persistent shelling, had failed to advance a yard out of Sanctuary Wood.

The Menin Road was a clean line on the map, drawn with a ruler. With only a map to go by you'd expect an easy stroll back to Ypres after the mire of the wood. Indeed, Jack had led the younger lads in his section to believe this, to encourage them. He'd been leading the platoon only for the last hour or so, since their officer, McLachlan, had been hit by shell fragments and badly wounded. No-one knew where the Sergeant was. A runner had come from Captain Snell, the company commander, to tell Jack that as Corporal he was to take over. They'd probably pass poor old McLachlan on his stretcher on the way back; the bearers were having an awful time of it, four of them to a stretcher instead of the usual two in their efforts to get the wounded to safety through the treacherous mud.

Jack walked ahead of the stragglers and drew level with Jimmy, who gave an expressive grimace, eyes rolling upwards. There was no possibility of conversation; it wasn't worth the effort to make yourself heard above the explosions which lit up the road ahead with eerie, flickering colours. The road was littered with broken limber wagons and gun carriages, and dead horses and mules – probably dead men as well if you cared to look. Occasionally, the surface was broken by a shell crater which had been hastily filled in with bits of rubble, broken wheels, stumps of trees and anything else which had been handy. The road had to be kept open so that the limbers could keep the front line supplied with shells and rations.

By the roadside, doctors and orderlies tended the wounded as best they could in makeshift field dressing-stations. They seemed to Jack to be horribly exposed to enemy shellfire. He'd been up and down this stretch of road twice, and each time he had felt that the whole area was far too easily overlooked. The Germans still held low ridges which looked down into the flat plain of the Salient from three sides, and they knew all about troop movements. Nowhere else on the Front could you be so far behind the line and yet still be in such constant danger from the German heavy guns.

He stopped again to make sure the last members of the platoon were keeping up, and then fell into step beside Jimmy, who trudged with head down and face blank as if unaware of the shell-bursts and the flares. Jack recognized the condition; after a while, you simply switched your mind off while your legs carried on walking, as if the rhythm lulled you into a sort of semi-consciousness. All you wanted was to find yourself in some hospitable farm or village, with a hot meal waiting, and somewhere dry to lie down and sink into oblivion.

Captain Snell, up in front of the company, quickened his pace as they approached Hell Fire Corner. Jack turned to hustle the stragglers through the notorious road junction on which enemy guns were always trained; the accuracy of German marksmanship was indicated by the piled remains of two gun-carriages by the roadside, and no-one with any sense cared to linger. The ruins of Ypres ahead of them looked like an Old Testament illustration of the wrath of God; the medieval city had been smashed and battered to rubble by seventeen-inch shells throughout the war. The crumbling tower of the old Cloth Hall stood out gauntly against the sky, fitfully illuminated in the flickering smoky light.

"Not far to Wipers now," Jack yelled at the last two boys. He was at most a couple of years older than they were, but they obeyed all his commands with a touching faith in his ability to shepherd them to safety – as if anyone could be responsible for anyone else in all this, Jack thought cynically. They'd certainly seen the Western Front at its most surly and unforgiving for their first outing. Still, they were alive, which was the best you could hope for. Jack didn't know how many of the Foresters were still out there, dead,

30

dying, half-submerged in the cold mud. To think it was August! – a month which conjured up memories of hot toil and an aching back at harvest-time, of the Greenstocks horses standing under the elms for coolness, of village cricket, and of the Bank Holiday fair at High Beach. The Salient seemed so cut off from ordinary human life that Jack could almost believe that the rain fell there alone, while back in Essex the crops ripened under skies of unclouded blue.

Two horse-drawn wagons were coming the other way – a ration-party going up to the front. The horses progressed hesitantly, frightened by the lights and the constant explosions – as well they might be, Jack thought, remembering the bloated carcases further up. He hated seeing horses at the front, whether they were officers' mounts or served humbler roles as pack animals. Mules were better, having more stolid temperaments and little imagination. But in either case, he thought it barbaric to drag animals into the war.

Jimmy laughed cynically whenever Jack remaked on this. "What's the difference? We might as well be bloody pack mules ourselves. Come to think of it, where the Army's concerned, a mule's probably a damned sight more important. You can't replace it as easily as you can a Tommy."

Jack saw the truth in this. If animals' lives were held cheap, so were men's; the casualty figures defied reckoning. Nevertheless, his Greenstocks training rebelled against the sight of thin horses shivering in the rain or hauling overloaded limbers. His working life before the war had been spent keeping the Greenstocks horses in what now seemed unimaginable luxury, with dry stables, deep beds of clean straw, and thick woollen rugs in winter. Strewth, Jack thought, if he saw a bed of straw and a horse rug now, he'd stretch out in it and sleep for three days round the clock.

They were close enough to the ruined city to see the ramparts sloping away at each side of the Menin Gate, and the dark glimmer of water in the moat. The ramparts had held, though not much else had been able to withstand the constant battering. It was a ghostly place, Ypres, inhabited mainly by rats, a few officers who skulked in their headquarters in the cellars and those unfortunate Other Ranks who'd been sent to bivouac in the cemeteries on the outskirts; the Belgian residents had been evacuated long ago. Once, Jack had looked forward to seeing the famous city, whose mere name conjured up visions of Belgian martyrdom and Allied gallantry. Now he couldn't wait to get through the dreary place and out the other side.

Twenty-four hours later, in the comfortable fug of a small estaminet in Poperinghe, it was easy to forget that the Menin Road was only nine or ten miles away. The troops liked being billeted in Poperinghe; it offered a variety of shops, cafés and estaminets, with the occasional evening concert for light entertainment. In Gasthuisstrasse, the Talbot House was one of the few places where officers and other ranks could meet on equal terms; Edward and Jack had once talked of meeting there if by some fluke they found themselves in Poperinghe at the same time. Well, there was no chance of that now.

The particular estaminet frequented by Jack and his friends, in a side street off the main square, did a satisfying line in egg and chips as well as house wine and Belgian beer. Jimmy, pushing his empty plate away and lighting up a cigarette, had just become aware of another pleasing feature of the establishment.

"What d'you reckon? She'll do, eh?" He nodded towards the young Belgian girl who was washing up glasses behind the bar.

Jack turned in his seat and looked across at the girl, narrowing his eyes speculatively. She glanced up, caught his eye and smiled, holding his gaze for a few seconds longer than modesty would have allowed; she was evidently used to appreciative stares. She couldn't have been more than sixteen or seventeen, Jack estimated, but nothing about her suggested innocence or bashfulness.

"Not bad at all," he confirmed. "Fancy your chances? I reckon you'll only have to try your luck along with five or six hundred other blokes."

"Oh, leave it to me," Jimmy said confidently. "Course, the old lingo's a bit of a problem out here. I was getting to be a dab hand at the old parly-voo, but with the way they jabber on in these parts you can't hardly understand a word."

"Just use the universal language of love, Jimmy boy." Charlie Jenkins leaned across the table for Jack to light up his cigarette. "But make sure her old man isn't around. With a daughter like that he's as fussy as an old mother hen. Keeps a closer eye on her than a brass hat with a whisky bottle."

Jimmy laughed. "He might look at it as a chance for Gallant Little Belgium to show its gratitude to the Allied heroes."

"Find out if she's got a friend," a private known as Victoria Cross said plaintively.

"For you, mate, I'll see what I can do. Who's for more van blonk, then?" Jimmy asked, standing up and stretching.

"I'll stick to beer, thanks," Jack said.

"Shall I come up to the bar with you?" Vic offered.

"No, you stay here. I'll put in a good word for you." Jimmy stacked the four greasy plates and shambled off towards the bar, a cigarette drooping from his mouth. Jack sat back in his chair and prepared to watch with interest. The girl continued to dry glasses briskly, her back turned on the drinkers, unaware of Jimmy's predatory advance. The other inhabitants of the bar were a noisy group of Canadians, engrossed in a hard-fought card game in a corner and oblivious to the charms of the patron's daughter.

"See the way she looked at you, Jack?" Vic remarked enviously. "I reckon you'd be in with a chance there."

Jack grinned, putting down his empty glass. "Not with Pa around, thanks. I saw him round the back just now when I went out. Great big bloke with huge shoulders. He was getting some crates out of a shed, so I reckon he'll be back in a minute."

"Well, I'd risk it," Vic said, with one eye on Jimmy's progress. "But I keep forgetting, you're a married man."

Jack slowly breathed out a cloud of blue cigarette smoke. He looked down at his hands and picked at a broken thumbnail. Charlie was looking at him across the table, one eyebrow raised.

"Truth is," Jack replied, "I keep forgetting it myself."

It jolted him to remember, particularly at times like this. Of all the changes the war had brought, this had been the most astonishing. He and Harriet had made love in the apple orchard last summer when he'd been home on leave – less than a year ago – and a baby boy had been the result. A hasty wedding had taken place in February, and the baby had been born in midsummer. Jack hadn't seen Harriet since the three days' leave he'd managed to get in June. Harriet was no good at writing letters; he got news of her and the child from his mother and elder sister, Emily.

"Cheer up, old lad," Charlie said. "It's not that bad, is it?"

"I wouldn't mind. It'd be nice to know you had something to go back to, when this is finished," Vic remarked. "For the rest of us, Jimmy and the like, it's hard to imagine ordinary life again after three years. We were just boys when all this started. We'll hardly be able to remember life without the Army."

Jack didn't know that he was any different, except that he'd have a wife and baby to provide for. He could remember, last year when they'd been in Béthune and Charlie had just joined them, thinking of Charlie as a much older man. He had a wife and children, responsibilities. Now Jack was in the same boat himself. But last year – before they'd been thrown into the shambles of July 1st – was an unchartable distance away. There had been a whole group of them from the village then, friends who'd joined up together in 1914. Now he and Jimmy were the only two left. Dick Twyford and Ted Briggs had died on the first day of the Somme fighting, and Harry Larkins had died of gangrene later. And others had come and gone: Corporal Woolmer, and Will Fletcher who had been blinded with a shell splinter through the eye, and Philip Morland, injured and safely out of the war, and Dolly Gray, killed, and Stephen, killed . . .

A burst of animated conversation at the bar jolted him out of these gloomy thoughts. The patron, coming back into the bar, had not been pleased to see his daughter giggling at Jimmy's efforts to converse. With a stream of incomprehensible Flemish and much waving of arms, he sent the girl back into the kitchen. Jimmy returned to the table with the drinks, looking rueful.

"You didn't fancy trying it on with the old man, then?" Charlie said drily.

"He's not such a good looker as his daughter. Just when she was starting to take a shine to me, as well." Jimmy sat down, aggrieved. "Oh well, Vic, we'll have to try our hand some other night. Got any more smokes, Jack?"

"Here." Jack pushed the tin across the table.

"Oh well, I think I'll be getting back." Vic looked more disappointed than Jimmy at the fading of the entertainment prospects; Jimmy's romantic conquests were usually more impressive at the boasting stage than in the carrying off. "Coming, anyone?"

Charlie got to his feet. "I'll come with you. I could do with turning in."

"But I've only just got these drinks in. You're not all clearing off, are you?"

"I'll stay on, now you've got me this beer," Jack said. "It's not late. See you blokes back at camp, then."

A cool draught wafted in as they opened the door to leave, freshening the stale, beery atmosphere in the estaminet. Jack's eyes were watering from the cigarette smoke that hung thickly in the air, and he was conscious of a painful cramp in his right foot, but all the same he was in no rush to leave. He was content just to sit drinking and chatting with no sense of hurry. Tomorrow, there would be parades and kit inspections and fatigues, the same the day after . . . eventually, they'd be sent up the line again, but Jack had learned not to think about that until the time came.

Jimmy was well into his bottle of white wine. He had a better head for alcohol than Jack, and could put away prodigious quantities without ill-effects. Jack had tried to keep up with him once, but had only ended up with his pay docked for returning drunk to his billet.

"Tell you what I was thinking," Jimmy said. "Now that you've got your stripes, why don't you try for a commission? Other blokes have got promoted from the ranks."

Jack looked at him with cynical amusement. "What, me be an officer? You must be joking. Can you see me eating in the Officers' Mess and talking with a plum in my mouth and having cocktails with the Brigadier and all that bull? – Not that they'd give me a commission anyway. No, thanks."

"It'd be a secure job, you having the nipper to think of, and all. You could stay on after the war, transfer to the Regulars," Jimmy persisted. "You might end up in India, playing polo and swimming in the Ganges . . ."

"What do I want to go to India for? No, it doesn't interest me. I'd end up neither one thing nor the other – not one of them, nor one of the blokes either. Why don't you try it yourself if you're so keen?"

"It's different for me. I haven't got a DCM, and I'm not Captain Snell's blue-eyed boy . . ." He ducked as Jack swung his fist round in mock anger, and put out a hand to steady his glass. "No, I'll go back to the Hunt, if there're any horses left after the Army's finished with them."

"Yes, well, I'll go back to the horses as well. Not as secure as the Army, but it's what I'm used to. And I'll be getting somewhere to live along with it, now that Philip Morland wants me to work for him."

"Are you really going to do it, then? Work for him? I thought you couldn't wait to see the last of him."

"It's a job." Jack poured the last of the beer into his glass. "We'll need a place of our own, me and the baby and Harriet. And I'll enjoy the work, if I ever get back in one piece. He's not like he used to be."

"Well, I hope you're right. What d'you reckon to our chances of seeing old McLachlan again? Was he bad?"

"He's been sent down to one of the base hospitals. I asked this morning at the Clearing Station. I hope he'll be all right, the poor sod. Badly wounded, was all they'd say. We could see that for ourselves. Stomach wounds are always bad."

"Oh, well. He might end up being nursed by your Alice, down at Eetapps." Jimmy drained his glass and stood up. "I'm just going out back."

Jack waited, staring down at the surface of his beer and thinking again about Philip Morland. At the start of the war, he'd hoped never to see him again; there had been a mutual disliking between them all the time Jack had worked at Greenstocks for old Mr Morland. Ironically, it had been on Philip's recommendation that Jack had got his Distinguished Conduct Medal after carrying Philip to safety during a trench raid. And the old grievances were long ago forgotten. Philip, like everyone else, had been changed by the war; the job would work out.

Jack remembered the two letters he'd received since coming out of the line. He took them out of his pocket to re-read them. The first was from Alice, thanking him for the birthday card and the small brooch he'd sent her and telling him about an outing with Lorna, meeting someone Edward knew. Poor Alice, he thought: hanging on to her memories. He'd sent her a note earlier to let her know he was safely out of the line.

The second letter was from Stephen's mother.

"Dear Jack," it read, *"Thank you so much for taking the trouble to write to me after Stephen was killed. We were both grief-stricken as you can imagine, but it was a comfort to know that our dear boy died painlessly – "* this was not quite true, but Jack had felt obliged to bend the facts a little – *"and did not linger on in hospital as so many of the poor young men do. I know that you and Stephen were special friends as he used to talk of you so much in his letters. I hope that if you are ever in London on leave you will find the time to call in and see us, as it would make us so happy to share our memories of him. I hope this finds you well and I am enclosing a little photograph of Stephen which you might like to have to remember him by. Yours sincerely, Mrs Ada Cartwright."*

Jack had already put the photograph in his pay-book, but he took it out now and looked at it again. The face in the picture was as familiar as his own: a high forehead with a strand of hair falling across it, frank wide eyes, mouth frozen in a self-conscious half-smile; Stephen was dressed in clean brushed uniform, and looked awkward at posing for the camera. The photograph must have been taken on his last leave. Private Stephen Cartwright, Third Epping Foresters, twenty years old, killed in action. Jack had seen the wooden cross which marked his grave. He still missed him painfully. His easy, companionable friendship with Jimmy went back for years, but Stephen had been different.

He put the photograph back in his pay-book and tucked it into his tunic pocket, and took a deep swig of his beer while he waited for Jimmy.

A Second Death

Yawning, Alice emerged from the fug of the ward into the damp air of a chill autumn morning. She had had some sandwiches and tea since finishing her spell of night duty; now her legs and feet ached, and she could feel waves of sleep numbing her brain in spite of the cold air. The grey sky looked sullen, promising nothing but further rain. Groups of nurses and orderlies picked their way along the paths which ran muddily between the tented marquees and wards; among them Alice saw Pauline Grey, the VAD who shared her hut.

Pauline hurried towards her, looking anxious. "Someone just came to the hut with a message for you – no, *no*, not a telegram," she added hastily, seeing Alice's stricken expression. "But it's Lorna Sidgwick. She's been taken ill during the night. She's in ward 6A. She sent a message to let you know."

"I'll go straight away." Alice turned back the way she had come, recovering from the momentary shock of thinking it was a telegram about Jack. It was not so long ago that she had opened the door of her hut to see Lorna standing bleak-faced with that other telegram . . . but it was bad enough that Lorna herself was ill. Hurrying past the mess-hut, Alice was sharply aware of how much she took Lorna's presence for granted, so much so that it was difficult to imagine her succumbing to illness, and so suddenly. Alice had seen her the evening before last. There must have been some sign, she thought, realizing that Lorna's air of overstrained animation had become habitual.

6A was a small section at one end of a main ward, temporarily partitioned off for sick nurses. Pausing in the doorway, Alice saw a Sister walking briskly towards her with a pile of bedding.

"Excuse me – can I see Lorna Sidgwick?"

The Sister stopped. "Are you her friend – Nurse Smallwood? She was anxious to see you. She's on the left, this side."

"Thank you. Is she very ill? I – I didn't know – "

"She fainted on the ward yesterday evening, and she's been feeling sick and dizzy ever since. One of the other nurses said she's had bad headaches and has fainted before, in her hut. It looks like nervous exhaustion to me. Yes, go and see her, but don't be too long. She needs to sleep."

It felt strange to Alice, used to the predominantly masculine atmosphere of the rest of the hospital, to enter a ward of females. There were four patients, most of them dozing, one muttering in her sleep. Someone had filled a jar with straggling Michaelmas daisies from the strips of flower beds outside, and there were mingled smells of cheap talcum powder and disinfectant. Lorna was in the farthest bed, propped up on her pillow, with her dark hair loose around her shoulders. She was gazing dully at the screen opposite, but she looked up as Alice approached, and smiled ruefully.

"Thank you for coming! I feel such a fraud, lying

here . . ." She moved her legs to one side so that Alice could sit down on the bed.

"Don't be silly! You've obviously been pushing yourself too hard. Why didn't you say anything about fainting before?"

"I didn't think much of it. I probably just stood up too quickly or something. Don't worry, I'll be all right in an hour or two. I'm back on duty this evening."

"You're not going on duty – don't be ridiculous. What use will you be if you faint again? You need to have a good long rest."

"But a big convoy came in yesterday – we're so busy on the ward – the theatre staff were operating all night – " Lorna's blue eyes flickered restlessly from side to side, slithering away from Alice's gaze. "I had to lay out a man on my ward as soon as I went on – a man who'd suffered horribly ever since he came in six days ago. Still, that's woman's work, isn't it? Patch them up, send them back to the front if they're fit enough, send them away on crutches if they're not, lay them out when they're dead . . ."

Her voice trailed away, and Alice looked at her in alarm. What Lorna said was undeniably true, but it was uncharacteristic for her to give way to such feelings of hopelessness. Alice groped for words of comfort, finding none to give. Lorna was lying back, her dark hair spread against the pillow and her eyes shadowed, looking so like her brother that Alice's imagination conjured a brief, vivid picture of Edward lying dead in the Casualty Clearing Station – the screens round the bed, the hushed voices, the strong young body being prepared for a hasty burial – *No!* She wouldn't think of it. They couldn't both sink into

43

despair, she and Lorna. But she couldn't think of a single encouraging thing to say.

"What's it like outside?" Lorna asked suddenly. "Have you heard any more?"

"The riots, you mean? Just the usual talk – no-one really knows what's happening. We're still confined to the hospital, and there are sentries on the gates. What's the matter with the other patients on this ward?" Alice asked, trying to channel the conversation into a safer area. She wanted to avoid agitating Lorna, who would be sure to have strong opinions on the subject of the riots in Étaples which were apparently threatening to break the iron grip of the military authorities.

"It must be highly embarrassing for the camp commanders," Lorna continued regardless. "They think mutinies are only for the French. But it's been coming to them. It's the limit, the way the troops are treated so brutally in the Bull Ring. You'd think the Army had to crush every spark of individuality out of the men, make them lose all their spirit."

"I know. And Jack said what makes it even worse is that the instructors never even go up to the front," Alice said, in spite of her resolve not to be drawn into the subject. "It's no wonder the men are resentful."

Lorna levered herself up to a sitting position. "God knows, the troops have enough to face when they're in the line. Why they can't be treated like human beings here, I'll never know. But I'm sure this rebellion will be crushed. There's talk of bringing crack troops back from the front line – "

The Sister, coming down the ward to replace a blanket which was slipping off one of the other beds, glanced at Lorna reprovingly. "Shh! Shh! I told you not to excite her," she told Alice. "She's supposed to be resting."

"I'm sorry. It's not Alice's fault," Lorna said wearily.

"Before I forget, Nurse Smallwood, you're to go to Matron's office when you leave here," the Sister added, tweaking the blanket back into place.

"Matron wants to see me?"

"You'd better go, then." Lorna lay back again as if tired by her outburst. "Sorry for going on at you."

"That's all right. You get some sleep now. I'll come back as soon as I can."

Alice wondered what the reason was for the summons. It was unlikely that she was about to be moved to different duties, since she had only just been taken out of the German ward and put on night shift. She walked along the corridor to Matron's office, mentally reviewing the last few days and wondering whether she had been caught out in some lapse of duty or inappropriate behaviour. The current Matron was fairly new, rumoured to be formidable. Alice found her sitting at her desk working at a pile of indents and duty rotas.

"Sit down, Nurse Smallwood," the older woman said, hardly looking up. She finished filling in a form in neat looped handwriting before putting down her pen and saying, "You're a friend of Nurse Sidgwick's, I believe."

"Yes, that's right," Alice replied. "I've just been to see her."

The Matron's grey eyes looked as tired as Lorna's. "I'm sending her home on sick leave," she said briskly.

"I can't spare the beds for sick nurses, to say nothing of the staff to look after them."

Alice was surprised. "I'm sure she doesn't want to go home. She was talking of going back on duty this evening."

"Yes, well, I haven't told her yet," Matron said, screwing the lid on her fountain pen with blunt reddened fingers. "That's why I've sent for you. There's no question of her going on duty, nor of staying here, as I said. She can be nursed by her family at home."

Alice, resenting the implication that Lorna was a nuisance, started to explain. "She's had a hard time. She's been out here for two years. Her brother was killed in April, and she was ill then, and insisted on coming back far too soon . . ."

Matron picked up another pile of papers. "Yes, I know. She's been overworked, like every other nurse here. But I've still no room to spare. I'll make the arrangements to get her to Boulogne tomorrow. You might let her know, and perhaps you could write to let her parents know she's coming."

"Yes."

"It'll probably be to Boulogne by ambulance, since there's no way of getting her to the station at Étaples as far as I can tell. The rioters are holding the bridge. Don't you think it's shameful to be afraid of setting foot outside in case we're set upon by our own men?"

Alice, considering an answer, saw that none was expected; Matron was already bent over her paperwork. She went back to the ward to tell Lorna the news, rephrasing what Matron had said into more tactful words. She expected another argument, but Lorna

46

submitted this time to the combined persuasion of Alice and the Sister.

"All right, I'll go," she said wearily. "But only on one condition. I'll go and stay with Dorothy and Mathilda in the East End, not back to the village. I couldn't stand it . . . seeing Edward's empty room again, and all his things . . . and if I go to them I can help out in the canteen instead of idling about all day."

"The *point* of it is for you to idle about," Alice said, uneasily sure that Lorna would merely exchange one kind of hard work for another. But Lorna was adamant, and eventually Alice went back to her own hut to catch up on belated sleep. At least Lorna would be in good hands; Dorothy and Mathilda, who had now set up their own canteen for the wives and children of absent troops, would make sure she didn't overtire herself, and the change might well do her good.

Lorna left for Boulogne the next day. Later that week, the nurses were informed that the "Battle of Eetapps", as the rebellion had become known, was over, and that they could go out of the hospital as usual during their time off. According to Mess Room gossip, the mutineers had got what they wanted – troops were to be allowed into town, and there would be no more Bull Ring. Alice found this quite unbelievable, but no further information was forthcoming, and she never saw anything in the newspapers about the mutiny.

"There's a man on my ward who's in the Fifth Epping Foresters, a Corporal," Pauline remarked over supper in the mess hut a few days later. "That's your brother's battalion, isn't it?"

Alice stopped eating and looked at her. "No, Jack's in the third, but Edward was in the fifth."

"Oh! I thought it was odd, because this man was saying he'd been wounded before, at Arras in April, and I didn't remember you saying anything about Jack being there. But wasn't that where – ?"

Alice nodded, putting down her knife and fork. "Did he say any more than that?" she asked.

"I haven't really spoken to him much. I just over-heard him telling someone else. You could go round and talk to him, if you liked. He might have been in Edward's company."

"Mm." Alice picked up her fork again and prodded at the congealing stew on her plate, wondering whether it would be wise to resurrect memories best left alone. She already knew, from a kind letter written by another Captain in the same battalion, how Edward had died leading his company in an attack. But at the same time she knew that she would go to speak to the man. If she didn't take the chance, she would always wonder what he could have told her: some fragment of conversation, some last sighting . . .

"Is he well enough to talk to?" she asked Pauline. "What's the matter with him?"

"He's had a foot blown off, and a facial injury. He was operated on last week, but he seems to be going on reasonably well. Are you going to eat that or not? I'll have it if you're not going to."

"Here, you're welcome to it." Alice pushed the plate across to her. "I *will* go to talk to him. Will you come with me, to show me where he is?"

48

"What, now?"

"When you've finished."

Pauline disposed of the last few mouthfuls with an appetite undiminished by the doubtful nature of the meat. She was well-known for her voracious eating. Alice wondered how she could look so vigorously healthy, in spite of the strain and the long hours. With her flushed fair skin and her hair swept back from a smooth brow, she looked as if she had faced nothing more than a vicarage garden party or a busy shopping expedition. Alice rarely spent long considering her own appearance, but brief glances into the mirror in her hut showed her a pale, grave face losing its girlish roundness, dark shadows under hazel eyes, and lank brown hair (it was difficult to wash it often enough, with neither time nor hot water to spare) escaping from its pins.

But the wounded men had worse problems to think of than tiredness or unwashed hair. The man from the 5th Epping Foresters wore no bandages on his face, and Alice caught her breath at the sight of the puckered inflamed scar which ran the whole length of one smashed cheek, pulling the eyelid down and the corner of the mouth up in a grotesque lopsided grin. Pauline should have warned her, for the man's sake. "You must always look a man straight in the face, no matter how dreadfully he's disfigured," Alice's first Sister had told the VADs on her ward. Alice knew that the men were particularly sensitive to facial injuries when the bandages first came off, watching the nurses to see how people would react to them when they left hospital. She tried to hide her initial shock, composing her face into a smile of greeting.

"Sandy, this is Nurse Sidgwick – Alice," Pauline said.

The man put down a week-old newspaper he had been reading and held out a hand. "Sandy Blatchford, Miss. Pleased to meet you."

Alice shook his hand, and Pauline said, "Alice knew someone in your battalion, Sandy. She wondered if you'd mind talking to her."

"No, I don't mind, miss," the man said. "I'm afraid I'm not much to look at."

"Oh, you've only just had your dressing off," Pauline said easily, "It'll get better."

But not much better, Alice knew. Sandy Blatchford looked about thirty-five, slightly built, with a shock of reddish hair and an air of resolutely making the best of whatever was flung his way. He would need it, she thought, to face the rest of his life with a shattered face and an amputated foot. The survivors weren't always the lucky ones.

"The surgeons are doing wonderful things now with faces," she said, not knowing how else to reply to such frankness. "They can rebuild noses and jaws, and even match hair for moustaches and eyebrows."

"So they tell me," the man replied with grim cheerfulness. "Who knows? I might end up a lot better-looking than I was before."

The introduction over, Pauline excused herself, saying she wanted an early night. When she had gone Alice hesitated, wondering whether she was being fair to this wounded man by asking him to recall memories which might well be as painful for him as for her. But it was too late now. He was looking at her with interest, waiting for her questions.

"So you knew someone in the Fifth?" he asked.

"Yes. Knew. Captain Sidgwick. Edward Sidgwick."

"Oh yes," the man said at once. He leaned forward for a moment, frowning hard, and then said, "I know who you mean. Got it now. Killed at Arras, wasn't he – badly wounded the night before the attack."

Alice stared at him. "Before? The night *before*? Are you sure, Corporal Blatchford?"

"The name's Sandy, miss. Yes, I remember it. A shell hit the officers' dug-out in the support lines. I wasn't in his company, but I was runner, and I'd only just left with a message when I heard the shell come over. Four of 'em killed outright – a bad do. Captain Sidgwick, he was the only one carried out alive, and they said he died soon after. He was new as company commander, wasn't he? Only recently made Captain, they said. Tall bloke, dark hair."

"Yes. But there must be some mistake . . . He died in the attack, leading his men. I had a letter . . ."

Sandy reached out and patted her arm awkwardly. "I'm sorry, miss. I hope I haven't said the wrong thing. But I am sure, I do know that. Saw him carried out with my own eyes. Was he a relation of yours, or a friend, like?"

"My fiancé."

"I'm sorry, miss," Sandy repeated. "You should have said, stopped me talking on like that. But I don't think he could have known much. When all's said and done, there's worse ways to go."

"Thank you. You've been very kind."

"Come in and see me some other time if you want a chat." He looked up at her and smiled as she stood up to go. The smile lessened the effect of

51

his disfigurement, the left side of his mouth lifting to match the right in what must once have been a charming grin.

"I will," she said. "And I hope you're soon well enough to be sent on home. Thank you again."

She walked back to her Alwyn hut feeling dazed by what she had heard. There must be some mistake! And yet Sandy had sounded so definite, describing Edward accurately. In the hut, she took a bundle of letters out of her trunk. They were all addressed in Edward's spiky black handwriting except for the last one, which was written in an elegant sloping hand in blue ink. She unfolded the letter inside and read:

". . . *Edward was commanding his company on the morning of April 11th, in a snowstorm. His men were held in reserve but were suddenly called on to reinforce A Company, which had been beaten back. Finding that A Company's commanding officer had been severely wounded, Edward gathered up the stragglers and led the renewed assault. He had made considerable progress towards his objective when he was hit by shell fragments and mortally wounded. I saw him when he was brought in to our front-line trench shortly afterwards, and I did not think there was any chance of his survival. I last saw him being carried down to the Aid Post. He had already been given morphia and I do not think he was conscious enough to suffer. He died next day at the Casualty Clearing Station . . ."*

There it was. Edward had died in action, leading his men, urging them on – the sort of gallantry that was mentioned in dispatches, might even have won him a Military Cross. But, all the same, there had been no mention, no medal . . . was this just a work of fiction, invented by Captain Addenham to make Edward's family feel better? Had he perhaps been confused, mistaking someone else for Edward? Or was it Sandy Blatchford who had made the mistake? Alice knew that grieving parents and wives were often deceived about the fates of their dead sons and husbands: a man was *killed instantly* who had hung on the German wire for days; someone who had jumped out of a shell-hole in a screaming funk had *died bravely*. For all her hospital experience, and knowledge of what the men endured, she could have been as easily deceived as the most gullible relative at home in England.

She tried to tell herself that it didn't matter; Edward was as irretrievably dead, either way. But she had pictured the events described by Captain Addenham so regularly that it was like remembering something she had read in a book. She had accepted that, and did not want to know of an alternative version. But if fact were fiction, where was the truth? Was there such a thing as truth, in the muddle of confused memories and kind intentions?

It was as if Edward had been killed a second time.

"It is very busy here," Lorna wrote two weeks later, *"with such a lot to be done, and I'm afraid I'm only a hindrance to Dorothy and Mathilda, although they are both very kind about having me to stay with them. Unfortunately I did get rather ill with a high temperature and fever soon after I arrived, but have recovered now sufficiently to do little jobs for them around the flat while they work at the canteen. I have decided that I really ought to go home to my parents for a few days at least;*

I wrote to tell them that I was in London, and they will be hurt if I don't go to see them.

One strange thing! I had a visitor the other day, and you will never guess who it was, so I shall tell you – Philip Morland! He was in the City on some sort of business for his father; my parents had told him that I was staying here, and so he called in, much to my surprise. He still limps very heavily with his badly set leg, and walks with a stick; apparently he has had the controls of his car adapted so that he can drive it. He wanted to know if I had any news of you and Jack, and told me all about the plan he has for Jack to work for him. He seems to want to get Harriet and the baby to move into the stables cottage straight away, as he says Harriet's parents' tiny cottage is no place to bring up a child. I must say it's kind of him to be so concerned.

I shall be back as soon as possible, but it occurred to me that you must be nearly due for some time off, since you've been out for nine months with only those few days' home leave in June. I know how busy it must be out there, but according to the papers a final breakthrough is imminent; if this present offensive does come to an end you might consider asking for leave. I'm sure you'd want to visit your mother and Emily, but perhaps you could stay here for a day or two. I'll look forward to hearing from you.

Lorna."

Alice read the letter through twice, lingering on the tempting suggestion to ask for leave. A week, perhaps, or even just a few days; time to call on Lorna in London, and catch the train out to Essex to see her mother and Emily, and Harriet and the baby . . . But it was impossible at the moment, she knew. Other VADs had been waiting for leave for far longer than she had, with little chance of having their requests granted while casualties of the push in the Salient were still arriving, trainload after trainload, to be allocated hospital space or sent on to Boulogne. The men spoke of hopeless losses, of mud like quicksand and unassailable German pill-boxes from which advancing troops were shot down with casual ease. The original aim of the offensive, back in July, had been to reach Ostend; the infantry had not so far reached the Passchendaele Ridge, less than ten miles from Ypres. Surely, Alice thought, with the weather so appalling and winter not far ahead, the attempt must either succeed or be called off. Superstitiously, she touched a letter from Jack in her apron pocket, knowing as she did so that his circumstances could have changed completely since it was written from a position of safety.

She wrote back to Lorna: "*I'm afraid there is no chance of taking leave at the moment, but perhaps later on, nearer Christmas . . .*"

Working Party

"Lieutenant Evernden," Captain Snell said.

Jack blinked, his eyes still adjusting to the dim light in the cellar that served as Officers' Mess. The young man who had been standing in the shadowy recesses moved forward into the bar of wintry sunlight which slanted through the doorway.

"Sir." Jack saluted smartly, the automatic response masking his surprise. The new second lieutenant, although as tall as Jack, had slim shoulders, and a fine-boned face above which the peaked officer's cap looked too large and clumsy. His skin was fair and unblemished.

"Pleased to meet you, Corporal Smallwood," the young man said, acknowledging the salute. He was very well-spoken. His uniform was brand new, every button and regimental badge polished to a high shine. God Almighty, Jack thought, noticing the smooth cheeks which would hardly warrant the effort of shaving, what were Headquarters playing at, sending up boys straight from school? This one must have been learning his Latin verbs and cheering on the rugger teams while Jack and the others had been in the front line. He could imagine what Jimmy and Victoria would say when they saw him.

"The men are parading at ten," Captain Snell said, "and Lieutenant Evernden will inspect Number

Eight Platoon. Sergeant Trotwood's still on the sick list, so I'll leave it to you, Smallwood, to tell the other NCOs."

"Yes, sir."

"Smallwood will tell you what you need to know about his section, Lieutenant. You'll find him very helpful," Captain Snell told the newcomer. "I'll leave you with him now. I've got to go and chase up some paperwork with the Medical Officer."

"Thank you very much, sir," the new officer said.

Both men saluted Captain Snell, who gave a final nod towards Jack and left. He looked a bit doubtful, Jack thought, as if making the best of what he had been sent. For the new lieutenant's sake, it would be as well if they weren't sent up to the front line for a bit – it would be too much for anyone, Jack thought, straight from Officer Training School, where battles consisted of planned objectives and orderly advances shown by arrows on a map, into the shell-torn quagmire of the Salient. But then he remembered Woodall and Trafford, the youngest privates in his section. They had been thrown straight in, no more aware of what to expect than this young officer.

They listened to the thud of Captain Snell's boots tramping up the cellar steps outside and away down the paved road. The brief silence which followed was broken by Evernden turning to Jack and remarking, "He seems awfully nice – Captain Snell, I mean."

"Yes, he is, sir. The men like him."

"Have you – had many officers since you've been with the platoon?" Evernden asked hesitantly.

"A few, sir, what with one thing and another."

The truthful reply would have been, "Yes, sir.

57

You'll be the fifth. Two of the others are dead, one's at home with a smashed leg and the other's in hospital, not likely to survive." However, Evernden seemed satisfied with Jack's answer, not pressing for further clarification. He took a handwritten list out of his pocket.

"It was all rather exciting coming up last night," Evernden said, "hearing the big guns for the first time. But I suppose you're used to it by now?"

"You could say that, sir. We'd only notice it if we *didn't* hear it."

"I suppose you don't take much notice . . . of shellfire . . . the risks of explosions and so on, when you've experienced it a few times?"

Jack hesitated. Evernden's look of enthusiasm had been replaced by an urgent probing for information, seeking reassurance. He was frightened, Jack saw, beneath the veneer of newly-acquired military competence. Jack remembered how he had felt, his own first time in the line – almost wanting to get on with it, to test himself, to find out whether he would be steady under fire. *Steady under fire* – there was a bloody stupid phrase! The Army didn't allow for ordinary human feelings. To be a perfect soldier, you'd have to have no imagination at all – then you'd have no trouble in standing up *steady under fire* like a target on a shooting range.

Well, he'd have to say something. He found himself parroting the empty phrases he had scorned others for using. "You'll be all right sir. The Captain'll look after you, at first especially."

"I hope so." Evernden seemed suddenly embarrassed at having given so much away. He looked down at the list in his hand and studied it for a few moments, then said to Jack more brusquely, "Here are the details I've been given. Perhaps you could tell me something about each man in your section?"

Jack looked at the list. Two of the names had been crossed off since the Company had come back from Sanctuary Wood, and two new ones added at the bottom.

"The last two, Evans and Griffiths, they've only just joined us, sir. Came from a Welsh battalion that was badly hit. Bachelor's fairly new, came into the platoon in May. Used to be a cab driver in peacetime. Cross has been with us since last autumn, joined up late on account of illness. Victoria, we call him."

"Oh." Evernden frowned at the list, looking baffled. "But why?"

"Well, sir, for a joke. Victoria Cross," Jack explained patiently.

Evernden stared at him. "Oh – oh, I see."

Jack gave up. Of course, it wasn't a particularly amusing joke when you had to spell it out. Strewth, he'd have his work cut out seeing that the blokes didn't run circles round this one. He thought of the approaching parade, and wondered who would be doing the inspecting.

"Jimmy Taplin," he continued, "one of the originals, comes from the same village as me. Worked at the Hunt kennels before the war. Had a bad wound in the arm last July . . ."

If Jack stopped to think about it, he expected to die. There was no reason why he shouldn't. It was pure fluke that he had survived so long – he had been in one place rather than another when a shell burst, a bit of shrapnel had scraped his arm rather than getting him in the chest, he'd fallen into a shell-hole out of the way of a burst of machine-gun fire. But his luck must run out, as everyone else's seemed to. Each time in the front line, there were more names to cross off the list; the men would shake their heads and say, "Old so-and-so copped it," and the newly-dead would soon be forgotten, rarely referred to again. He could hear the others saying, "Poor old Smallwood's gone west, then? Shame – he was a decent bloke, when all's said and done," and then someone would ask if there were any spare fags going, and that would be that. Jimmy would probably write a soothing letter home, and Alice would get another telegram at the hospital . . . You only hoped that when your turn came it would be quick, and that you wouldn't be left screaming in agony in a shell-hole beyond the wire or retching your lungs up in hospital.

If Jack thought about the months to come, stretching into winter – the numbing cold nights, the endless hours waiting in sodden trenches, the lice, the pain of frozen limbs, the futile attacks – his brain reeled, he knew he would be unable to endure it. But he had trained himself not to think beyond the next twenty-four hours. That was as much as he could cope with, as much as anyone could.

Sometimes he thought of the vague time called *after the war*. He thought of Greenstocks – the fit horses clipped out for the winter's hunting, the harness-room smelling of clean leather and metal polish, the ring of hooves on the road at morning exercise. It was his past as well as his future, if he had a future.

He and Stephen used to spend hours together talking about horses. It was their way of escaping. But now Stephen had gone. Jack felt his emotions had been dulled and blunted by the death of his closest friend; no other death could ever affect him in the same way again.

But he was aware of a superstitious fear that his own luck was due to run out. Each time he returned safely from the line it seemed that the dice were loaded more firmly against him; the law of averages must come into operation soon. It was like a voice in his head, sneering at him. *Next time, next time.*

Orders were given out a few days later – night-time working parties up past Hooge, repairing communication trenches. They moved up into makeshift billets in a ruined farm near Zillebeke, ready to march up to the front each night and back at dawn.

It already seemed that the few days' rest had never existed; the Salient claimed them back. The inevitable fitful rain spattered into the men's faces as they sploshed up a pitted track, grumbling under their burdens of duckboard, shovels, planks and corrugated iron.

"Bloody hell. Might as well try digging porridge."

"They'd do better to send the ruddy Navy."

"Give me a choice an' I'd have frost and snow rather than this rain pissing down . . ."

"Gorblimey, I hoped we'd seen the last of this lot. I bet I'll be bloody well pushing up daisies within a week," a man near Jack remarked with morose relish.

"No, you won't," Jimmy replied confidently. "I

61

can tell you for certain you won't be pushing up any damn' daisies."

The man who had spoken turned on him belligerently. "What d'you mean by that? How'd you know?"

Jimmy turned his head to the left and the right, surveying the dismal surroundings. "Where the hell d'you think you'd find a single bloody daisy in the middle of all this?"

Jack grinned, momentarily forgetting his soaked feet and the rain coursing down his face. Trust old Jimmy.

"Close up, there," Evernden ordered sharply. He had become increasingly edgy since the Company had moved up from the safety of Poperinghe. Earlier, soon after leaving the farm, some of the men in another section of the platoon had starting singing an obscene song, and in the end Jack had told them to stow it, knowing that Evernden would get a sharp reproof from one of the other officers otherwise. It was a fairly quiet night, but still the occasional shell came arching over. Several times Evernden winced in an almost visible effort to refrain from throwing himself down on the muddy track, while the men had carried on trudging, unconcerned.

"You need to listen out for the way they burst, sir," Jack told him. "You can tell how close they are."

"I bet you're fed up with playing at nursemaid, eh?" Jimmy said when Jack fell back into his place in the line. "Who's supposed to be in charge of this platoon? We could do without someone who's still wet behind the ears."

"Give the bloke a chance. He'll learn, same as we

did," Jack replied shortly. He felt suddenly irritated by his mediating role, trying to save Evernden from losing face with the men, at the same time wanting the camaraderie of joining in their grouses and grumbles. "You can't wait for him to make some daft mistake, can you?"

"What's up with you, then? Don't bite my head off."

Jack didn't answer. He resented Jimmy's cynicism, which had the effect of making him feel unexpectedly protective towards the new lieutenant. Evernden represented much that Jack disliked – privilege, unearned status, old-school superiority – but he had enough to cope with as it was, without people waiting for him to land flat on his face. But, earlier on, Evernden had reprimanded Jack for allowing Jimmy to call him by his first name: "As an NCO, you shouldn't permit such slackness." Jack didn't need a bloke two years his junior to tell him the rules, but he thought of all that Regular Army stuff as old hat. The officers could keep their upper lips stiff if they liked, but he wasn't going to pull rank with his oldest mate over something so unimportant. It was like having Philip Morland over again, using the last letter of the rule book to cover up his own insecurity. Perhaps a spell at the front would knock some of that out of Evernden.

The line had been pushed forward since the battalion had left Sanctuary Wood. The track had soon petered out, and they were trudging up a slight incline over land which had been fought over since the beginning of the war; it was pitted with shell craters full of stinking stagnant water and littered with military and human debris. The mud sank squelchily underfoot, grasping the legs in a cold embrace. Occasionally Jack's feet encountered something less yielding beneath the surface, and he didn't like to give too much thought to what might be down there. The whole Salient was a graveyard; British, Germans and Colonials alike lay rotting in the deep mud, so that sometimes it seemed they weren't so much fighting each other as struggling against the destructive forces of nature.

"Bloody hell, how much further is it?" someone complained.

"Not long now," Jack said, not really knowing.

At last, the men in front stopped and dumped their burdens, and Jack's platoon did likewise, realizing that the shallow indentation they had been following was actually a communication trench. The main action was on the slopes up to the Passchendaele Ridge, further to the north, from which direction the artillery rumbled steadily; this sector was quieter, although there was enough spasmodic shelling to keep the working parties alert. The rambling, inadequate trenches had become channels for seeping water, occasionally blocked by mounds of earth from shell-bursts. The men looked around dispiritedly; in these glutinous conditions, they were expected to throw up parapets, deepen the trenches, reinforce the sides and dig sumps. Occasionally, a flare soared up over the front line ahead and fizzed as it dropped back to earth, making Jack think of a joke currently in circulation: "What colour flares will they use to signal the end of the war?" The answer: "Black lights against a night sky."

"All right down here?" Captain Snell, having come back from the front of the column, showed Evernden his platoon's length of trench. "And don't forget to relieve your sentries every hour."

Evernden divided the men into small groups, each with its own length of trench. Jack was relieved to see him pick up a shovel and start digging, instead of merely standing directing operations – the men preferred an officer who was willing to muck in.

"I'll go down the far end, shall I, sir?" he asked. "Trafford and Woodall and the two Welsh lads could do with a hand."

Evernden nodded. "I can send a runner if I need anything."

Jack started to wade back down the waterlogged trench. He had gone only a dozen yards or so when he heard the purposeful whine of a shell, not going overhead this time – his instincts told him to throw himself down, but before he could do so he heard the final rush as the shell ripped into the trench behind him. The blast of hot air lifted him off his feet and sent him sprawling. Clods showered him, and he found himself half-buried in wet earth, with mud in his face, in his mouth, in his eyes. He tried to struggle to his feet on legs weak with the shock of the explosion. Someone pulled him upright and started knocking the debris off him. The rest of the salvo had screamed harmlessly overhead.

"I'm all right – "

Jack tried to push the man away, only one thought in his mind. He tried to climb over the mound of earth and splintered wood which blocked the trench, fell over as his legs gave way, struggled up again. He scrambled past the obstruction, catching his tunic on a projecting plank end; something ripped. He came face to face with Williams, the runner, who stared at him wildly and clutched at his sleeve.

"Don't go any further up, Corporal – nasty mess along there – the new officer, a direct hit – "

Jack pushed past. The flickering light of a flare showed him emphatically that there was no point in calling for the stretcher bearers. He turned back to Williams, trying to suppress an insistent urge to vomit. He swallowed with difficulty and took a deep breath.

"The other lads that were working here, they're round further up in the sap," the runner said. "Managed to get theirselves out of the way in time. I was with them. A bit shaken, but no worse. We shouted to Mr Evernden, but it was on us so sudden . . ."

Jack trusted himself to speak at last. "Get up to Captain Snell, quick as you can," he told Williams. "Tell him what's happened. I'll have to clear up here. Miller, you'd better help me," he called to the nearest man.

The runner set off, and Miller approached reluctantly. "Christ. Not much left of him to bury, is there?"

Jack said, "I'll get a sack. See if you can find any belongings, identification disc, pay book. God Almighty – " The last two words exploded from him. He felt a barely controllable desire to lash out at something, hit someone, to give vent to his sudden futile rage at the pointlessness of it all. He had had no personal liking for Evernden, had hardly known the poor bugger, but what a sheer bloody waste! Straight from training camp to an abrupt violent death without even having seen the front line! Giddy with anger and shock, Jack stumbled along the trench, realizing that he'd never come so close to losing control of himself. At this rate he'd be running out over the top, getting himself blown to bits . . . where was he going? . . . to get something . . . to get a sack. Down at the other end where he'd been going in the first place. Someone yelled something at him, but he pushed past, not answering. Shells were plopping softly to either side, and he could smell hay – hay that had got wet in the barn and was spoiled, no good for the hunters now, it'd make them cough, they must have only the best . . .

"*Gas!*" The eyes of the man in front of him were bulging with fear. "They're gas shells!"

Jack snapped back to alertness. What had he been thinking about, for God's sake? It wasn't hay, it was phosgene. "Sound the gas alarm!" someone was shouting to Jimmy, who was sentry. Jimmy grabbed the handle and began swinging it, producing a loud, nerve-twanging rattle. The men nearby were unfastening their masks from around their necks and pushing them hastily over their heads; Jack pulled himself free of the man who was trying to restrain him, and hurried down to Trafford and Woodall. The pale fumes were already drifting along the trench, flowing into hollows and swirling in deadly currents. He felt for the fastening of his own respirator, his fingers clutching at nothing. Where the hell was it? God Almighty, it must have been torn off him when he'd blundered into those planks – he'd heard something go . . .

67

Woodall and Trafford already had their masks on, looking like grotesque clumsy insects. The stuff was in Jack's eyes and mouth and throat, he could feel it burning, corrosive, his stomach heaving in protest. He bent double and retched, gasping for air, gulping down more of the lethal fumes. He choked helplessly as hands grabbed his arms and hauled him upright. The faces of giant insects loomed over him; he heard the cry of "Stretcher bearer!" and knew that this time it was for him. The faces were disappearing, obscured by a dark film over his eyes – he was sinking blindly into a black hole, drowning, slipping thankfully into unconsciousness.

He had to get to Evernden, tell him to put his gas mask on . . . but he was sinking in the mud . . . there was no-one else . . . Evernden wouldn't know what to do. He was swimming up the trench, uphill, floundering in the stinking mud, the ooze filling his mouth and nose, drowning him. The runner was trying to stop him, but he swam round the corner, and there was –

His yell of fright jerked him into wakefulness, still gasping for breath. Someone was close to him, clamping a smelly rubber mask over his mouth and nose. He fought and struggled, pushing the vile thing away.

"Shh! Shh! You're dreaming," a female voice said. "Take deep breaths. It's an oxygen mask. And try to calm down."

Jack obeyed, realizing that he was no longer in the trench but propped up in a bed in some sort of room; the voices around him had an indoor sound to them. The opaque film over his eyes blurred and cleared

68

as he blinked, till he could make out a high ceiling above, and a white-uniformed figure bending over him. The face was a pale blob.

"Can you see?" the girl's voice asked.

Jack nodded beneath the mask. He felt sick and his eyes stung painfully. Confused impressions came back to him . . . lying on something face upwards to the rain, with a voice saying "This one doesn't look too good" . . . his head swimming as he was driven in some sort of motor vehicle rocking slowly up an uneven road . . . Now he opened his eyes for long enough to see that he was in some sort of hospital ward, with brick walls and a beamed ceiling, and a narrow wooden staircase going up to the next floor. He remembered that Evernden had been killed, and turned his head away from the nurse into the pillow, but was overcome by another fit of choking. Between racking coughs he gulped uncontrollably, and the nurse held the mask over his face again. He was soaked in sweat, and shivering at the same time.

"Where am I?" he asked, as soon as he could gasp out the words.

"At the Casualty Clearing Station in Vlamertinghe. You've been gassed. Now don't try to talk. It'll make you start choking again."

"Can't I lie down properly?"

"No, you've got to be propped up. It's easier for you to breathe that way."

The girl's hands, smelling of soap, were soft and cool as she smoothed his hair back and arranged his head more comfortably on the banked pillows, but she had no further time for him; the patient in the next bed was calling out urgently. Jack's blurred eyesight distinguished wild eyes and foaming lips in a face white with pallor. He wondered whether he looked as grotesque.

Shortly, another nurse came up to his bed, an older woman this time, accompanied by an orderly with a bowl of warm soapy water and several flannels. He realized that he was still wearing his filthy uniform, reeking of mud and gas and sweat. The nurse started to unfasten the buttons of his tunic, chatting to the male orderly.

"I can do that by myself," Jack said, embarrassed.

The nurse laughed cheerfully. "I'd like to see you try! You're in no state to sit up, let alone do anything else."

Jack had to submit to being undressed and washed all over, and put into pyjamas and into the bed, beneath the harsh brown Army blankets. It was pleasant to feel clean again, but he was glad it hadn't been the soft-voiced younger girl – he wouldn't have known where to put his face. And when, gripped by a painful stomach cramp, he asked where the lavatory was, the nurse told him not to be so silly, and fetched him a bed-pan. He had no choice but to use it, but felt ashamed, hating the indignity.

He soon found that the nurse was right about his condition. He had to devote all his attention to breathing; each lungful of air was a deliberate effort, and his chest hurt so much that he thought his heart was affected. He observed his symptoms with fascinated horror. He had never been seriously ill in his life, and he hated the thought of his body being out of his control, reacting in its own unpredictable ways to the poison. His eyes hurt too much to keep them open for long, and all he could do was lie there concentrating on breathing. When taking each breath became an intolerable struggle, a nurse would clamp the oxygen mask over his face. The minutes passed slowly, slowly into hours, broken by the relief of sleep. But three more times he woke up, sobbing for breath and fighting the blankets, from the same nightmare.

In the morning, there were screens round the next bed, and when they were taken away the boy who had lain there was gone.

Philip Morland

Alice sat on the lower deck of the bus looking out at the drab streets of East London. Undernourished children were scavenging in pig-bins, and there were long queues outside the food shops; it was almost as if the same people had stood there patiently since Alice's last visit in June. As then, rubble from the latest air raids was screened off from the pavement by makeshift hoardings. Two begrimed figures were unloading sacks of coal from a dray in Bow Road, and only when the bus drew alongside did Alice see that they were women; they wore thick-soled boots like men's, and had their hair twisted into turbans. The air was heavy with smoke when Alice stepped off into the street, so that she felt briefly nostalgic for the clean, pine-scented air of the Canche estuary.

She found the address Lorna had given her, a big dilapidated Victorian house in a residential street near Maryland Point. A hand-painted sign above the bay windows of the ground floor read "Cost-Price Restaurant", and inside Alice could see a large room where women and children sat eating at long benches. She thought that it looked rather similar to the canteen run by Sylvia Pankhurst in the Old Ford Road, where Lorna's friends had worked be-fore moving away to set up their own similar establishment. A notice on the front door gave the opening hours; Alice had arrived at one of the busiest times.

She joined the customers who were filing through the front door. Inside, a plump woman who was sorting out meal tickets and money at a table in the hallway looked curiously at Alice's VAD uniform.

"I've come to visit Lorna Sidgwick," Alice explained. "She's expecting me. Is she in the kitchen?"

"No, love, she'll be upstairs in the flat. I'll take you through to Mrs Braithwaite, shall I? Leave your case here a minute."

The woman led the way through the dining-room, which was filled with the smell of cooked meat and potatoes and vegetables, making Alice realize how hungry she was after her day's travelling. Women, children and the occasional elderly or wounded man queued at the servery, holding trays. In the kitchen at the back of the house, six women were working, either attending to saucepans and baking tins at the cookers which lined the back wall, or doling out portions of food at the hatches which linked with the main room. They all wore blue overalls and large caps which hid their hair, so that Alice couldn't immediately distinguish either Dorothy or Mathilda. The plump woman spoke to one of the cooks, who turned and looked at Alice and crossed the kitchen to greet her. Having met Dorothy only two or three times, Alice remembered her stylish clothes and her thick brown hair swept up with casual elegance; she looked very different now, her ample figure concealed by the shapeless overall, her hair flattened under the cap and her face perspiring in the steamy atmosphere. She clasped Alice's hand affectionately.

"My dear! How good to see you again. You must be exhausted after your journey – Mathilda! Alice is here!" she called to her sister-in-law, who turned from the serving hatch and waved a fish slice in greeting. "You'll have to excuse us, I'm afraid," Dorothy continued. "As you can see, we're rushed off our feet. Lorna told us you were coming unexpectedly – how did you manage to get leave?"

"I swapped with another girl whose plans were changed at the last minute," Alice explained. "She wants to take her leave in January instead, so Matron agreed that we could exchange dates."

"You look as if you could do with a few days' off. I know how hard you work out there," Dorothy said. "Why don't you go upstairs and see Lorna? She can show you where you're sleeping, and you can have a wash, and then we'll send up a meal for you. Mrs Hawkes will show you where to go."

Rather puzzled by the references to Lorna upstairs, Alice said, "I was expecting Lorna to be down here. Is she still not well, then? From what she wrote, I thought – "

Dorothy frowned. "Didn't she tell you? She's had a touch of pleurisy – not serious, but the doctor has diagnosed complete rest. You know what Lorna's like, though, and how hopeless it is to persuade her to rest even for a day – she's taken over the accounts and the letters. I must say it's very useful for us, and it keeps her indoors. But there's no question of her spending another winter in those freezing huts at the hospital. I think she's resigned herself to staying here

74

until the spring. Go on up and find her – we'll see you later on."

Alice followed Mrs Hawkes back to the entrance hall to collect her case, and went up to the first floor. She found Lorna in a sitting-room-cum-office, prodding at the keys of a typewriter.

"*Alice!* You're here!" She was on her feet at once, enveloping Alice in a hug. "How are you?"

"More to the point, how are you?" Alice stood back to examine her friend critically. "Why didn't you say you'd had pleurisy, in your letters? But you do look better than you did, I must say."

"I would have come to meet you at Victoria otherwise," Lorna said. "No, I'm fine, really – almost over it. But what's your news? Are you still just as inundated in your ward? And have you heard from Jack?"

"He's still up in Belgium, but he was behind the lines when he last wrote."

"The newspapers are saying this latest push must be coming to an end, with the Canadians having taken Passchendaele. Let's hope they're right for once. But let me show you where you'll be sleeping, and then we can have a meal. It's only a camp bed in my room, I hope you don't mind – the other rooms are either being painted or being slept in by helpers. I hope you won't be too uncomfortable, but it's only for two nights – didn't you say you were going on to the village on Thursday?"

"Yes, that's right – Ma and Emily are expecting me. Of course I don't mind having the camp bed. I'm glad you could put me up at such short notice."

Later, when Alice had washed and tidied herself

and they had had a meal brought up to the upstairs sitting-room, Lorna took her on a tour of the house.

"You'll be amazed how much they've done – all the ground floor rooms have been knocked into one big one, with the kitchen enlarged at the back, and fitted out for large-scale catering. And I must show you the top floor – come on." Lorna was already on her way up the second flight of stairs. "Look! I think we could convert these rooms into a self-contained flat for ourselves, after the war, and rent it from Dorothy and Richard."

"Would they mind?"

"Of course not. They're interested in the work I want to do, campaigning, writing, public speaking – we'd all be involved together. I've already discussed it with them. Look, there's a small bathroom up here already, and this room would be a living-room, and we could divide this one up into two small bedrooms – we'd only need to get this bit converted into a kitchen. We'd have everything we need."

Alice looked approvingly at the well-lit rooms. Lorna, her characteristic optimism having returned, made it sound as if the war would end tomorrow, dispelling Alice's own visions of staying in France, tending endless streams of wounded men into her old age. "That would be marvellous, to have something already organized," she remarked.

"I told you Richard's involved with the No-Conscription Fellowship, didn't I?" Lorna said. "And Geoffrey's in the RAMC. He's still working on his poems – he's trying to get them published as a volume. Now, come and look at the main rooms on the first floor. You'll recognize a lot of the pictures and things, from Hillbank House . . ."

Alice slept heavily that night, and awoke in the morning thinking she had overslept and was late for duty on the ward. The unfamiliar room came slowly into focus, and she remembered where she was; Lorna's bed was empty and already made. While she was still contemplating getting up, Lorna, dressed and with her hair pinned up, brought her in a cup of tea.

"You slept well – it's gone nine! I'll bring you some hot water. Come and have some breakfast when you're ready. I put out some of my clothes for you – I thought you might prefer it to wearing uniform. The skirt will be too long, but you could hitch it up with a belt."

"Oh, thank you," Alice said gratefully. Nurses serving abroad weren't allowed to have civilian clothes with them, so she had no choice but to arrive in uniform; today, though, she was far happier to put on mufti. She would probably help out in the canteen, she supposed, unless Lorna wanted assistance with the office work.

"By the way," Lorna said casually over breakfast, "Philip Morland said he might call in this afternoon."

"Really?"

"He comes up to London on estate business sometimes. When I saw him the first time I suggested that he brought us a few crates of vegetables from Martlets Farm if he had room in the car – we're always short. He's been calling fairly regularly since, and usually comes up for a chat."

Alice thought about this information during the morning, while she filed papers and sorted invoices for Lorna. Really, Philip Morland was the last person she wanted to see, particularly here, where she was treated as a social equal by Lorna and the others. She had been a servant in Philip's parents' house since she had left school, for almost three years before the outbreak of war. She had lit the fire in his room, fetched his tea and hot water in the mornings, made his bed, picked up the clothes he had dropped on the floor, cleaned grass-stains off his cricket flannels and sewn buttons on to his shirts, in a relationship at once intimate and remote. Philip had had very little to do with her on a personal level, certainly not as much as his sister, Madeleine, and Alice would have no reason to dislike him if it hadn't been for his frequent clashes with Jack. She knew that Jack was at least partly to blame, but Philip had often gone out of his way to create difficulties for him; there was a collision of personalities there, each of them as stubborn as the other. And now Philip wanted Jack to work for him, with the horses . . .

Lorna ripped a sheet of paper out of the typewriter with an exasperated humph. "I just *can't* get on with this machine!" she complained. "I haven't got the patience. I'm typing more mistakes than correct words – look at all this wasted paper!" She glared at the waste-paper basket, which was half-full of crumpled sheets.

"Why don't you do the filing for a bit, and let me have a go?" Alice said. "It's just copying, isn't it?"

"Well, all right, if you don't mind. You're probably more careful. Look, you've got to copy the amount shown here, and type the address there, and then do an envelope. You use this lever here to go down a line – like this – and that bar for the spaces between words."

They changed places, and Alice started to type very slowly and carefully, placing a ruler on the invoice beneath the row of figures she had to copy. While her fingers and half her brain were occupied, her thoughts drifted back to Philip Morland, and this surprising connection with Lorna. She supposed they must have known each other reasonably well, before the war – the Sidgwicks and the Morlands frequently dined at each others' houses – but both Edward and Lorna had been away at university, and neither of them had ever spoken much about Philip. Lorna was two or three years older than Philip, and there was no obvious common ground in terms of attitudes or experience; it was puzzling that Philip should call so often. She wondered whether he had a romantic interest in Lorna. Well, stranger things had happened . . . but what about Captain Aldridge? Lorna hadn't mentioned him, and she didn't like to ask.

She had to contain her curiosity about Philip until the afternoon. Lorna brought him up to the sitting-room, and Alice heard the irregular *thump*-step of his laboured progress up the stairs. She had last met him in June, shortly after Edward's death, when Mrs Morland had invited her to tea at Greenstocks. It had been difficult to behave as a guest in the Morlands' house, and Alice thought that she would find it only slightly less awkward to meet Philip in these different surroundings. But she remembered how much changed he had seemed, and this was her renewed impression as he entered behind Lorna, leaning on a walking stick and dressed in a well-cut tweed suit.

It was hard to see in him the handsome, arrogant schoolboy he had been when Alice had first started work at the house. He was now in his mid-twenties, but looked older; his cheeks were hollowed, he had grown a moustache (which suited him, Alice decided) and his manner was almost apologetic as he held out his hand to her.

"Hello, Alice. It's good to see you here. Have you got many days' leave?"

"A week altogether." She shook his hand, unsure how to address him – in the old days it would have been Mr Philip, to distinguish him from his father, but she was no longer a servant. Philip seemed too familiar, while Mr Morland was too formal – or should it still be Lieutenant Morland, in spite of his having been invalided out of the Army?

"Do sit down. I'll make us some tea," Lorna called out, disappearing into the adjoining kitchen.

Alice sat down in one of the armchairs facing Philip, who lowered himself with difficulty to the sofa and perched on the edge with his right leg stuck out stiffly. She wished she had dashed out to make the tea herself, instead of being left alone with Philip, who sat looking at her intently in just the way she remembered from their last meeting. His eyes were a pale blue-grey which, together with his very upright bearing, had always made him appear haughty; Alice could imagine him as the rigidly correct subaltern Jack had described.

"I expect you'll be going home to see your family?" he said after a few moments.

"Yes. I shall take the train home tomorrow morning."

Philip frowned at his brown brogue shoes. "I wish I'd known. I could have arranged my visit for tomorrow instead of today, and driven you back myself. I didn't know you would be here until Lorna told me downstairs."

"It's very kind of you, but I really don't mind going by train – "

He looked up at her with sudden enthusiasm. "But look here, why don't I drive you back with me tonight? I've got a couple of appointments to keep in the City after I leave here, but I could easily be back here for six."

"But – " Alice looked helplessly towards the kitchen doorway, willing Lorna to come back. He seemed so anxious to do her a good turn that she didn't like to disappoint him. But, on the other hand, what on earth would she talk to him about, during the long car journey into Essex? She had no idea at all how long it would take. "Well, you're very kind, but I only arrived here last night, and I've little time to spend with Lorna as it is. And I wouldn't want to bring you out of your way, though I do appreciate your offer. Have you any news from the village?" she asked, to move the conversation on.

"Oh – food shortages, tea and butter especially just now . . . Lord Calderdale's eldest son's been killed – Andrew, who was in the Royal Flying Corps . . . we've just lost another groom to the Army, Harriet's young brother Alfie – "

"Alfie?" Alice repeated in surprise. "Goodness! Is he old enough to join up?" She thought of the scrawny boy of fifteen who had taken Jack's place at the Greenstocks stables; there wouldn't have been an Army uniform small enough to fit him, the size he had been then.

Philip smiled ruefully. "He's eighteen now, the same age Jack was when he enlisted. I know; it seems that a whole new generation is taking over where people like myself left off . . ." He broke off, looking down at his injured leg. He seemed regretful, Alice thought, not overjoyed to be out of the fighting as many men in his situation would have been. She thought of Edward, who had been affected by the war in a different way, becoming increasingly angry and embittered by the futility of expending thousands of lives in an advance over a stretch of desolate ground measured in yards, not miles. The change in Philip was just as marked; he seemed to regard his injury as evidence of personal inadequacy and failure.

"Have you seen Harriet at all, and the baby?" Alice asked, as Lorna came back into the room with the tea things on a tray.

"Oh yes. The baby looks fine, growing fast," Philip said. "I've told Harriet that the stables cottage is empty, ready for her and Jack as soon as they want to move in. She's still with her parents now, but it'll be too crowded in that small house when Jack comes home. Mr and Mrs Sedley have moved out into the gardener's cottage – it suits them better, being smaller. We've got no full-time gardener now, of course."

"That will be lovely for Jack and Harriet," Lorna

said, pouring milk. "And what about you? Have you made any plans for yourself?"

"I'm waiting to have another operation on my leg, to give me more flexibility," Philip said. "If it's successful I should be able to ride a horse again, at any rate. And I've applied for a post at the War Office. I'm still doing estate work, meanwhile. I'm afraid my father's health isn't too good, and the constant worry over farm workers isn't helping, so I feel I'm paying my keep."

Lorna handed him a cup of tea. "Would that mean living in London, if you were appointed to the War Office?"

"I'd probably stay up in London during the week and go home for weekends. It would be possible to drive up and back daily, but it'd be more convenient to stay in town . . . I was just saying to Alice that I could easily drive her home tonight, to save her a train journey tomorrow."

"Oh, but – " Alice was about to repeat the objections she had made earlier, but Lorna said, "That's a good idea. You could always come back again and stay here on the last night of your leave, to make up for not staying tonight."

Alice's reproachful look went unnoticed by Lorna, who was pouring more hot water into the teapot. While Alice was about to refuse Philip's offer again, feet could be heard pounding urgently up the stairs, and then there was a pause during which heavy breathing could be heard outside the door, followed by a brisk knocking.

"Come in!" Lorna called.

Mrs Hawkes stood at the door, flushed and panting.

"Telephone call – for – Miss Alice – Smallwood."

"Telephone call? For me?" Alice got up quickly, unable to think who it could be. No-one, apart from her mother and Emily, knew she was here. Not bad news, *please* . . . She followed Mrs Hawkes downstairs and picked up the earpiece reluctantly.

"Hello?"

"Is that you, Alice?" It was her mother, speaking very slowly and loudly, unused to telephones. "I'm at Dr Sidgwick's house. It's bad news about Jack, love, I'm afraid. He's in hospital in France."

"In hospital?" Alice repeated. "Where? What's happened to him?" She felt dizzy, clutching at the newel post for support – shock or relief, she didn't know which – Jack wasn't dead, he wasn't dead . . . but . . . her mind was filled with lurid pictures of all the things that could have happened to him.

"In Boulogne – he's been gassed. We got one of those field cards in the second post, just a few printed lines, *I have been admitted into hospital, sick* – nothing personal. And in the same post we got a letter from a Captain Snell. It says that Jack was gassed and sent down to a Casualty Clearing Station and then on to Boulogne. Seriously ill, it says."

"Does it say which hospital?"

"Yes, I'll read it out to you. Here it is. Number Thirteen General Hospital, Boulogne. I hope that won't be unlucky thirteen. Captain Snell says he found that out knowing Jack had a sister in France who might be able to go and see him."

"Number Thirteen Base Hospital. Yes, I'll go straight back. I can be in Boulogne by midday tomorrow, perhaps even tonight."

"Does that mean you won't be coming home?"

"Yes, I'm sorry. I'll try again as soon as I can, but – I must see Jack. I'll write to you to let you know how he is. Give my love to Emily and the children."

"Yes. It's a shame we won't be seeing you – but, well . . . Give our love to Jack, and find out whether there's anything he wants sent to him."

Back upstairs, Philip and Lorna were all concern on hearing the news, Lorna helping Alice to pack her bag, Philip insisting on driving her to Victoria Station. She changed back into her uniform, bade hasty farewells to Dorothy and Mathilda, who were in the kitchen chopping onions for the evening meal, and got into Philip's Daimler outside the house. Well, she would be driving with him after all, although under entirely unexpected circumstances.

"Write as soon as you can!" Lorna called from the pavement. "I hope – " Her last words were lost as the car pulled away.

Philip drove confidently, weaving in and out of the traffic in Mile End and the Bow Road. Even so, the journey seemed interminable to Alice, who was wondering whether she would be able to get to Folkestone in time to board a ship that evening.

"What will you do if you can't get a ship out tonight?" Philip asked, as if reading her thoughts.

"Oh – I suppose I'll have to find a hostel or something in Folkestone."

"I know a couple of places. I'll write down the addresses for you when we get to the station. Have you got enough money? And any French currency, for when you get back?"

She nodded. "I think so, thank you."

"It might be better to book in somewhere – otherwise, if you get on a boat late tonight, you'll arrive in Boulogne in the early hours of the morning with nowhere to go. Don't let me forget to give you the addresses before I leave you."

She appreciated his emphasis on the practicalities of travel, which took her mind off her anxieties. At Victoria, he parked the car and carried her bag into the ticket hall for her.

"I hope Jack isn't too badly off," he said as they waited at the ticket office. "Gas cases can be dreadful, I know, but at least he's been moved on to a Base hospital. He can't be desperately ill, or they'd have kept him at the CCS."

"Yes, that's true," Alice said, grateful to hear someone else confirm what she had already tried to tell herself.

Philip took a diary out of his pocket, wrote down some addresses and tore the page out to give her. "Here are the names of those places I mentioned. And you will drop me a line, won't you, to let me know how Jack is? My parents will be anxious to know, too."

"Yes, of course."

"Well, I'd better say goodbye here. I'd come to the platform with you, but I don't like to leave the car for more than a few minutes."

"No, don't worry. Thank you so much for bringing me here. It's very kind of you. I hope you get the job you want at the War Office – and I hope your operation is a success."

He shook her hand. "Thank you. Goodbye, Alice, and good luck. Perhaps we'll meet again soon."

She watched him as he walked back through the crowded station, turning to give her a final wave. The terminus was packed with troops, and families in little knots delaying the moment of departure; a group of Queen Alexandra's nurses drank tea by the Red Cross stall. Philip, on his own in the midst of all the comings and goings, had an air of intense loneliness.

No.13 General Hospital

Folkestone harbour was crowded with troop ships, hospital ships and supply ships; to the west, the coast-line stretched away in a placid sandy curve, away from the military arteries of shipping lines and railways. Alice stayed on the deck for most of the voyage, in spite of the cold wind, reluctant to go below because of U-boats. She watched as the familiar white cliffs, topped by smooth downland with a thin chalky foot-path winding up to a summit, gradually faded into a smudge far behind the churned wake of the ship. She had never seen England from the sea until she had left for France at the beginning of the year. The pale coastline dwindling into obscurity against the heaving grey swell gave her a new perspective; it seemed such a small island, vulnerable and isolated in the vast seas which surrounded it. But she knew that it was this very isolation which protected it from invading armies; borders between countries were less easy to agree over and defend than the clear demarcation of coastlines, as the recent fates of France and Belgium testified.

The blurred grey shape ahead clarified into the headland of Cap Gris-Nez, and soon the huddled buildings of Wimereux came into view, the shallow cliffs to the north, and the low hills behind Boulogne, crowded with tents and huts. A thin rain was falling as the ship docked, and Alice huddled into her coat, waiting behind the crowds of disembarking troops. It was nearly midday. Most of the hospitals allowed visitors in the afternoons only, but she wanted to find out where No.13 General was and make sure that Jack was definitely still there, even if she couldn't see him until later in the day.

She found out the location from a pair of Queen Alexandra's nurses. "We're going back there," one of them told her. "If you want to come with us, we'll show you the way."

It was not far to walk from the harbour to the sprawled collection of buildings. Alice's guides directed her to the most likely ward, where another Sister told her that yes, Jack was there and was recovering as well as could be expected.

"But you can't see him yet, I'm afraid. Come back in an hour and a half."

Much relieved to hear that Jack's condition hadn't worsened since the letter had been sent, Alice went back into the town, where she warmed herself in a small restaurant, drinking coffee and eating brioches. Her journey over, she had nothing to do but think of Jack. Since hearing the news about him, she had tried not to think of the worst gas cases she had seen arriving in the convoys, choked, blinded and terrified, coughing up their burnt lungs in clots. Jack couldn't be that bad, she told herself . . . but with luck, he'd be ill enough to be sent home for a convalescent period, out of danger for the time being at any rate.

At last the time came when she could return to the hospital. She found her way back to the ward, where the Sister led the way between the rows of beds and advanced on a sleeping form.

"Wake up – you've got a visitor come to see you!"

Jack raised his head drowsily from the pillow and looked at her, unrecognizing.

"Hello, Jack," she said, approaching the bed.

In spite of her mental preparation, she was taken aback by the bluish pallor of his face and his bloodshot, heavy-lidded eyes; she had half expected to see the sunburnt country boy of three years ago. He seemed to have lost weight, and the pyjama jacket hung loosely on his shoulders as he struggled to raise himself.

"Alice? How did you – " Before he could say any more, he began coughing convulsively, and she stooped to help him into a more comfortable position. "It's all right," he gasped after a few moments, "not nearly so bad as it was – it's only that I've just woken up. You can hug me properly now, only not too hard."

She did so rather gingerly, not wanting to start him coughing again, and he kissed her cheek.

"Oh, Jack! How long have you been here?"

He grinned weakly. "I don't know what day it is, to tell you the truth. Two or three days, I suppose. This is a surprise, though – how did you know where to come?"

"Captain Snell wrote. He thought I might be able to come up from Étaples. Although as it happened I was in London with Lorna when I heard."

"Do they know at home, then?"

"Oh yes. I expect you'll get letters from them in a couple of days. But how are you? Has it been awful? Are there any complications?"

"Well, it hasn't been a cake walk, that's for sure. It could still turn to bronchitis, so they say, but I feel a hell of a lot better than I did when I was brought in. And I've been lucky compared to other blokes – you should have seen some of the poor blighters down at the CCS . . . but you must have seen enough gas cases yourself. What about you? Did you have to cut short your leave, then?"

His voice sounded strained, and he broke off at intervals in fits of harsh coughing. Alice, deciding to take over the talking, told him about her brief stay in London, about the Braithwaites' house, and about Philip Morland's visit.

"He said the stables cottage is empty for you to move in whenever you want to," she finished. "That's nice of him, isn't it? You must be looking forward to seeing Harriet and the baby again. Perhaps you'll be sent on to a London hospital soon, and she'll be able to come and visit you."

She saw the bleak look cross his face.

"Yes, I suppose so," he said, without enthusiasm. "The baby's nearly six months old now, isn't he? He won't know me at this rate."

"Perhaps you'll have a nice long convalescence."

"Yes, perhaps. What are you going to do with the rest of your leave? Will you cut it short and go straight back?"

"No! I shall find somewhere to stay here in Boulogne and come and see you every day."

"That'd be grand," he said, cheering up a little. "These hospitals fair get you down. Never known the time go so slow, even when you're asleep more than you're awake. But it won't be much of a leave for you, though, spending half of it in a hospital."

"I don't mind," Alice said. "I can look at all the bed-pans I don't have to empty . . . Have you read about the Italians' retreat at Caporetto?"

"Yes, I saw a bit about it in the paper."

They talked of war news for a bit, but Jack was already looking wearied by the effort of talking, and soon fell into a doze. A VAD nurse brought tea, and was very helpful when Alice asked if there was a cheap hotel nearby. When she left Jack, promising to come back the next day, Alice exchanged all her English money and booked herself into a small attic room which suited her purse better than the more comfortable hotel Philip had recommended at Folkestone. It had a gas fire, she noted gratefully, looking out of the dormer window at the grey wintry sky.

For the next few days, she fell into a routine of sleeping late, breakfasting at a café in town, writing letters, then walking around the old town or along the coast towards Wimereux, and visiting Jack in the afternoons. On the second day, while Jack was dozing, she cornered the ward sister to ask for details of his condition.

The Sister hesitated, and then her glance fell on the red efficiency stripe on Alice's sleeve. She said, "Well, I expect you've seen gas cases for yourself. According to the card he was very bad when he was first taken to the CCS. But he's past the most dangerous period now. With these lung irritant gases, most deaths occur within the first day – after that they're more than likely to make a full recovery. He's breathing on his own all the time now, without the Haldane mask."

"Is he likely to be sent back to England soon?"

"We might think about it in a few days' time, if he continues improving," the Sister said. "But he keeps waking up with a bad dream – not that he's the only one, of course. Last night he kept shouting out the name Stephen. Is Stephen someone who was with him when he was gassed?"

"I don't know. He's probably dreaming about his friend who was killed six months ago," Alice said. "He was very upset about it."

"Well, see if you can get him to talk about what happened. It often helps them, to get it off their minds, so to speak."

"I'll try," Alice said doubtfully. She remembered Edward's moody silences, and the impossibility of knowing what dreadful memories he was suppressing. Jack, however, told her what had happened in the trenches near Zillebeke as soon as she asked, describing the gas attack and the death of Evernden in a flat, emotionless tone. Alice listened without interrupting, realizing why the incident had brought back vivid memories of Stephen's death. Stephen had been killed by a casual shell, just as Lieutenant Evernden had. Her nursing experience had already shown her that there was no cure for nightmares, and she suspected that Jack would recover from his physical weakness long before his mind would blot out the brutality he had been exposed to.

On the last day of her leave, he told her that he was to be shipped back to London the next week. To her surprise, he seemed dejected at the prospect.

"But you'll be nearer to home, and you'll soon be well enough to go to a convalescent hospital," she told him.

"I know."

"Well, aren't you pleased?"

"It's just that – oh, I don't know – you get so used to Army life that it's hard to think about anything else, especially knowing you'll most likely come back . . . I'd almost rather be back with the blokes. Convalescing – it'll feel like lead-swinging."

Alice laughed. "No-one in their right mind would think so. You obviously won't get past a Medical Board for some time yet. And Ma and Emily will be able to visit, and Harriet can bring the baby to see you . . ."

"I don't know." Jack brought out an envelope from under his pillow and handed Alice one of the pages inside. "I got this today in with a letter from Ma. It's the second letter she's ever written to me. The first one was to tell me she was expecting."

Alice unfolded the sheet of paper and read, "*Dear Jack, sory to hear you are in hospitle, hope you wil be out soon. Harriet.*" She looked at Jack, uncertain of the reaction he expected from her. She said slowly, "Well, it's not exactly . . . affectionate, I suppose, but obviously Harriet hasn't got much of a way with words, not in writing. I'm sure she's looking forward to having you back at home, really."

Their relative situations were ironic, she thought. Jack, even though he had always been devoted to Harriet, had become a husband and father without consciously having planned either development, and was now facing all the difficulties that went with it. She, on the other hand, who would have positively welcomed the chance to bear Edward a child, was left with neither husband nor baby, from which position she rather envied Jack's circumstances. She had had misgivings about his marriage at first, never having thought Harriet good enough for him, but her doubts had been at least partially dispelled when she had seen them together last June, with the new baby. Jack had seemed so delighted with the baby Stephen that she was surprised by his indifference now. It would be difficult to adjust to domestic life, obviously, but then how soon would that be necessary? Three years, four more years of war?

"Anyway, there's not much point in worrying about it now," she said lightly. "It'll probably be all right when you get home. Just concentrate on getting yourself well. Have you heard anything from Jimmy since you've been here?"

Stephen

Jack was beginning to feel bored. Convalescing was all very well, but he was finding time heavy on his hands. The early part of the day was governed by routines like those of an Army camp – you had to get up at a certain time, shave every day whether you needed to or not, and stand to attention by your bed, if you were fit enough, when the Medical Officer came round in the morning. After that, Jack spent the rest of his days in chatting with other patients, strolling round outside on a mild day, helping to take round meals and cups of tea, and looking at the newspapers. This was all right as far as it went, but he'd never had so much time to himself before. He wasn't much of a reader, there were only so many letters to be written, and his eyes were still red and sore, needing to be bathed every day.

Each morning when he woke up, he thought of Jimmy and the others, wondering whether they were behind the lines in a cushy billet, or in some foul cesspit of a front-line trench. He supposed he'd get back eventually, though the cold winter weather affected his breathing, and the pain behind his breastbone reminded him of the damage to his lungs. He was given convalescent clothing, a blue suit worn with a white shirt and red tie; he felt peculiar in it, used to the familiar khaki he had worn for the last three years.

"Course, you can't tell where you'll end up," Robbie Atkison, the man in the next bed, told him. "I was wounded at Thiepval, a nice Blighty, got myself sent home for a couple of months, then when I went back I got sent to a battalion of leftovers scraped together from every regiment you could think of. Had everything in it but the Girl Guides."

Jack realized that his chances of being sent back to his own platoon were remote, even if it still existed in any recognizable form by the time he was fit. The thought depressed him; such stability as he found in the Army was represented by Jimmy and Victoria and Charlie, and Captain Snell. It wouldn't be at all the same with a bunch of strangers.

His mother and Emily came to see him once or twice every week, and Harriet rather less often.

"Here's Mrs Smallwood to see you," the orderly told him the first time she came, and he looked up expecting to see his mother. Instead, Harriet was walking towards his bed – of course, she was Mrs Smallwood now. It made him feel odd, as if he'd grown up suddenly. She looked healthy, round-cheeked, as wholesomely pretty as he remembered her when she had been a kitchen-maid at Greenstocks. Her softly-curling hair was pinned up becomingly beneath a maroon felt hat with a black ribbon. She smiled at him rather coyly, and he heard a wolf-whistle from one of the other patients. He stood up and embraced her, and she kissed him back and giggled and looked round at the ward, readjusting her hat.

Jack fetched her a chair and sat down facing her, feeling as awkward as if she were a stranger.

"Well, how are you then?" she asked.

"I'm getting on well, thanks. Soon be out of here I expect, at a convalescent camp. Didn't you bring Stevie with you?"

"No, my mum's got him. Didn't want to take him with me on the train."

"I'd have liked to see him. Can't you bring him next time?"

Harriet didn't look eager. "He'd probably cry on the train, or mess his nappy. You can come home and see him soon, can't you?"

"I hope so. How is he, anyway?"

"He's fine. Getting quite big now."

Jack tried to picture the boy he remembered as a tiny baby. "Well, what does he do? Sit up? Stand? Talk?"

Harriet looked at him with scornful amusement. "Course he doesn't talk. He's just a baby. It's easy to see you don't know anything about babies."

"Well, I've never had one before, have I?" Jack retorted, disappointed by her reluctance to enlarge. "Haven't you even got a photograph of him to show me?"

"Where would I get a photograph from?"

"Oh, I don't know. Just an idea. But I haven't even seen him since he was born. Who does he look like most, you or me?"

Harriet considered for a moment. "Much more like me, I think."

"Well, that's probably best for him."

She looked at him for a moment and then smiled, evidently deciding that this was a compliment. "I'm going to start work again next week," she told him. "Mum doesn't mind having Stevie at home."

"What, back at Martlets Farm?"

"No, at Greenstocks. I'm going to be a proper Land Girl. Alfie's in the Army now. They've only got old Sedley left, and he's getting stiffer and more grouchy every day. There's already two other girls working there, Doris and Marjorie."

Jack digested this for a few moments. "Are you short of money then?" he asked, concerned. "I thought you wouldn't be too hard up with what I send, especially as you're with your mum and dad."

"It's not just the money. I get fed up with being stuck in with the baby all the time. It'll be fun to meet some other people for a change."

"But are you sure it's all right to leave him? Isn't he too young to be left?"

He heard her sigh faintly in exasperation. "Don't go on at me, Jack. I told you, Mum doesn't mind. I'll be there every morning and every night, for goodness' sake."

Her attention was already slipping away from him; she had turned slightly, so that her chair faced the middle of the ward, and she was watching the comings and goings. Robbie Atkison was returning from a stroll in the grounds, and he looked at Harriet with interest as he approached.

"Is this your wife then, you lucky blighter? Going to do me the honour?"

Jack introduced Harriet, and watched her as she exchanged a few remarks with Atkison. He found himself hoping that next time she'd come with his mother and Emily; it'd make conversation a lot easier.

After tea had been brought round by a Red Cross helper, he suggested a walk outside. Harriet agreed, and he took her arm as they went out into the chilly afternoon. The hospital grounds were not extensive, comprising lawns with benches, some bare cherry trees and evergreen shrubs. A few men in wheelchairs were taking the air, pushed by visiting relatives.

Harriet shivered, took a deep breath and exhaled slowly. "I don't know how you can stand it in there. It'd get me down. I hate illness."

Jack looked at her in amazement. The ward was full of patients who were almost ready to be discharged; as the last stage of his slow journey from the front, the ward was positively cheerful, with a gramophone playing, vases of flowers brought in by visitors, groups of men sitting about chatting or playing cards, and plenty of Red Cross volunteers bringing round urns of tea or distributing the mail. How on earth would Harriet react if she were suddenly to be confronted by a convoy of wounded straight from the aid post – the stench of sweat and filth and blood, the animal groans and cries? This was like a luxury hotel in comparison. But, he thought, he shouldn't be surprised by Harriet's remark. She had seen nothing of the war, knowing only of its effect on the village community. And with her marked lack of curiosity about his experiences, her happily ignorant state was unlikely to change.

He made no reply, and they walked on in silence for a while. He wondered whether she felt as peculiar as he did, supposedly on intimate terms with someone so distant. But Charlie had told him that he had similar problems when he went home on leave: he looked forward to seeing his wife for months on end, and then, when he did see her, could hardly think what to say. It took a good day or two for them to get used to each other again, he had said.

Out in Belgium, stuck in some rain-sodden reserve trench and bored to distraction, Jack had often thought fondly of the evenings he had spent with Harriet in the orchard, remembering the warm grass, the woodsmoke in the air, her hands touching him, stirring him, her body smooth and soft beneath her working clothes. Things would be easier when he got back to the village, he thought. She would be more herself there. And there was Stevie, the baby: the only good thing to come out of the war so far.

As Jack's condition improved, he was encouraged to leave the hospital during the afternoons. It felt strange to have time to spare in London; till now he'd only passed through, on his way to Victoria for the boat train or out to Essex in the opposite direction. On his first outing, he and Robbie Atkison took the tram to Piccadilly. Jack held out his fare to the conductress, and was surprised when she walked straight past.

"No need, dear," she called over her shoulder. "Wounded soldiers don't have to pay."

"That's right. We can go anywhere on public transport for nothing," Atkison confirmed. "Mind you, I reckon you need an arm in a sling or your head bandaged if you really want to do well in London. Look at us – not a scratch between the two of us. My mate who was out on crutches reckons you get free beer, tips, girls, the lot, if you've got part of yourself bandaged up."

It was nearly Christmas, and the cafés and restaurants were already festooned with bunting; in Piccadilly, a brass band played Christmas carols, and women sold flags for the Red Cross. A tattered sheet from a newspaper billboard flapped against Jack's legs, and he bent down to disentangle it and read *Tanks Victorious at Cambrai*. The current headline on the newsvendors' boards was *Civil Strife in Russia*. Well, it was good to know that there was a victory somewhere, for once in a while, Jack thought. But how would the Russian situation affect the war as he knew it? If the Germans were able to remove troops from the Russian front and bring them down to Flanders . . .

"This'll be the fourth Christmas of the war, d'you realize?" Atkison said. "Let's go and have ourselves a drink somewhere, and hope it'll all be over by *next* Christmas."

The next time Jack got a pass to go out, he decided on an impulse to visit Mrs Cartwright in the East End. He still had the letter she had sent him, with the address: 26 Ladysmith Road, Mile End. He took a tram to Mile End station, where he stood on the pavement and looked at the map one of the nurses had sketched for him, assimilating his first impressions of this unfamiliar part of London. Stephen had probably got off the tram at just this spot when he'd returned home on leave, and walked along the drab street Jack was crossing now. The air, thick with the mingled smells of sulphur and coal-dust, clogged Jack's lungs, making him cough. Ladysmith Street was shabby, consisting of rows of terraced houses with doors opening straight on to the pavement of broken flagstones, where litter spilled from overflowing dustbins to be caught by drifting eddies of wind. An elderly woman swathed in a black shawl looked at Jack curiously, and a cat with matted fur opened its mouth in a pink triangle to miaow at him from a windowsill. How could Stephen have lived here? Jack wished he hadn't come; he should have left his memories undisturbed. Stephen should have come from a country village. To Jack, used to Epping Forest and the copses and meadows of Essex, the rows on rows of begrimed narrow streets seemed as claustrophobic as a prison. It was baffling to him that Alice actually wanted to live in this part of London.

He found No.26, and knocked on the door reluctantly, almost hoping no-one would be at home. But he heard movement inside, and then the door opened. The woman who stood inside was younger than his own mother, in her early forties, he judged. Her greying hair was pinned back into a bun, and she wore a black skirt and thick blouse with a flowered apron over the top.

"Mrs Cartwright?"

"Yes?"

"I'm Jack Smallwood . . . Stephen's friend. You wrote to me not long ago . . . you said to call in if I was in London . . ."

The woman's mouth fell open. "You're Jack? Come home from the front?" She stared at him for a few moments as if he were a ghost; then she recovered herself quickly, and opened the door wider. "Oh, I'm sorry – you did give me a start – but what am I doing, keeping you here on the doorstep? Come on in, dear. Are you on leave, then?"

Jack explained as he stepped into the small sitting-room. Mrs Cartwright had been ironing, and a pleasant smell of steam and freshly-washed cotton filled the room.

"Do sit down, Jack. So you've been ill? Do you think you'll get out to France again?"

Jack answered her questions, noticing meanwhile the resemblance to Stephen in his mother's heavy straight hair and widely-spaced eyes beneath a broad forehead. Like her son, Mrs Cartwright had little trace of an East End accent, but there were hints of a rural upbringing in the broadness of her vowels. Jack knew very little of the family background, other than that Stephen's father – like his own – had died young. There was a younger sister, he remembered.

"But you must be tired, coming all the way from the hospital like that, and me not even offering you a cup of tea! Let me get the kettle on – " Mrs Cartwright brushed past him into the kitchen, and he was left sitting in an armchair and looking round the room. It was neat and tidy, with antimacassars over the chair-backs and a faded but well-brushed carpet; there was a pile of folded garments in a basket by the ironing-board. For all the urban squalor of the street outside, Jack was reminded of the cottage he had lived in with his mother and Alice before the war. A few Christmas cards stood on a polished dresser, and a meagre fire burned in the grate, just sufficient to warm the small room. He stood up to look at a row of framed photographs on the mantelpiece. Most were of Stephen: a grinning schoolboy; a new recruit in uniform; another picture identical to the one Jack had; Stephen at the seaside, trousers rolled

104

up, standing ankle-deep in the waves with his arm round the shoulders of a laughing fair-haired girl. Jack recognized her from the photograph Stephen had kept in his pay-book. Even if he had not, he would have assumed from the strong likeness between the two that the girl must be Stephen's sister.

"I'd just enough sugar left to bake some biscuits earlier," Mrs Cartwright said, "so you've called at the right time. I don't take it in my tea and neither does Sarah, but I expect you do? Stephen said most soldiers did to drown the taste of the tea."

Jack nodded, and said, "That's Sarah in the photograph, isn't it?"

"That's right. She's working in munitions down at Woolwich. You must come again, now that you know where to find us. We feel as if we know you already, Stephen used to write so much about you in his letters. Here's your tea, with plenty of sugar. Have a biscuit with it."

"Thank you. That's grand." He sat down and sipped the hot tea, and his gaze returned to the row of photographs, the brief summary of his friend's short life. He thought of Lieutenant McLachlan's random decision to post Stephen, rather than someone else, as sentry in the precise place where a shell was destined to drop. Soldiers were superstitious about such things, the apparently trivial sequence of events which led to someone being in one place rather than another when disaster struck. One man in Jack's section always put on his left boot and puttee before the right and did up his tunic buttons starting at the bottom, sincerely convinced that these procedures could influence the firing of a heavy gun by a

German artilleryman half a mile away. Jack, rather scornful of this sort of meaningless ritual, couldn't help thinking of the chance impulse which had sent him down the trench the night he had been gassed, instead of waiting with Lieutenant Evernden. But then a less kindly Fate had decreed that he should lose his gas mask . . . It didn't pay to think about things too carefully. The German who had fired the shell that had killed Stephen had no idea of the shock waves reverberating back to this East London house, just as Jack's own actions in the front line must have reached back to families in Germany, unknown to him. It was something he preferred not to think about. In the heat of the moment, you concentrated on putting a machine-gun out of action or toppling a sniper from a concealed hide; there was no time to consider the human consequences of your action. You did what you had been trained to do.

Mrs Cartwright ate a biscuit thoughtfully, subdued after her initial chattiness. Jack wanted to talk about Stephen, to bring him back to life, however briefly, but wasn't sure whether it would be tactful to do so. However, after a few moments, she looked up at him and said, "It was true, wasn't it, what you wrote about how he died? I wouldn't like to have a wrong picture in my mind."

Jack assured her that it was, but she wanted him to tell her the whole story over again, enlarging on the details he had given in his letter. By the time he had finished, she had taken a handkerchief from her apron pocket and was dabbing at her eyes.

"I'm sorry, Jack. I hope you didn't mind me asking. It must have been terrible for you as well, seeing him die – but look, I'll show you something more cheerful, if you'll wait here a minute."

She hurried up the stairs, and returned with a sketch book in her hands.

"Did he ever show you any of his drawings?"

Jack frowned. "No – no, I'm sure he didn't. I would have remembered."

Mrs Cartwright turned over the pages of the book lovingly, and then passed it to Jack. "He used to like drawing the horses at the brewery, even before he went to work there. He always loved horses. The recruiting officer told him he could have applied to the Royal Horse Artillery, but he didn't want to – he didn't think it was right to use horses in the war. He never showed me any pictures he'd done while he was out there – perhaps he never did any – but he drew some of these on his last leave."

Jack put the sketchbook on his knees and turned the pages slowly. The sketches had been drawn in thick soft pencil by an untrained hand, but many of them had caught the strength and dignity of the huge Shires, the graceful arch of the neck, the great muscled hindquarters straining. There were close studies of the horses' heads too, with their manes and forelocks plaited and beribboned, each sketch labelled with a name, "Duke" or "Baron" or "Princess". Jack examined each one with intense satisfaction, picturing Stephen leaning over the page, concentrating hard on conjuring the animal's personality in the angle of the ears or the shape of the eye. Here was Stephen as he wanted to remember him, rather than as the shattered form on the stretcher. Not particularly bright, not outstandingly brave or resourceful, not witty or amusing;

just an unassuming, kind-natured boy, rather bewildered by the events he found himself caught up in.

Jack's recollections were interrupted by the turning of a key in the front-door lock and a female voice calling out, "Mum! I'm home!"

The girl who came in wore the brown tunic and trousers of a munitions worker, with her hair tucked up inside a shapeless hat. As she saw Jack sitting in the armchair, she stopped dead just inside the doorway, her gaze fixed on him. He could only stare back; she was so astonishingly like her brother.

Her fleeting expression of delighted bewilderment faded to one of utter weariness. She raised a hand to her eyes and said unsteadily. "I'm sorry. For a moment I thought you were Stephen. He used to sit there just like that."

In The Front Line

"Votes for women at last!" Alice said, putting the newspaper down on the mess table. "It's amazing how little notice anyone's taken. In peace-time it would have been cause for a great celebration."

"It's a start," Lorna agreed, "but we mustn't think of it as the end of the struggle. The vote's only being given to women over thirty, and then only to those who own land or are university graduates, and the wives of voters. Men get the vote at twenty-one – it's still unfair!"

Alice nodded. The Representation of the People Bill would leave her as voteless as before. "But think of the satisfaction it'll give you to vote when you're thirty. And those women who will be able to vote can support other changes in the future."

"I suppose so. But haven't we proved ourselves enough in the war? Is there anything women *haven't* done, short of actually fighting?" Lorna said fiercely.

"It's not me you need to convince. Come on, let's go and have coffee in the Nurses' Club."

It was good to have Lorna back. It was early spring, the days were lengthening, and green daffodil shoots were already spearing the raked earth alongside the mess hut. The mild weather brought Alice bitter memories of the previous spring; it had been on a day like this, nearly a year ago, that Edward had appeared unexpectedly at the ward, and they had spent what proved to be their last brief hours together, before he had had to go back to Arras. She appreciated Lorna's presence; their shared sorrow would make the approaching anniversary of Edward's death more bearable.

"Did I tell you I saw Patrick Leary?" Lorna remarked, settling into an armchair. "You know he's engaged to a girl called Siobhan, who was working as an ambulance driver in London? Well, she's transferred to the motor ambulance convoy here in Étaples. I wonder if we could track her down? It'd be nice to meet her."

"The Irish girl?" Alice remembered the attractive dark-haired girl in the photograph Captain Leary had shown her. "Have you met her before?"

"No, but I've heard a lot about her. Patrick's obviously completely besotted with her. I bumped into him in the Strand last month. She was already out here then – he was due to come back the next day, and was hoping to be able to see her more often now that she's in France."

Alice felt briefly envious of the young couple. "Did you see anything of Captain Aldridge?" she asked.

Lorna's expression changed. "Oh . . . no. I had a couple of letters. He's probably too busy to write much. I saw Philip Morland quite a few more times – you know he's at the War Office now. His operation was a success – he's only got a slight limp now, hardly noticeable. He invited me out to dinner just before I came back."

"Really?"

Lorna looked at her and laughed suddenly. "Alice,

110

don't look like that! He's just become a good friend, that's all. It's been difficult for him, the last year . . . his family really don't have much idea of what he's been through, and they insist on treating him as a wounded hero. But his confidence was badly shaken by what happened – he feels that he let himself down, and the men he was commanding, too."

"He told you all that?" Alice said, amazed.

"I don't think there was anyone else he could talk to," Lorna said slowly, "especially not at home. His uncle's a Lieutenant-Colonel, who comes to dinner and talks about the glorious history of the regiment and the fine fighting spirit of the men, as if nothing had changed since the beginning of the war. And the rest of the family seem to have no more idea than that."

Alice thought of the isolated figure at Victoria Station. "Poor Philip. It must be hard to live up to that."

"Mm. Families can be very difficult . . . What about Jack? Have you heard from him since he got back to his unit?"

"No, just the letter I got to say he'd been passed fit and was coming back. Nothing since," Alice said. "I wish he could have stayed at the convalescent camp for a few more weeks, but I knew he wouldn't stay in England longer than he had to."

It was a tense time, with talk of a major German offensive at any point on the whole front. One day, according to rumour, the attack was expected in the Ypres sector; the next, it was confidently expected that the push would be against the French. There had always been rumours of one kind or another, but these seemed to have more substance than most. The Medical Officers, in their tours of the wards to decide which patients could be sent to England, weren't sending back any officers, commissioned or NCO, who were at all likely to recover; such men were to be kept in hospital until they were fit enough to go to convalescent camp in France and back to their units. One young Corporal in Alice's ward had been discovered weeping under his bedclothes after being give a "Blighty ticket" and then having it taken away again at the last minute.

The last week of March saw convoys arriving in ever-increasing numbers, train after train pulling up in the hospital sidings. Every meal seemed to be interrupted with whistle-blasts and shouts of "Convoy in!", and the distinctions between day and night-shifts became meaningless. The casualties arriving were exhausted and filthy, their eyes glazed from lack of sleep, their wounds only hurriedly dressed or sometimes not even covered.

Alice, one Sister and an orderly were in charge of a whole ward full of newly-arrived wounded. Surrounded by stretchers, heaps of filthy bandages, bloodstained blankets, mud-encrusted discarded boots, and the men who looked up at her so patiently, Alice fought down rising panic – more casualties were still arriving, stretchers being dumped down in any available floor-space . . .

"We haven't even got the supplies to deal with all these. Where shall we start?" She tried to quell the rising note of hysteria in her voice.

Sister Thomas told the orderly, "You'd better go along to the repository and get as much lysol, saline, gauze and bandages as they'll give you. And be as quick as you can – we haven't got enough here to deal with more than a few. Smallwood, you'd better start putting all these soiled bandages and dressings into a bucket."

Alice heard an outraged shout as Sister Thomas yanked a dried-hard dressing off a wound. There was no time for gentleness; the men simply had to be processed like items on a factory production line. And Alice had never seen such despair before. Normally, at least some of the men arriving at the base – the less seriously injured – were pleased to find themselves in hospital, away from the fighting. Now, they were unanimous in speaking as if the war was lost.

"The Germans'll be here in a few days' time," they told her. "Jerry's breaking through and nothing's going to stop him" . . . "Never 'eard anything like their barrage, even after three years in the thick of it. When our guns opened up in reply you couldn't even 'ear 'em against the din" . . . "They'll be at Buckingham Palace this time next week."

Field-grey columns marching down Birdcage Walk – no! It couldn't happen, the bitter losses turning out to be all for nothing, the hundreds of thousands of lives thrown away . . . But the men told of Peronne and Bapaume being retaken; the Germans had swept over the Somme battlefields with derisive ease, striding through Martinpuich, Guillemont, Contalmaison, Beaumont Hamel. The names were familiar from the dreadful summer of 1916, representing ground gained at such enormous cost, yard by desperate yard . . . Alice could have wept, but there was no time to do anything other than work, stripping off dressings, cleaning up wounds, passing the more urgent cases on for surgery, making the men as comfortable as possible, clearing away the debris littering the ward. There was no time to have proper meals, just a quick bite at a sandwich between one patient and the next.

The days passed and still the wounded poured in, talking of positions overrun, disorderly retreats and guns abandoned to the enemy. Alice couldn't understand it.

"Why have the Germans been able to advance so far so easily?" she asked a slightly-wounded gunner who was doing his best to help her with the round of dressings.

He shrugged. "So many of them, so few of us . . . we've run out of reserves, but they seem to have more and more reinforcements. Where I was, near Peronne, they were coming at us in hundreds and we had hardly any ammunition left. I don't know how we got out."

Peronne, by now, was miles behind the German lines. It seemed hopeless – the front line was falling back closer and closer to the coast; the British would be driven into the sea soon, Alice thought. It was rumoured that the Germans were shelling Paris with an enormous heavy gun placed seventy or eighty miles away. It must be only a matter of time before the war was lost. It couldn't be happening . . . the whole British Army in retreat? But it *was* happening. And where was Jack, in all this confusion? Alice's anxiety for him became a gnawing certainty that she would never see him again. Another spring, another loss – the omens were bad.

Very late one evening, Alice returned to her hut to hear a faint snoring inside. Pauline was on night duty, and the hut in darkness; as Alice entered, she tripped over something large and solid on the floor, and crashed into one of the beds. Stumbling to her feet, she lit the candle-lantern and stared in astonishment as she saw that the hut was occupied by two strangers. One nightgowned figure raised its head and blinked at her, while whoever was in Pauline's bed continued to snore.

"Oh, is this your hut?" the girl asked drowsily.

"Well, yes – or at least it was!" Alice saw that what she had fallen over was someone's trunk. "What's happening?"

The other girl yawned hugely. "Sorry. We've been moved up from the Casualty Clearing Station at Dernancourt. The Germans were getting so close, we had to pack up and move out . . . wounded, beds, stores, everything. We went up to Doullens, and then some of us were told to come on here. We were sent to these huts and told to double-up with the VADs using them – one to sleep while the other's on duty. But someone's obviously got that wrong, haven't they? I'd better let you have your bed back." But her voice trailed away as she sank back against the pillow.

"Wait a minute. Did you say Dernancourt? Is that on the far side of Albert?"

"No . . . no . . . this side," the girl mumbled. After a few moments it was clear that she had fallen back into a deep sleep. Alice hesitated, her sense of injustice at being displaced from her own bed fighting with her reluctance to send the exhausted girl out into the

115

night. She wondered briefly whether to go to Matron and make a fuss, or whether to try to find a spare bed in another hut where someone was away on night duty. But it was all too much effort, now. She washed quickly, found her spare blanket, wrapped herself in it and lay down on the floorboards, with her winter coat thrown on top.

She expected to fall asleep straight away, but the hard floor and the cold draught kept her awake. She thought over what the other girl had said. If the Germans were already close to Albert, they would soon be in Amiens, frighteningly close . . . the hospitals might have to be packed up, somehow, and everyone evacuated, an immense move that defied organization . . . maybe she would wake up tomorrow to hear the thud of German boots outside. With the Casualty Clearing Stations falling back, the hospitals themselves were almost in the front line . . .

At last she dozed, but was suddenly wide awake again, her heart pounding. A loud noise, close at hand. She listened, straining her ears, making out the sound of an aircraft overhead. She heard the whine and screaming descent clearly this time, followed by a sickening crash – close, but how close? She scrambled up from her makeshift bed in horror as she realized that it must be *German* planes overhead – they were bombing the hospitals! She grabbed her coat and pulled it on.

"What is it?" The girl in her bed was awake too, sitting up.

"German planes overhead – "

Her words were cut off by the deafening shriek of an explosion, and the boards of the hut seemed to tremble under Alice's feet. She dropped to the floor with a cry of alarm, hands over her ears.

"Gracious, that was close," the other girl said calmly.

"I didn't hear that one drop – " Alice was shaking, pulling on her boots with difficulty. So this was what it was like to be under bombardment – the dreadful silences between explosions, the taut straining of nerves as if your whole body yearned for flight . . . How did the troops bear it, time after time?

"You never do hear the one that gets you." The other girl spoke as if she were quite accustomed to air raids. She stood up, putting on her coat. "Come on, we'd better go and see what's happening."

How could she act so normally? Alice was conscious only of a desire to crawl under the bed and stay there until the danger had passed. The drone of the planes overhead was punctuated by the booming of anti-aircraft guns and the staccato rattle of machine-gun fire. Outside, she expected to see the wooden buildings on fire or smashed to splinters, but to her amazement there was no apparent damage. Someone shouted, "They fell in the village," and then above the din she heard the bugle calling everyone available to the wards. Ashamed of her fear – what about the patients, many of them unable to move? – she hurried to the nearest ward where someone was shouting for help, the other girl running with her. People were screaming and yelling inside; Alice pushed the tent-flaps open and found herself wrestling with a man desperate to get out. He threw her to the ground, shouting something about a dug-out. She struggled up, getting entangled in the canvas flaps, while an

117

orderly and a Sister dragged the man back to his bed. He continued to kick and shout, and the Sister called to Alice, "Are you all right?"

Alice nodded, and the Sister continued, "Come over here and restrain this man while I do something for the others."

"All right, all right, mate, it's all over now. They won't be coming back," the orderly was saying, again and again. Alice didn't think the man could hear. His eyes were tightly closed, he was drenched with sweat and his limbs twitched convulsively. Alice pressed his arm and shoulder firmly to the bed, her own terror sharpening as she saw the effects of the bombing on these shell-shocked men.

"There's a few of them going berserk, setting each other off," the orderly told her in an aside. "It's the last straw for some of them. All right, mate, all right," he continued to soothe. "They won't be coming back, it's all finished . . ."

But the planes *were* coming back – Alice could hear the stutter of the engine as she strained her ears to hear above the shouting and the anti-aircraft fire. She heard the plane circling low, heard the tearing whine, and then the shock wave of the explosion rocked the tent, the walls billowing inwards with the blast of hot air. Screams and yells sounded from close by. In the renewed pandemonium in the ward, there was no chance of rushing out to see what had been hit, but she knew, this time, that it must have been one of the wards.

The urgent need to calm the renewed hysteria in the ward had the effect of helping her to control her own fear. There was nothing to do but to copy the girl who had come in with her, assuming a calmness she didn't feel, moving among the beds with deliberate slowness as though nothing out of the ordinary had happened. One of the men sat huddled on his bed, his shoulders heaving, looking through her as she approached. "It's all right – they're going away now," she told him, trying to persuade him to get back into his bed. It was true this time – the planes *were* going, the roar fading to a distant hum, the night unnaturally quiet in the aftermath of the raid. At last the man climbed into bed and lay huddled there, and another patient said, "I'll stay with him now, miss."

"Some of these men will need sedating," the Sister told her, "but I've got nothing left. Go outside and see if you can get an MO to come in, will you?"

Alice pushed through the tent flaps and hurried along the line of huts, the smells of burning and high explosive acrid in her nostrils. She caught her breath as she saw figures moving about in the haze from the most recent explosion, carrying stretchers or armfuls of bedding, or lifting smashed pieces of timber away from a ruined hut. Pauline's ward! A jagged hole had been blasted in one side, and part of the roof was open to the sky – through the splintered boards Alice could see distorted iron bedsteads and split mattresses with the stuffing spilling out, and churned earth thrown upwards through the smashed boards of the floor. The last dazed victims were being evacuated, carried on stretchers or stumbling out led by nurses and orderlies – but surely they couldn't all have survived such a blast? Alice looked around wildly, her eye lighting on three shrouded figures lying neatly in a row on the ground, blankets pulled right up to hide the faces . . . patients, or nurses? One of them could be Pauline –

But while her jolted brain was still registering the possibility, she saw Pauline being led out of the ward, her face blood-spattered. Pauline detached herself from the orderly and walked shakily towards Alice. Tears ran down her face, mingling with blood from a long gash, and she was shivering uncontrollably as she blurted out, "Sister's dead – killed outright – and two patients . . . Sister Robertson, dead," she repeated, staring at Alice as if she expected her to deny it.

"She's badly shocked, miss," said the orderly, a haggard-faced man who looked as if he should be having treatment for shock himself. "Come along now, miss," he said to Pauline more loudly. "We must get that cut treated, and get you wrapped up warm."

Alice remembered that she was supposed to be finding a Medical Officer. She told Pauline that she would come and find her later, and resumed her search, at last tracking down an MO and returning with him to the tented ward only to find that sedatives had already been procured from somewhere else, and that all was relatively calm. The girl who had been in her bed – their conversation seemed to have taken place days ago – was still there, and she left with Alice to see what help was required at the bombed ward. The bodies had already been taken to the mortuary, and people were beginning to disperse. A weary MO stood in the wreckage, looking hopelessly around at the debris.

"We've done as much as we can for the time being. The rest of the clearing-up can wait till the morning," he told the two young women. "I suggest you get some sleep. We can't have the entire nursing staff up all night. It'll be duty as usual tomorrow."

Alice found out that Pauline had had her cut face treated and had been taken to the nurses' sick-bay to spend the night, so she and the other girl returned to the hut in the first glimmer of dawn light. They both stared incredulously as Alice pushed the door open.

"Well, would you believe that!"

The girl who had been asleep in Pauline's bed was still there, still snoring peacefully, apparently having slept through the entire raid.

They looked at each other and grinned suddenly, stifling giggles. After all that had happened that night, Alice was amazed to find that there could still be something to laugh about, however crazily.

"Well, it must be your turn for the bed," the other girl said, throwing off her coat. "I don't mind having the floor. I don't think a bed of nails would keep me awake tonight."

The air-raid had claimed eight victims in all, it was confirmed next day; one of the bombs dropped on the road near the village had struck an ambulance, killing the driver and all four passengers. And engineers were currently labouring to rebuild the railway bridge over the Canche, which had been smashed, severing the rail link to the south. The hospital staff listened, subdued, as procedures for future air-raids were explained. *One* raid, Alice thought, could be got through somehow – but to lie in bed night after night listening for the sinister drone of enemy aircraft, prepared at any moment to rush outside to face God only knew what horrors, or to hear the shriek of a bomb plunging through the roof of whatever hut you happened to be in – how long could ordinary human beings tolerate such strain, she wondered?

"We'll be wearing helmets and digging ourselves into trenches at this rate," someone remarked cynically as the assembled staff left the meeting.

A special burial service was held for the Sister and two patients who had died in the raid, and Alice went down to the cemetery with Lorna and Pauline. Pauline still had one side of her face bandaged – the cut had been stitched and was likely to leave a permanent scar. Alice thought regretfully of her friend's previously unblemished good looks. Well, she had been wounded in action as honourably as any soldier; if decorations for valour were awarded to nurses and doctors and orderlies, the authorities would have to dole them out in handfuls for last night's efforts. Work in the theatre, where Lorna had been assisting a surgeon who had operated for more than twenty-four hours without a break, had continued without a pause throughout the raid. With all the purposeful activity around her, Alice felt that she had done little more than dither hopelessly, of little use to anyone, but was uncomfortably aware that she was likely to have ample opportunity to put this to rights within the next few weeks.

The cemetery seemed larger each time Alice saw it, rows upon rows of stark crosses sweeping down from the road towards the sand-dunes of the estuary. Trees and scrub were gradually being cleared from the edges to make new graves, and it was here that fresh sandy soil had been dug for today's burials. It was a calm day, the light slanting through a gap in the clouds

122

to illuminate a strip of sea on the horizon. Clumps of early violets grew among grass and pine needles at the edge of the wood, and the fresh green of the larches was beginning to show along the dark knobbly twigs. Alice thought of her surprise on first arriving in France to discover that the trees and wild flowers and birds were much the same as in England. She couldn't remember now what she had expected in her ignorance, as if France were the other side of the world instead of merely separated from England by a narrow strip of sea – great exotic orchids? palm trees? flocks of tropical birds? She brought her attention painfully back to the words of the burial service. It was all too familiar; Alice, like all the nurses, had become a professional mourner at the funerals of soldiers who had died alone in hospital, far from their relatives and comrades-in-arms.

Pauline was crying; she had worked with Sister Robertson since being posted to France eighteen months ago. Alice had known none of the victims, but she thought of the dead patients, men who had survived injury and the comfortless journey back to the base only to die so violently. An Army chaplain read the funeral service, the drone of his voice echoing meaninglessly in Alice's ears. She had been a regular churchgoer before the war, like most people in her village, but she had been influenced by Edward's cynicism; he had seen the soothing words of ministers as, at best, a panacea, giving the illusion of comfort where none existed, at worst a weapon to justify the unjustifiable . . . pulpit progaganda, he had called it. The service was nearly at an end, the shrouded figures lowered into the graves, the earth showering in on top.

And now the bugler was blowing the haunting notes of the Last Post, which more than any wordy ritual had the power to move her to tears.

She turned away from the group by the gravesides. Fresh earth on the opposite side of the cemetery, and bundles of spring flowers, showed where another burial had taken place that morning. A figure stood by the new crosses gazing out to sea, khaki uniform dark against the pale sand of the dunes beyond. The mourners began to drift away, back to the hospital. The solitary officer was walking back too, and Alice saw him snatch a handkerchief from his pocket and rub his eyes angrily. Finding himself about to converge on the group from the hospital, he veered away, not looking up, and walked off quickly in a different direction. Alice noticed that Lorna was gazing after him, her face suddenly pale.

"What's the matter?" Alice asked.

Lorna didn't answer for a moment, then spoke so quietly that Alice could hardly hear her reply. "That's Patrick Leary."

"Oh – " Alice stopped walking and stared at her as she realized the significance of this. "Oh, Lorna, you mean – "

Lorna nodded. "The ambulance driver who was killed. It must have been his fiancée."

Spring Tide

The Flanders countryside was alive with the renewal of spring. There were fresh leaf-shoots in the beet fields, and the squat Belgian cattle, which Jack thought looked more like pigs, roamed in the greening fields. It was very different from the shell-swept, uniformly mud-coloured landscape Jack associated with Flanders, but the rustic peacefulness was deceptive; at every turn in the road he expected to see the field-grey of German uniform sweeping towards him in serried ranks. The news seemed darker at each stage of the journey. The Germans had retaken Armentières, and had swept on to capture Bailleul and the Kemmel Ridge. The celebrated *Mademoiselle from Armenteers* would be dispensing her special brand of comfort to German troops now, Jack supposed, rather than to the British who had sung her praises for so long . . . The realities of the situation were too dreadful to contemplate: the trampled corpse-strewn acres, held through all the bitter months, falling to the enemy within a matter of days. He was shocked to realize that the Allies seemed about to lose the war. After so many months of stalemate, it seemed impossible that the war could ever be won by either side.

Reporting to the Railway Transport Officer at Boulogne the day before, he had been sent on to join a depleted battalion near Hazebrouck. To his annoyance, his companion for the journey was a man he had met before and disliked intensely: Frank Whitfield, a Regular Army Corporal who had served briefly with Jack's company in the Third Epping Foresters back in 1916. With them went a draft of newly-trained privates, and Jack wondered what they could expect to find at the front, if indeed there was still anything resembling a front.

The unit the newcomers were posted to was billeted in a farm on the outskirts of the town. As he had suspected, it consisted of survivors salvaged from the ruins of battalions overrun in the recent fighting; most of the men were exhausted, and were being kept in reserve to rest and await reinforcements before struggling back to stem the flow of the German advance. Jack had no idea what had happened to his old company. Jimmy had written to him back in February, but anything could have happened to them since – they might all be dead, or be German prisoners by now. He couldn't think about it.

He and Whitfield were put in charge of sections in a platoon commanded by a Lieutenant Rupert Drummond-Lacy. Jack, who had formed certain preconceptions on hearing the name, was pleasantly surprised to find Drummond-Lacy eminently likeable. In his early thirties, he was a barrister in civilian life, a very tall man with an air of being mildly entertained by whatever happened around him. Whenever not actively engaged on duty, he could be seen sitting under a tree or in a corner of a barn engrossed in a red-bound book he always carried with him.

He continued reading even when a German Fokker flying low overhead was engaged in aerial combat with a pair of Camels, and every other man within earshot stood craning his neck up at the sky until the Fokker was harried off.

"Poems, I'll bet. He looks the type," Whitfield remarked caustically, as if such choice of reading matter were diagnostic of moral weakness.

"What if it is?"

"He's a four-letter-man if ever I saw one," Whitfield said.

Jack guessed that he meant homosexual rather than merely unpleasant. "Why d'you say that?"

The other man grunted. "Tell it a mile off."

Jack dismissed this as maliciousness – Whitfield had always been the type of bloke who enjoyed spreading gossip. Drummond-Lacy was slender in build, with a thin bony face, long tapering fingers and slim wrists and ankles. This slight femininity of appearance, coupled with a tendency to make flamboyant gestures when talking, was anathema to Whitfield, who was of the bluff, seen-it-all-before-when-you-was-wet-behind-the-ears Regular Army type. Later, reporting to the Lieutenant as orderly corporal, Jack found him sitting by a ditch with his book, and read over his shoulder: "*The purple sandpiper (calidris maritima) frequents rocky coasts and shores. Its dark plumage and plump build distinguish it from other members of the sandpiper family.*" Well, it took all sorts. Some blokes played Crown and Anchor to take their minds off things, or got drunk. Drummond-Lacy read a bird book.

"It's a bird book," he told Whitfield with quiet

triumph when he returned to the store to allocate the rations. "Not poems."

Whitfield shrugged. "Makes no odds to me."

"He did all right down at Estaires, when the Germans took it," said Jack, who had been talking to some of the survivors. "A lot of the blokes panicked and were ready to surrender, either that or run out in the open where they would've been shot down. He got them in order and managed to lead most of them out of it."

"Told you that himself, did he?" Whitfield said.

Jack, lifting tins of bully beef out of a packing case, chose not to continue the conversation further.

Compared with the men around him who had been deprived of sleep and food for days on end and were now virtually comatose, Jack felt almost ashamed of his own conspicuously fresh condition. He had made a good recovery from his illness, and the weeks in convalescent camp doing press-ups and physical jerks and night manoeuvres had left him feeling as fit as ever. With most of the battalion resting, he had little to do beyond allocating rations and helping the platoon Sergeant to drill the newcomers into shape; the most difficult problem he had to face, for the time being, was cutting a ration loaf into eight equal pieces. With no particular friends in the ranks, he spent much of his spare time talking to Drummond-Lacy, who was temporarily the only officer and seemed glad of the company.

To Jack, whose knowledge of the war was derived from his own immediate experience, whatever rumours were being bandied about at the time and the

128

occasional flick through a newspaper, the other man seemed remarkably well-informed about the overall situation.

"The German generals have handled this advance cleverly," he told Jack, "driving a wedge between the British and French armies. They know that when it comes to a crisis the French will fall back to defend Paris, whereas the British Army's main concern is to hold the Channel ports. But now that Foch has become commander-in-chief, we might be able to get together a better resistance – if there are enough troops left in England to replace those we've lost in the last month."

"But surely we can't hold out, can we, sir?"

"It's hard to say from where we're sitting. The appointment of Foch may have come too late for any large-scale co-ordination of resistance." He could have been discussing the possible outcome of a cricket match, Jack thought, impressed by his detachment.

The fact that Drummond-Lacy had taken a liking to Jack gave Whitfield further ammunition for insults.

"I'd be careful if I were you, all these cosy chats. Don't turn your back on him," he remarked when Jack went back to the outhouse they shared. He accompanied his words with a graphic gesture which made his meaning unmistakable.

"Oh, for God's sake – " Jack found the repeated taunts irritating beyond endurance. "Haven't you got anything else to think about? You've got him all wrong anyway."

"Well, you would stick up for him, wouldn't you?" Whitfield persisted.

Jack felt his anger rising. The only time Whitfield showed any sign of animation was when he had his knife in someone. His face was creased into a knowing leer, his mouth sneering beneath the clipped black moustache, showing teeth discoloured by tobacco.

"What do you mean by that?" Jack demanded.

Whitfield laughed unpleasantly. "Well, it's obvious, ain't it – remembering how pally you used to be with that fair-haired lad . . ."

"You filthy-minded bastard – "

Jack stepped closer, and Whitfield laughed in his face. "That hit home, didn't it, eh?"

"That's my best mate you're talking about," Jack said through gritted teeth, "and he's dead now. I've had enough of your mouth."

"Oh yes? What're you going to do about it, eh?" Whitfield jeered.

Before Jack knew it they were grappling fiercely. Whitfield was still laughing contemptuously as Jack seized his arms and tried to push him against the wall. But Whitfield was the heavier and stronger of the two; he brought his knee up with a sharp jerk and twisted himself free as Jack doubled over in pain. Jack rushed at him again, his anger fired by that mocking grin. Locked together, they overbalanced and crashed against the wall of the outhouse in a clatter of pitchforks and shovels, falling heavily against a rusted chaff-cutting machine. Whitfield gave a grunt as he fell, but he rolled over first and sat up, pinning Jack down.

"Your best mate, eh? Well, there's another name for that – "

Jack, savage with indignation, wrenched his right arm free and swung it wildly, clobbering the side of Whitfield's face with all his strength. Whitfield bent forward, stunned by the impact, raising a hand to his face as Jack struggled to extricate himself from underneath him. Suddenly aware of a pair of legs standing in the doorway, Jack froze, mouth open, and stared up into the appalled face of Drummond-Lacy. There was a brief, startled pause.

"What the hell's going on here? Get to your feet, the pair of you," the lieutenant ordered.

Jack scrambled up, brushing bits of chaff and spider's web from his tunic, acutely aware of the ridiculousness of the situation, while his grievance still rankled. Whitfield got up more slowly, panting, and Jack saw with satisfaction that there was blood streaming from his nose. But Drummond-Lacy was looking far from amused.

"Good God." He eyed them both with distaste. "What on earth do you think you're doing, scrapping like schoolboys? What's this all about?"

Jack said nothing, feeling that he couldn't begin to explain to the lieutenant, of all people. Drummond-Lacy's glance passed impatiently on to Whitfield, who was stemming the flow of blood from his nose with a khaki handkerchief. "Well? I asked a question. Whitfield, what were you fighting about?"

"Just a bit of a disagreement, sir," Whitfield mumbled indistinctly.

"A *disagreement* – good God! You're both NCOs, for goodness' sake, you're supposed to be setting an example to the new troops – an *example*, God help us – just look at you!" His gaze swept up and down the dishevelled pair in bafflement. "You'd better be thankful we're in this dire mess, with the Germans just over the hill – in normal circumstances you'd be reporting to your Commanding Officer in the morning, and you'd certainly lose your stripes for this, both of you. As it is – well, report to me when you've cleaned yourselves up."

He turned abruptly on his heel and marched away, stiffly correct. Whitfield didn't look at Jack; he bent to pick up his cap and walked out without a word, still holding the bloodstained handkerchief to his nose. Well, he'd deserved that, the bastard, Jack thought, not sorry at all; he was concerned only that he'd let himself down badly in front of an officer he liked.

Later that night when he settled down to sleep on a pile of sacks in a barn – having pointedly removed himself from Whitfield's vicinity – the fight replayed itself in his mind. He realized that the intensity of his anger had sprung from the partial truth of Whitfield's words. Close friendships were common enough between soldiers – between officers, too. "I don't know why you two don't get married" was a joke frequently made to an inseparable pair, said quite without malice. But there had been a time, during the reprieve from the Somme fighting, when Jack had been anxious about his feelings for Stephen. Soon afterwards, when he'd been home on leave, Harriet had made her intentions obvious, and his enthusiastic response had convinced him that he had nothing to worry about; but he recognized now that he had loved Stephen, had been closer to him than he would ever be to Harriet, and that Stephen in return had loved him more than Harriet ever would. Whitfield would never understand something like that, he thought, pounding his greatcoat into a more comfortable hollow for his head. Whitfield had the sort of mind that reduced everything to coarseness. Jack turned over restlessly, fully awake now. Every time he closed his eyes he saw Whitfield's face grinning at him.

Two days later, standing on parade in an orchard loud with birdsong, Jack listened to the words of the newly-arrived Colonel. The speech was delivered in a bracing tone, intended to stiffen up the troops about to move to the front. Their rest was over. They had been fattened for the kill.

"You will face all manner of challenges as we move forward. The German advance is continuing, and I must remind you of the words of Sir Douglas Haig, in the special Order of the Day for April the twelfth. *'There is no course open to us but to fight it out. Every position must be held to the last man: there must be no retirement. With our backs to the wall and believing in the justice of our cause, each one of us must fight to the end.'* Brave words, bravely spoken; the British Army has responded magnificently. But in spite of all our endeavours over the last few weeks, we *still* have our backs to the wall as the German advance continues. I believe we can stem that tide, and I know that I can rely on every man of you to do his best in the next few days."

Many of the men the Colonel faced were seasoned troops who had been beaten back from Meteren and Bailleul and Estaires. Jack wondered what fighting spirit they could possibly have left; backs to the wall again, as if it had ever been any different.

The Colonel dismissed the parade, and the men prepared for the march. Drummond-Lacy would be leading the company, having been appointed Captain. He had told Jack that he didn't want the promotion and knew that it had little to do with merit; it was simply that no-one else was available. They passed through the outskirts of the town and marched along a dusty tree-lined road. Occasionally, serving as a reminder of how close the German artillery was, one of the treetops had been lopped off by shellfire. A group of peasants came along the road pushing a handcart with furniture and belongings stacked in it, topped by a cage full of cackling hens, and two children prodded sticks at an unconcerned cow which ambled slowly along. And all the while, walking wounded and ambulances were going back towards Hazebrouck.

"Good luck, mates," some of the retiring troops called out, and "Jerry's over the next ridge. He'll be here in time for breakfast."

What would it be like if the Germans did break through, Jack wondered? Most of the troops – himself included – were so used to trench warfare that the notion of fighting in the open was new to them. It would be a different kind of game altogether, he thought, recalling manoeuvres practised at training camp. But then they had been rehearsing British advances and breakthroughs. Here, they would be on the receiving end. The pale sun broke through thin patchy cloud, and Jack wondered whether he would still be alive to see it set in the evening.

By late afternoon, they reached a small village deserted by civilians and with enough brickstacks and piles of rubble to provide cover. But this was not to be the end of the day's march; Jack heard the Colonel, who had ridden up on his horse, giving further orders to Drummond-Lacy.

"The division on your right have got their flanks in the air. You must bridge the gap at all costs. Get forward to the line of trees on that ridge. There won't be any artillery support, I'm afraid: we can't get the guns up in time."

"Yes, sir."

At all costs – well, Jack could see what that was likely to mean. If there had been a temporary gap in the line, the reinforcing troops could easily move on forward only to find that the Germans had got round behind them; they could end up encircled and cut off. But Drummond-Lacy was getting the situation under control, looking at the slight slope ahead through field-glasses, getting machine-gun teams organized to give covering fire. For all his detachment in quiet moments, there was nothing hesitant about him now. He was scanning the ground, assessing the degree of cover afforded by the gradient.

"Hatherleigh, take your section up there to the right, using the cover of that ditch. Smallwood, straight ahead here to the right of the track. Whitfield, on the other side of the track, and the Sergeant and I will be on your left aiming for that clump up there. Watkins and Woodhouse, keep your sections down here in case Jerry works his way round our flank."

All was quiet ahead – too quiet, Jack thought, creeping through the grass of the meadow. Pity it

135

wasn't a month later – the grasses would have been longer then, giving better cover . . . Dandelions tickled his nose, and he stifled a sneeze. Surely the Germans would have taken advantage of the gap and moved forward to the line of trees? His eyes were trained on the saplings ahead, alert for any sign of movement. He could hear the soft tread of the men behind him . . . boys of eighteen and nineteen, most of them, from the new draft, about to see action for the first time . . . There was something huddled in the grass in front of him, and he heard the boy behind him catch his breath as he saw that it was a dead German, shot through the head, blood congealing over the side of the face and flies already gathering – the division to the right must have been able to enfilade the advancing enemy troops as they came through the gap, but that meant there would be others . . . A shot rang out behind him, and a swiftly muffled shout. Grenades exploding in the brickstacks; he glanced back over his shoulder and saw the plumes of red dust. There must be Germans down in the village, hiding in the ruins – not too many, he hoped, or they really would be surrounded. But if Jerry had got down to the village, he certainly had the ridge as well, Jack thought, concentrating on his task. A sudden flash in the trees ahead, something catching the light – the enemy had the disadvantage that any movement on the ridge was visible in silhouette agains the skyline.

"Get down!" Jack whispered hoarsely to the men behind him, pressing himself face down in the grass just in time as a machine-gun rattled out from the ridge

136

ahead. He heard bullets singing harmlessly overhead; the curve of the ground was enough to give them cover, provided they kept low . . . the machine-gun was traversing from left to right, and Jack heard a shriek as someone in Lieutenant Hatherleigh's party went down. From the shots and yells behind him, he guessed that there was hand-to-hand fighting in the village. He raised his head cautiously and looked along the ridge. The flare of light betrayed the position of the machine-gun – just one, he thought, although there could easily be snipers hidden up there as well. A slight indentation in the ground ahead would give him the chance to creep up closer.

He wriggled round to face the lads behind. "We'll creep up that small gully and see if we can put that machine-gun post out of action," he told them. The faces looked at him, some frightened, some excited; the boy nearest him, Jones, had bitten his lower lip until it bled. Jack felt horribly responsible as he led them slowly up towards the ridge; they had no idea what to expect, depending on him for guidance. The ground flattened out towards the summit, and he didn't dare go on – the machine-gunner would pick them off at close range – but they were near enough to throw bombs. He called four of the others to come up close to him, and told them what he intended to do.

"See that holly bush along there, and that dead branch sticking out like a letter V? They're just in the middle there, behind that mound. Got the Mills bombs, Sanders? Jones and Partington, give covering fire . . . And don't show too much of yourself when you throw, or he'll have you – look out for snipers – Ready!"

He pulled the pin out of his own bomb and threw it. The other four followed suit, throwing most of the bombs wide in their excitement. Jack ducked, listening for the explosions. The machine-gun was still traversing – and the gunners knew where they were now . . . a couple of potato masher grenades came over, falling well behind them . . . Jack turned himself into the ground to avoid the blast. Earth showered down on his back, and he heard a quickly-stifled cry of alarm from one of the others . . . but he was only frightened, not hit. Now they must move fast. If they didn't get the gunners this time, there'd be more of those coming over, and they'd eventually find their mark.

"And again! Aim carefully . . ."

Again the bombs hurtling through the air, the series of explosions, and this time there were yells and screams, and the machine-gun was silent. Sanders collapsed to the ground beside Jack, wincing in pain and clutching his arm.

"Sniper – to the left of the machine-gun . . ."

"All right," Jack said. "Keep your heads *down*, unless you want to stay here with friend Jerry back there," he snapped at Jones and his friend, who were elated by the success of the bombing and were craning their necks to see what had happened.

He took off his helmet and carefully raised it above the edge of the hollow he was lying in. Within seconds, the helmet was spinning crazily, ringing with the impact of the sniper's bullet, the reverberations reaching down to Jack's arm. But someone else had seen the movement; a shot rang out across the field, followed by the crack of branches giving way under the sniper's weight as he fell.

"Come on. But slowly. And if anything happens, get back to this hollow."

He crept forward, ears and eyes straining, half-expecting the hammer-blow of a sniper's bullet. He had no idea what to expect when he got to the ridge; there could be massed divisions of German infantry for all he knew, heavy guns aimed and ready to let rip. The grass at the top of the slope was thin, riddled with rabbit-holes – a good place to bring ferrets, Jack thought irrelevantly. He was almost at the trees now, Lieutenant Hatherleigh bringing his men up on the right. He risked a look over into the fields beyond. No Germans, no guns – scattered farm buildings, a few dishevelled barbed-wire entanglements, the remains of an ammunition dump, an observation balloon a good way back, and apart from that just a quiet sun-warmed meadow with dandelions flaring in the grass, and larks singing above. It was impossible.

Drummond-Lacy had brought his men up to complete the line. "Well done. Well done. Only a few casualties, mostly back in the brickyard." He lay down flat among the rabbit-holes and scanned the valley with his binoculars. "I think Jerry must have dug in behind those buildings and along the line of that farm track. But we've got a good position here, if we can hold it. It looks as if they've outrun their support. That's a good sign."

Jack had had himself perfectly under control during the advance up the field, his responsibility for the younger men leaving no room for fear. Now, the immediate danger over, his throat was dry and his head ached. He looked at the remains of the German machine-gunners, sprawled bodies, a trickle of blood in the dust, a hand clawing at tree roots. He felt sickened, weary. *Thou shalt not kill*, he thought, until it was wartime, and then *Thou shalt kill*. One of the dead Germans lay with a pale face turned up to the sky; he had sandy eyebrows and lashes, and blue eyes staring. Jack felt as if he were looking at someone he had known. But there was no time for thinking; there was Sanders' wounded arm to be seen to, and hours of work after that: digging in, consolidating the new line. Drummond-Lacy was already sending a runner back to the Colonel, bringing the Lewis gun teams up, showing the officers and NCOs where the wire should be placed. When darkness fell they'd go out and get the German machine-gun and turn it round so that it faced down into the valley. And the dead Germans would have to be buried. Supply lorries would already be coming up to the village, Jack thought, with sandbags and trench stores, and food and water for the men. They would dig in and wait for further orders, or for the next bombardment, when the Germans inevitably brought up troops and artillery.

He was sent back down the field with Jones and Partington to bury the dead German they had passed on the way up, a task he loathed. But, in spite of his tiredness, he felt more optimistic about the day's events than he had thought possible that morning. He was alive and unscathed, and he had brought his section through with only Sanders wounded. And

140

from what he had seen – even though, admittedly, it was only a tiny sector of one part of the front – it looked as if the German advance may have reached its limit. They must be as stretched as we are, he thought; they can't have unlimited reserves. Perhaps, like an abnormally high spring tide, the advance would soon be on the ebb.

Home

Alice looked at the letter curiously. The envelope was addressed in a hand she didn't recognize, and it had an Epping postmark. Opening it, she looked at the signature first and found that it was from her brother-in-law, Emily's husband Tom. He had never written to her before, and something must be amiss for him to write now, she thought, turning to the beginning of the letter.

"*Dear Alice,*" she read. "*I am very sorry but I will have to ask if you can possibly come home. I know you are doing important work out there but there is no-one else I can turn to. Your mother is very sick and so is Emily and now Mary going down with it as well after she was nursing them at first, they all have influenzer. They really need some one to look after them and you will see I cannot stay away from the farm just now with it being harvest time. Dr Sidgwick is very worried about your mother what with her weak heart and now he thinks this could turn to newmonia, so you will understand why I have to ask you, it was Emily's idea. Hope you will write to let me know you are coming, we had a letter from Jack yesterday and he is all right, Yours sincerley Tom.*"

"Well, you're due for your six-monthly leave," Lorna said when Alice showed her the letter. "Of course you must go. You'll only worry about your mother if you stay here."

142

"But a week won't be long enough, will it, not if she's that ill?"

"Go and see Matron," Lorna said. "She might be able to help you to get a long leave. You do have a good reason, after all."

But the Matron, although sympathetic, did not think an application for extended leave would be successful. "Not with this push still on, I'm afraid. The only alternative is for you to break your contract. You do have the excuse of a crisis at home, so I imagine you'll be given clearance."

Alice had no choice but to apply. She was glad that the series of air-raids seemed to have come to an end; otherwise she was sure others would think she was inventing a crisis to get herself out of danger.

Another farewell, another departure – but this time it was Lorna who stood waving by the hospital entrance, and Alice who was driven off by a helpful RAMC man to catch the train at Étaples. She looked out of the window at the familiar coastline with a sense of nostalgia. The sunlight glinted off the sea so strongly that it hurt her eyes to look at it. Swallows were swooping down to the mud flats by the side of the river; the dunes beyond were afire with the brilliant yellow of flowering gorse. She wondered whether she would ever come back. Now that she had left, she would have to do a spell in a London hospital before re-applying for foreign service. VADs who broke their contracts were not looked upon favourably.

A column of troops marched away from the station, singing loudly, sleeves rolled up, tunics unbuttoned. Alice knew they were Americans – no British commanding officer would have allowed his men to march in such an informal way. The American troops were noticeable for their size and fitness, their strange drawling accents and – most striking of all – their air of happiness, as if the war was a splendid party they had been invited to. But their arrival in France had made all the difference to general morale.

"Doughboys," the driver said. "Think they've come to win the war for us."

Walking the last half-mile to the village, Alice had a sense of stepping back in time. Ahead of her was the church in its huddle of yew trees, the weatherboarded cottages straggling away from it along the twisty lane. The wheat had already been cut in the fields by the river, but the banks were luxuriant with meadowsweet and the purple spires of willowherb. She paused on the stone bridge and looked down at the plumy blue-grey of the willows by the trampled place where the cattle came down to drink. It was a still evening, the silence broken only by the throaty cooing of woodpigeons in the elms.

She had stood here with Edward, the day he had asked her to marry him. She remembered it so clearly that she almost expected to turn round and see him standing beside her, tall and immaculate in his officer's uniform, his face set and anxious as he frowned down at the river before asking the question which had so surprised her. She hadn't agreed immediately, had kept him waiting, not through indifference but because she hadn't wanted him to make a rash decision . . . incredibly foolish, it seemed now, to have wasted a single second of their time together. They could have been married immediately . . . losing a husband rather than a fiancé couldn't have made her loss any harder to bear. She picked up her bag and walked on, leaving Edward's ghost behind.

"Dr Sidgwick thinks Emily should be over the worst within a day or two," Tom told her when she arrived at the cottage. He had been working on the harvest at Dairygrounds Farm, and seed-husks clung to his white shirt and his eyebrows and hair. "But it's your mum we're most worried about. He thinks it's a new strain, this influenza, worse than he's seen before – brought back from London, he says. Ten or more people in the village have gone down with it, and some of the mothers are keeping the nippers indoors so they don't catch it. But with our Sammy, we reckon he's better off at school than here."

Alice dumped her bag and went upstairs to see the invalids. Her mother was asleep in the small back bedroom; not wanting to wake her, Alice went into Tom and Emily's room. Emily was awake, but had a high temperature and a sore throat, and said that she ached all over.

"Isn't there any treatment for it?" Alice asked.

"Not really. Dr Sidgwick left some medicine, but I don't think it does much good. All we can do is rest and drink lots of water. It's Ma who's got it worst. She's got a high fever and she's delirious with it a lot of the time. The doctor says the next few days will tell." Emily propped herself up and dabbed at her forehead with a towel. "Ooh, but it does make you ache. I'm a mass of aches and pains from head to foot. I hope you don't go down with it. It was good of you to come home."

145

"And Mary's got it too?"

"Yes, she's in the attic room, but we'll have to put her in with Ma now you're here so you can have the attic to yourself. Sammy's having to sleep downstairs in the hope that he won't get it."

Emily's daughter Mary had been a schoolgirl of thirteen when Alice had left home. Alice had not seen her for over a year, and realized that she must be sixteen now. She had started work at Greenstocks as a housemaid, Emily told her.

Alice was disappointed. After all that had happened, after all the changes the war had brought, particularly for women, Mary was simply taking over from Alice herself, dusting the same shelves, sweeping the same stair-carpet, probably wearing the same uniform. "Doesn't she want to do something different – find a job with better prospects?" she asked Emily.

"Not really. She's still young," Emily said. "She doesn't want to leave home like some of the young women have. And the Morlands have been good to us."

Nothing had changed. When she and Jack had left the village, Alice had imagined that the link with Greenstocks had been severed, never thinking that Jack would want to go back there. But, it seemed, the Morland family would keep its hold over the Smallwoods, keeping them in their place. Alice resented it.

Dr Sidgwick called regularly to see her mother, whose fever reached its height shortly after Alice's arrival. Alice sat by her bedside as much as she could, helping her through the spasms of coughing, and listening to her ramblings when she was awake. Her mother was confused; she recognized Alice, but didn't seem to remember that she'd been away, and she kept asking if Jack was home from the stables yet.

"The next few days should see an improvement. It's lucky it isn't winter," Dr Sidgwick told her, "or we might have seen it worsen into pneumonia. You never know what form this new virus will take. Just try to keep her temperature down by giving her plenty of fluids, and give her this medicine every four hours."

He had aged since Alice had last seen him, his thin figure stiff and bent, and he walked down the stairs with difficulty, placing his feet with extreme care on the narrow steps. It was odd to think that he would have been her father-in-law if Edward had survived. She had always liked Dr Sidgwick, who was kindly and approachable, unlike his sniffy, well-bred wife. Alice had never been able to imagine Mrs Sidgwick as her mother-in-law, and couldn't quite understand how someone so forbidding could have produced Edward and Lorna.

She fell into a routine of domesticity and nursing, changing beds, making milk drinks for the invalids, shopping at the village stores and sorting out the complexities of the new ration books. She made breakfast for Tom and Sammy in the mornings and saw them off to work and school, and cooked their suppers when they came home. Catering for the family exercised all her ingenuity, with so many foodstuffs in short supply. Meat was rationed, and the butcher's shop in the village opened for only

147

an hour each day while people queued in the hope of securing a small scraggy joint or a pound of offal. Alice stewed the meat with whatever vegetables she could get, or made nourishing soups with the stock. The only bread obtainable was the Government Regulation kind, made with maize or oats and with potato added to the flour; Emily usually baked her own bread for the family, but Alice hadn't the time, with so much to do.

Tom spent the evenings watering and weeding his vegetables in the back garden, or picking runner beans or blackcurrants. He had been invalided out of the army with permanent damage to the tendons of his right hand, which had left him unable to fire a rifle. The injury made farm work difficult, but at least he was alive; Emily was lucky to have him safely at home with her, Alice thought, and to know that the children wouldn't be left fatherless.

Emily and Mary were slowly recovering from the influenza, but Dr Sidgwick warned that the illness would leave them run-down and susceptible to further infections. Mrs Smallwood would take longer to regain her strength when the fever finally abated, he said. She had never been in good health for as long as Alice could remember, and had been semi-invalid for years. Looking at her mother's frail figure on which the clothes seemed far too loose, Alice felt guilty for having neglected her during the war years. If it hadn't been for Emily, she wouldn't have been able to leave at all. And yet she knew that, in spite of her regrets, she would leave again as soon as her mother was fit enough.

She found it hard to adapt to village life. One part of her, grateful for the unhurried days and the memories of happier times, battled against the part which wanted to rebel against the narrow-minded backwardness of so many village people. In the village shop, Mrs Riley stood gossiping to the postmistress just as she had for as long as Alice could remember. Other customers waited patiently while she gave vent to her feelings about the price of butter and the scandal of having German prisoners working on the farms, and how indecent it was to see the Land Girls wearing breeches. Evidently these outrages were far more important than the Allied advances across the Marne and the black day of the German army. Those people who did talk about events in France seemed confident that the war would soon be over, and that the Germans would be forced to ask for peace terms. With the newspapers heralding triumphant advances and quoting impressive numbers of prisoners taken, it was easy to overlook the casualty lists on the inside pages. Alice knew that advances, even successful ones, were infinitely more costly in terms of lives than stagnant trench warfare in quiet stretches of the line.

"The Germans are on the run, Emily says," Mrs Smallwood said. "It's good to think it'll soon be over and we'll have our Jack home again." The worst of her fever had passed now, her temperature had dropped, and she was able to sit up in bed and talk lucidly.

"Yes, let's hope so," Alice said. Jack wrote home spasmodically, sometimes a brief letter, more often a field postcard with all the printed lines crossed out except "*I am quite well*" and "*I have received your letter*". Alice worried about him constantly, keeping her fears to herself, for she did not want to disturb her mother's confidence. If anything did happen to Jack . . . God forbid . . . she knew it would give her mother a blow from which she might never recover.

One afternoon, walking back to the cottage with her shopping, Alice came across Sammy and a group of other boys from the village school playing at soldiers, rushing against a wall with imaginary bayonets and cries of blood-curdling ferocity.

"Filthy Hun – stick him in the guts! Finish him off!"

Alice was furious. She rushed over and caught Sammy by the sleeve, pulling him round to face her while his friends looked on astonished.

"Don't you dare play games like that. The Germans aren't filthy Huns. They're just people, the same as you or me."

Sammy stared back at her unabashed. "No they're not. Everyone knows they're filthy beasts. They kill babies and gouge out people's eyes. Georgie's brother says so and he should know."

"You shouldn't believe it. The German soldiers are ordinary men like Jack and your Dad. Jack doesn't hate the Germans."

"Yes he does. He's a soldier. All soldiers hate the Germans."

"She's soft in the head. A Hun-lover," one of the bigger boys muttered.

"And you're old enough to know better," Alice retorted.

She insisted that Sammy came home with her; she wouldn't leave him to his violent game. He marched angrily beside her, head held up, resentful of being told off in front of his friends. Indoors, he ran straight upstairs to his mother, and Alice heard his voice raised in protest.

"Don't waste your energy. You'll never stop them playing war games," Emily said later when Alice went up to see her. "Boys will be boys."

· Alice felt too dispirited to argue. Sammy was only nine, after all, and his attitude was merely a visible demonstration of the views held by many adults in the village. It was all so simple at this distance from the war. The British were heroes. The Germans were filthy Huns. The Allies would win because they had been destined to win from the beginning.

She was beginning to feel restless, bored with her domestic routine. Her mother was recovering steadily, well enough to get dressed in the afternoon and to sit out in the back garden on fine days. Emily was up and about again, and Mary was talking about going back to work at Greenstocks, although Dr Sidgwick advised a few more days' rest. They had been lucky; the influenza was of a particularly virulent kind, and there were reports of people dying from it.

"I don't suppose you'll be needing me for much longer," Alice remarked to Emily as they sat in the afternoon sunshine shelling peas for supper.

Emily looked up at her in surprise. "What, are you thinking of going away again? I thought you'd stay at home for good, now you're here."

"No, it's been nice to stay for a short while, but there's more need than ever for VADs, especially experienced ones. I saw it in the paper yesterday. And Lorna said in her letter that this influenza epidemic is in France now – there are almost more men ill with it than there are wounded. I shall write to Devonshire House and see if I can get posted to a London hospital."

"Well, if you're sure. I thought you'd have been glad to get away from all that gloom."

Dr Sidgwick called later and pronounced himself well pleased with Mrs Smallwood's progress. "You must come to tea, my dear, now that you're less busy with the invalids," he told Alice. "Why don't you come on Saturday? Madeleine Morland is coming to see us then – Mrs Montjoy, I should say of course, now that she's married. She'd like to see you, I'm sure."

"Thank you. It's kind of you," Alice said. She probably wouldn't go, she thought, remembering the ordeal of making polite conversation with Mrs Sidgwick, but it was thoughtful of him to offer. She'd have to remember to make some excuse beforehand.

She wanted to call on Harriet and the baby, but was afraid of the baby catching influenza. Next day, though, she met Harriet's mother in the village street, pushing her grandson in a very smart perambulator. "Mrs Morland gave it to us – it's her old one," she told Alice. "Kind of her, wasn't it?"

Alice was more interested in the baby, who was looking around alertly, one fist clutching a small woolly dog; he had plump round cheeks and wispy brown hair. "Oh, he's lovely, isn't he?" she exclaimed. "He must have got his blue eyes from Harriet – Jack's are brown. He looks bursting with health, doesn't he?"

"He's nearly sixteen months. Aye, he's a good little chap," Harriet's mother said proudly. "You know our Harriet's a Land Girl now? Works up at Greenstocks."

"Yes, Jack told me. I'll write to tell him I've seen the baby."

After so much contact with sickness and injury and death, Alice felt infinitely cheered by the sight of Jack's son so obviously fit and well cared-for. Jack would forget the doubts he had expressed about his marriage as soon as he saw him, she was sure.

When Saturday came, she remembered her invitation to tea with the Sidgwicks.

"Why don't you go?" Emily said. "It'll do you good to get out of the house for a change. I can look after Ma."

"Well – all right. If you're sure you don't mind."

The Sidgwicks' parlour was exactly as Alice remembered it: a floral padded seat in the bay window, plush velvet curtains, small tables adorned with numerous ornaments and vases and framed photographs. Mrs Sidgwick greeted her in the hallway; she seemed far friendlier towards Alice now that there could be no possible prospect of their becoming relations by marriage. Alice sat down in a chair by the fireplace to find Edward looking at her from an ormolu frame on the mantelshelf. She should have been prepared for it, but all the same the frisson of recognition left her momentarily stunned. It was a photograph

153

she hadn't seen before: he was in uniform, holding his cap under his arm, and was looking directly at the camera, his mouth lifting in the beginning of a smile as if the photographer had said something to amuse him.

She looked away hastily, her gaze dropping to another group of photographs on a low table beside her. Lorna in VAD uniform . . . Lorna and Edward as small children riding ponies . . . Edward as a schoolboy in cricket flannels standing next to someone who looked familiar – Alice looked more closely. Broad face, thick dark eyebrows . . . someone she had seen recently . . . Of course, it was a very young Patrick Leary, she realized in surprise. Dr and Mrs Sidgwick must know Patrick; she wondered whether they knew about the death of his fiancée, and decided that now wasn't the time to mention it.

She gathered her wits together in time to greet Madeleine, who arrived in a shiny new Napier motorcar and swept in full of the confidence of being newly-married and having a husband who was not fit enough to be in the Army.

"Alice! How lovely to see you!" She crossed the room in a fragrant drift of perfume and scented face-powder, and gave Alice a sisterly peck on the cheek.

She was as well turned-out as ever, in a fitted suit of kingfisher-blue crêpe, and with her fair hair pinned up under a small black hat with a curling feather, so that standing next to her Alice felt tired and dowdy in her old navy blue serge jacket and skirt. The blouse she was wearing was one given to her by Madeleine herself, four years ago. Although she saved some of her wages, she had had little time to buy new clothes for herself.

They sat down, and the Sidgwicks' maid – a girl of about Mary's age – brought in tea. Madeleine talked about the town house she and her husband had bought in Epping and were having redecorated, and then Alice asked about Philip.

"Oh, he's got a staff job now, as a liaison officer. We hardly see him. He spends half his time at the War Office and half in Montreuil. Of course it's tremendously exciting at the moment. I'm sure he wishes he were at the front again."

Alice, who was equally sure that Philip wished no such thing, reflected on the change in her relationships with the Morlands since she had worked as their servant. Then, she had preferred Madeleine to her brother, charmed by the older girl's easy friendliness and engrossed by her accounts of dances and parties, eligible young men and the latest fashions. She found Madeleine rather irritating now, with her chatter about curtain fabric and the difficulty of engaging suitable servants, and the frequent references to her "war work" which Alice knew consisted of serving tea once or twice a week, becomingly dressed, to troops billeted in the area. Alice felt far more sympathetic towards Philip, the only one of the Morlands to have been significantly affected by the war. She wondered if either Madeleine or the Sidgwicks knew of his growing friendship with Lorna.

"I expect you'll be thinking of going back to nursing before long, Alice, now that your mother seems to be on the mend?" Dr Sidgwick asked her.

"Oh, really? I thought you'd have been pleased to get away from that dreary hospital," Madeleine said. "A friend of mine is a Red Cross helper at Broadlands Hall, and she says some of the things she has to do almost make her faint."

"No, I shall go back as soon as I can," Alice said firmly. "I've already written to ask for a place in a London hospital, and I shall try to get out to France again." The more she saw of the village, the more determined she was to escape.

Later, turning down the offer of a lift home in Madeleine's Napier, she walked back through the village. The street was almost deserted, and she smelled woodsmoke on the air. Late summer was turning slowly to autumn; the chestnut trees behind the schoolhouse were heavy with conkers in their spiked green shells, and outside Emily's cottage the shrubby roses had formed plump orange-red hips, like tomatoes. In spite of her resolve, Alice felt suddenly sorry that she would soon be leaving for the London streets and the wearying routine of another hospital.

The letter from Devonshire House came, asking her to attend an interview. But the same evening, troubled by a nagging headache and a feeling of intense tiredness, she went to bed early, putting her ailments down to a heavy period. Next morning she awoke feeling worse, with a dry painful throat. Her head reeled when she stood up.

"Of course it's not just a cold," Emily said when she mentioned her symptoms. "You're going down with the influenza. You'll have to write to that nursing headquarters place and say you can't go after all."

November 11th

Jack crouched in the bottom of the shallow trench, his heart pounding against his rib cage. Alongside, their faces distorted with fear, were the young men of his section, some of them under bombardment for the first time. Jack had experienced heavy shelling many times, but that didn't stop him from being just as terrified as the younger lads. Unlike them, he had seen what happened when one hit directly.

A trench mortar swished overhead and exploded behind in a great crash, sending earth and stones showering into the trench. Partington, next to Jack, was bent forward, hands clasped over his ears, while Jones shouted something at him, Jack couldn't hear what. Steel fragments shrieked overhead, the sound tearing at Jack's nerves. He thought he could last out one more minute before he gave way to sheer gibbering terror, and when he thought that minute was up he braced himself for another minute, and then another; that way he stood some chance of keeping himself under control. He had long ago given up the idea that he could save himself by quick thinking or initiative; the shells screamed down in their final rush so fast that you couldn't hope to get yourself out of the way. It was just a matter of chance whether you lived or died. And even if you survived now, you'd be shelled again some other time, and again, until finally you were killed or went mad.

He had no idea how long the barrage had been going on; it could have lasted for hours, or only minutes. It had been just before dawn when the shelling started, and now he wasn't sure whether the hazy diffused light was autumnal mist or the smoke of the barrage. Their own artillery was answering – heavy booms from half a mile back made the ground shudder. Jack glanced along the trench to make sure everyone was prepared, rifles loaded and ready. This bout of shelling could easily be shielding an attack; a wave of grey-clad figures might already be close at hand behind the curtain of lead, ready to leap into the trench with bayonets fixed.

A shell thudded into the trench and rolled against Jack's feet. He stared at it mesmerized, waiting for the blast that would tear his body apart, strangely without fear, almost resigned to it . . . then slowly he realized nothing was happening . . . it was a dud. Thank God . . . Partington was staring at it too, his eyes enormous with fear like a stoated rabbit's. Jack managed to grin at him as he picked up the shell and lobbed it out of the trench, but he could hardly control the shaking of his hands as he gripped his rifle again.

There was no attack. An unnatural silence fell over the waning of the barrage, like a blanket muffling the ears. Jack, hearing nothing, wondered whether his eardrums had actually been shattered by the din, until he made out sounds of moaning further along the trench, and frantic digging. The mist lingered, sun filtering through hazily – it was impossible to tell what was going on. Jack had a look through the periscope

158

and saw the tangled roots of a tree thrown out of the ground by an explosion in front of the trench; he could make out nothing beyond but the concealing mist. He heard the drone of a plane overhead, a German one probably, trying to see how successful the barrage had been. The pilot wouldn't see much today, Jack thought, but the fact that he was flying at all must mean it was clearer overhead; this must be a ground mist, which would clear before long as the sun got up.

The men were exchanging anxious glances and shifting on cramped limbs, unnerved by the sudden quiet. If the attack wasn't coming now, it would only come later. Captain Drummond-Lacy was making his way along the front, checking for damage and casualties, setting men to dig where earth had collapsed into the trench or to go out under cover of the mist to reinforce the wire. The men in Jack's section, although badly shaken, were uninjured apart from minor cuts caused by flying debris, but there were worse casualties . . . stretcher bearers were coming up, and the walking wounded were making their own way back with field dressings clamped to their heads.

Order was slowly re-established, and the men started to boil up dixies of tea or to eat their portions of ration-loaf. Drummond-Lacy continued to prowl about, looking uneasy, gazing through his binoculars at a partly-smashed wooden barn half way between the lines. Later in the morning, he called Jack, Corporal Whitfield and Lieutenant Hatherleigh into his makeshift dugout.

"The Colonel wants prisoners," he told them in his precise tones, "so that we can find out whether

159

the Germans are planning to attack here or whether they're concentrating their forces on the action further south. We're to mount a raid tonight to get some. I think there's a machine-gun post in that ruined barn – possibly snipers as well. We'll go out tonight as soon as it's fully dark and see what we can find."

From the way he talked, you'd think he was describing a bird-watching expedition, Jack thought. Well, he wouldn't be seeing any purple sandpipers tonight. Not snipe but snipers. Dismissed, he left the dugout with Lieutenant Hatherleigh to choose twelve men for the raid. He wondered what the night would bring. He'd had one lucky escape already today, that shell being a dud – perhaps that was a good omen; or perhaps on the other hand it was a bad one, signifying that he'd used up his share of luck. He remembered that he had scorned other men for being superstitious, and made his way back along the trench.

Towards dusk, Drummond-Lacy called the raiding party together for a briefing. He wouldn't be going with them after all, he told them, the Colonel had forbidden it; Sergeant Horne would be going instead, with Hatherleigh leading. Jack saw Whitfield smile sardonically at this piece of information, as if the Captain hadn't proved himself often enough during the months he'd been commanding the company. The raiding group was to split into two, approaching the barn from both sides. There was to be no barrage; the aim was to surprise the inhabitants of the barn and to avoid drawing fire from the German front line.

"If it all goes smoothly, you should be back here within a few minutes," Drummond-Lacy concluded.

The men assembled, wearing knitted balaclava helmets, their faces and buttons blacked with mud. They had been given a tot of rum each, and Jack could still feel the smooth warmth of it in his throat and stomach. There was movement behind the German lines; in the stillness of the night, he could hear the rumble of wheels on the pavé, and muffled hooves. It sounded so close, and he was going to be even closer in a moment. It was familiar, this feeling of keyed-up eagerness to get on with it, alternating with stomach-cramping fear.

"Right!" Lieutenant Hatherleigh, very tense, motioned the raiding party forward. Jack scrambled over the parapet, turning to check that his group was with him. He could smell the grass, damp with dew; dead leaves crackled underfoot as he crept forward. The barn was at the edge of a wheatfield, uncut, but trampled by many feet as the line had passed over it first one way and then the other. Hardly a stalk remained upright, the unharvested grains mashed into the ground. Jack had spent the afternoon studying the ground carefully through the periscope and memorizing every shell-hole that might provide cover, but it was difficult to find his bearings in the dark . . . a green flare soared up and fizzed back to the ground, casting a strange underwater light and making the men freeze in their crouched positions. Rattle of machine-gun fire, further up the line . . . the flare had been enough to show Hatherleigh exactly where the barn was, straight ahead; they were too far to the right. Jack followed as he corrected his line, crouching and dashing, waiting for the stragglers to catch up, working his way round to the cover of some low bushes along the track that led to the barn. Whitfield should be in a similar position at the other side by this time . . .

They were close to the barn now, close enough to hear a startled German exclamation from inside, and then the machine-gun burst into abrupt fire, shattering the taut silence. Jack heard screams as someone was hit, and then the machine-gun traversing – another yell . . .

Hatherleigh turned round to make sure everyone was with him. "Ready? Now – "

They were clambering over boulders and fallen planks of wood across the barn's entrance, spreading out inside, bayonets fixed. The barn smelled of damp hay and apples and explosives. Figures moving against the faint light . . . how many of them? . . . spinning round to face the intruders . . . Hatherleigh saying something in German . . . Shellfire outside, red lights flickering against the plank walls of the barn, against which Jack saw hands raised above coalscuttle helmets. "*Kamerad . . . Kamerad . . .*"

"*Raus*," Hatherleigh ordered, gesturing with his revolver. "Smallwood, get that rifle. See if there are any more."

Jack picked up the rifle and groped about in the dark as the prisoners filed out, five of them. Partington was leading, the other men herding the machine-gunners with their bayonets. Jack put the gun out of action by cutting the ammunition belt with his knife, and followed on, stumbling over the smashed timbers, out into the open. The prisoners had had no time to send up SOS flares, but a sentry had seen movement; Jack heard the *phut* of a rifle bullet

162

spitting into the ground by his feet, and a second one tore through his sleeve, grazing his arm. The prisoners were hurrying across the trampled field, prodded by bayonets; Jack could hear one of them sobbing . . . then the *crack* of another rifle-shot, the unmistakable thud of a rifle bullet hitting flesh and bone, and Jones was down . . . Jack ran up to help him, but as he bent down the boy gasped and his limbs quivered and then he lay still. The bullet had struck him cleanly between the shoulder-blades. God, Jack thought, sickened, one of his own section, a boy of eighteen . . . he thought briefly of the telegram home, the stricken relatives . . . but he must concentrate, or his own family would be getting a telegram too . . .

The rest of the party was approaching their own trench now, calling out the password, *"Weather"* – chosen because it was practically unpronounceable by Germans. They slid down behind the parapet, the prisoners with them. Jack hurried across the last few yards and slithered down into the trench. He took a few moments to get his breath back and then followed the party along to Drummond-Lacy's dugout.

The prisoners were already standing to attention. Jack stared at them, seeing in the lantern-light that three of them were mere boys, thin, trembling, with girlish unshaven faces, two of them crying . . . they looked no more than sixteen or seventeen. God, Jack thought, these were the Huns, the anonymous sinister figures in field-grey, the Kaiser's invincible army. Frightened children.

Drummond-Lacy spoke in fluent German to the older man who appeared to be the leader of the group. The man, who had been staring stony-faced and impassive, relaxed visibly and replied at great length, with much gesticulation. Drummond-Lacy appeared to understand, nodding in satisfaction and saying, "*Ja, ja,*" at intervals.

"He doesn't think the attack will come here," he translated. "They've hardly any reserves, and he says they're desperately hungry. He seems pleased to be taken prisoner, in fact. Sergeant, get them some bread, and then choose two of your platoon to escort them down to the Colonel. Hatherleigh, any casualties?"

"Two killed, sir, by the barn – Winterthorpe and Miller. And – ?" He looked across at Jack.

"Jones, sir. Killed outright," Jack said shortly. Three men were dead, but the Colonel had his prisoners.

They were on the march, moving forward, forward, virtually unopposed. The Germans were retreating as fast as they had advanced in the spring, and the columns moved across the debris of their occupation, abandoned camps, blown-up ammunition dumps, the burnt-out wreckage of a Fokker aeroplane, dead horses, dead men. Civilians waved and cheered as the marching columns entered villages freed from German occupation. The villagers were returning to their homes, bringing back their meagre belongings, sometimes cadging lifts on army supply lorries. The soldiers were billeted in farms, schools, churches; each day they stretched stiff limbs and marched on across open countryside.

"Do you realize," Jack remarked to Partington as they sat by a roadside eating their sparse midday meal, "people at home will be looking at their newspapers and seeing a black line going further and further across

France and Belgium. Well, that's us – we *are* the black line."

Partington was impressed. "Coo, it makes you feel important, don't it?"

The weather had turned cold and wet. Civilians were predicting the end of the war, but the troops were so cold and exhausted from the endless marching and the inadequate rations that they hardly cared. People had been saying that all along, Jack thought. The war would end by Christmas – next Christmas – perhaps the Christmas after that. Soon, he thought, they would come across a fortified line where the Germans had dug in and brought up new reserves, and the tide would sweep the other way once again.

He heard the Colonel talking to Drummond-Lacy about the likelihood of an armistice. Armistice? What did it mean, he wondered? He asked the Captain later.

"Armistice – it's a word derived from the Latin *arma*, arms, and *stitium*, stand. As in solstice, *sol* of course meaning sun."

Jack grinned. The man was like a walking diction-ary, when all he wanted was a simple answer. "Arms-stand?" he repeated. It sounded like a new word for stand-to, or else some kind of gymnastic feat.

"It means an end to the fighting."

"Is it really going to happen, then?"

"Perhaps. It seems the Germans are asking for peace terms. It won't be the end of the war, though," Drummond-Lacy explained with typical caution, "just a truce while terms are negotiated."

It was the second week in November. They were still moving on, marching each day with aching legs, their packs heavy on their shoulders, covering greater distances than had ever seemed possible in the endless stagnation of trench warfare. They marched along railway lines where the Germans had destroyed bridges as they retreated, and they slept in draughty barns where rats ran over their faces in the night. The supply wagons struggled to keep up with the advance, and rations were short: no breakfast, a damp Army biscuit at midday, a tin of bully-beef to be shared amongst a whole section. Drummond-Lacy and the Colonel must have got it wrong, Jack decided. The war would never end. They would go on forever, marching in the rain. The men grumbled, their ankles twisting on the cobbled roads, their feet blistering.

"Close up, there," the Sergeant bellowed. "Step up, look smart. Come on, you there, no falling out."

Sometimes the retreating German artillery turned to aim defiantly at a cross-roads, and the rumble of heavy guns was never far ahead; there were still occasional casualties, and outbreaks of hand-to-hand fighting with small groups of enemy stragglers. Most of these were glad to surrender and be sent down the line under escort. Germany was in the throes of civil strife, Drummond-Lacy told Jack; the people were fed-up with years of hardship, and now the chronic food shortages and the influenza epidemic were trying them beyond endurance. The Kaiser would be forced to abdicate, he thought.

Another morning; Jack got his section ready to line up for the march and they stood ready for orders, flexing stiff knees, loosening aching shoulders. The Colonel was standing ready to address the column. He was holding a piece of paper, and smiling – Jack couldn't remember ever seeing him smile before. He read aloud to the troops: "Hostilities will cease at eleven o'clock today November the eleventh. Troops will stand fast on the line reached at that hour . . . defensive precautions will be maintained . . . There will be no intercourse of any description with the enemy . . ."

The troops stood listening, some faces incredulous, some disbelieving, some elated. Eleven o'clock – four hours to go until the Armistice! A truce while peace terms were negotiated, Drummond-Lacy had said – not really an end to the war; but regardless of the precise definition of the term, Jack thought, it meant the end of the war as far as the troops were concerned. He could hardly take it in, convinced that a stray shell would knock him for six before eleven o'clock arrived. The march was going ahead anyway, and they could still hear shelling ahead of them, and the occasional crack of a rifle bullet. Evidently, hostilities would not cease until precisely the allotted hour.

At two minutes to eleven the Captain gave the order to fall out by the roadside. An explosion sounded in the distance, and Jack wondered whether some poor blighter had copped it at almost literally the last minute. Eleven o'clock, and some of the men around Jack were cheering, some, like him, numb and silent with disbelief. The shelling had died away, and he tried to take in the idea that there would be no more bombardments, no more raids, no more pushes, no more gas attacks. It seemed impossible. The war had dominated his life for the last four years.

They reached a small village, where the Belgian inhabitants came out to cheer and wave and press

167

withered flowers into the soldiers' hands; the area had been occupied by Germans only twenty-four hours ago. The march ended here, and the men were directed in groups of six or seven to billets in various houses. Jack, Whitfield and another NCO were put together in a house owned by a man in his sixties and his daughter, a young woman in her early twenties. She spoke no English and the troops understood only a word or two of Flemish, but she managed to convey by a mixture of French and eloquent gestures that her husband had been killed early on in the war. She showed them to a cellar, where mattresses and blankets had been thrown down on the floor. Germans had slept there last night, Jack thought, looking at a notice on the wall in the peculiar curly Teutonic script. While he was trying to read it, Whitfield snatched if off the wall and crushed it to the floor beneath his boot.

The men were to be allowed to rest for the remainder of the day. The field-kitchens would catch up by evening, Drummond-Lacy promised, and there would be a decent hot meal; meanwhile, there was time to sit about smoking or chatting, to have a good wash-down, or to find a quiet corner for a doze.

"Trust our luck to be stuck in this backwater instead of in a big town," Whitfield grumbled. "If the end of the war isn't a good reason for a skinful, I'd like to know what is."

The villagers did their best. Quantities of beer and wine were procured from places where they had been concealed from the Germans, and after the men had had their dinner everyone crowded into the local estaminet, locals and troops together. Hatherleigh turned out to be an accomplished pianist, playing tune after tune to which increasingly rowdy choruses were sung.

Jack joined in with the rest, but was aware of a vague mood of anti-climax. He couldn't analyse his feelings. This was the day everyone had dreamed of for months, for years even, and yet he sat in the middle of the laughter-filled room holding his glass of beer and feeling almost subdued. The war was over and he supposed he would be going home soon – he would be a civilian again, wearing his own clothes, sleeping in a proper bed, pleasing himself about what he did in his leisure hours. He couldn't make this a convincing picture, unable to imagine clearly the life he would be going back to. It seemed quite incredible that he could have survived the war, and not only survived, but had come through without losing an arm or a leg, or his eyesight, or his sanity. Thousands hadn't been so lucky, but he had. And he thought of the friends who wouldn't be going back: Harry Larkins and Ted Briggs from the village, and Jones who had died just the other day, and Evernden, and Edward (what would Alice be thinking now?) and Stephen; they would stay here in their graves. It didn't seem right that he had survived when they had not. It was as if his survival had been paid for at their expense. He felt dirty, unworthy of the sacrifice. He should have died too.

The combination of tiredness, beer and the stuffy atmosphere of the estaminet was making him sleepy. He decided to walk about outside in the fresh air for a bit and then make his way back to the billet. The damp coolness outside refreshed him, and he was glad to be on his own for a few moments. Lights in the estaminet shone from uncurtained windows – no need to be careful now – and on the edge of a vegetable garden nearby someone had lit a great celebratory bonfire; he saw dark figures moving against the leaping flames, and gold sparks flying upwards. He went along to have a look, leaning over the fence, and soon became aware that someone was standing next to him and plucking at his sleeve. He turned, recognizing the young woman from the billet. In gesture, she asked him whether he were going back, and he nodded.

She fell into step beside him. After a few moments she pointed at him and said, "Nom?"

"Jack."

"Zhack," she repeated.

"No, *J*. Jack."

"Zhack. Zhack," she said again.

He laughed. It sounded so delightful, the way she said it, so different from the workmanlike name it was. He pointed at her. "And you?"

"Marie."

"Marie."

"Non, non." It was her turn to correct him. "Ma*hrrie*."

He tried to copy the way she said it, rolling his tongue around the *r*. At last he reached an approximation, and she laughed and clapped her hands in appreciation. When they reached the house, she opened the door to the parlour and motioned Jack inside. He really wanted to go to sleep, but unsure how to explain and not wanting to offend, he followed her inside. There was only one armchair in the room, and she motioned him to sit in it while she took off her coat and fetched a bottle of wine and glasses from a cupboard in the wall. Seeing that there were only two glasses, he wondered where her father was.

"Er . . . père? Papa?"

She indicated by pointing in the direction of the estaminet, miming drinking and then hands whizzing round a clock that he was likely to be celebrating with his friends for some while yet. She poured out a glass of wine and handed it to Jack, and stood by the fireplace, in which the remains of a fire glowed. Jack looked around the small room. There was not much furniture, just the chair at which he sat, two upright chairs and a table, and a rag rug on the slate floor. On a shelf above the fire was a photograph of a moustached man in Belgian army uniform. The young woman saw him looking at it.

"Mon mari – mort." She touched the stripes on Jack's sleeve. "Caporal?"

He nodded, and she pointed to the photograph and nodded to show that her husband had been a corporal too. Her hand moved down Jack's arm to touch the two wound stripes. She looked at him enquiringly, but he didn't have the vocabulary to begin to explain how he'd got them. He noticed that she was really very attractive, with warm colouring, and lively dark eyes in a high-cheekboned face. The wine was going to his head; he felt pleasantly warm and hazy sitting in the comfortable chair. Marie refilled his glass, and sat down beside him on the chair arm, close to him; that was pleasant, too. Nothing seemed quite real to him. She smelled cleanly of soap and cologne, and she was leaning so close against him that her soft hair tickled his face. Soon, when the bottle of wine was empty and she stood up and pulled him with her and led him upstairs, that seemed like a very good idea. She led the way into a small bedroom and pulled the curtains and closed the door behind. Then she came to him and put her arms around him, lifting her face to his.

"Zhack . . ." She murmured something he didn't understand. But, befuddled and slow-witted though he had been, he needed no further encouragement. His arms tightened around her firm body and he kissed her face and her throat. After a few moments he sat down on the bed and pulled her down beside him, and she began undoing his tunic, and he unfastened the buttons on her dress. It took so long for him to get all his uniform off, unwinding the endless puttees and unlacing his boots, that soon they were both laughing at the ridiculousness of it. At last he turned to her gratefully. He had forgotten his melancholy weariness of earlier in the evening; he was only aware of his sharpened senses and the woman watching him, wanting him. He pulled her to him, and lost himself in the scent of her flesh and the warmth of her embrace.

In the morning he felt dreadful. He woke up in the cold cellar to the sound of snoring from the others, and remembered what had happened. Marie had pushed him out of her bed shortly after they had heard her father tramp slowly up the stairs and close his bedroom door. It had been unfortunate that just as Jack emerged from the back door of the house, carrying his boots by the laces, Whitfield and Corporal Smith had appeared round the corner making for the cellar steps. That would give Whitfield fuel for gossip, and no mistake. Jack realized that he had got himself into an awkward situation. How long would they be billeted here, he wondered? Today was to be a rest day, so they'd be staying at least one more night.

He lay staring at the cobwebbed ceiling until Whitfield stirred and got up from his makeshift bed and went up the cellar steps to fetch water from the outside tap for washing and shaving. Seeing that Jack was awake, he started whistling the tune of "*Who were you with last night?*" It hadn't taken him long to change his tactics.

"Enjoy yourself last night?" he taunted. "I hope you'll be all right at the next short-arm inspection."

"Oh, leave off," Jack said, turning over so that his back was to Whitfield. "What you mean is, you hope the opposite."

"Well, with German officers being here up till two days ago, you don't suppose you're the first, do you? There's a special hospital down at Eetapps, I've heard. It'd be a shame to end up there, eh, when the rest of us are going off home? The treatment's very painful, they say."

Jack gazed at the wall. This aspect of the encounter was something he hadn't even considered last night – he hadn't considered anything, really; it had just happened. He didn't think Whitfield was right in his insinuations, as Marie had given him to understand that she hadn't been with another man since her husband had died, but the thought was worrying all the same. And most disturbing of all was the realization that he hadn't even thought about Harriet, not for a second. He had been unfaithful to her – the word sounded in his head like an accusation. It was daft, he thought; when he had first been out in France, before he had married Harriet, there had been ample opportunity to go with other girls, but he hadn't wanted to then, thinking only of her. Now that he was married – and a father as well, to make it worse – he had given way to the first temptation, forgetting that she existed.

Well, he wouldn't get caught again. He wasn't sure how he was going to face the young woman or her father, knowing what had happened. He wondered whether Marie would expect last night's amorous encounter to be repeated, and whether she would be upset if he made no further advances. He didn't want to hurt her feelings; he hoped the problem would be solved for him by the battalion moving elsewhere. He was aware that he had used her, in the same way a man might use a bottle of whisky or a shot of morphine. However, reason told him that she had used him in the same way; he was simply a soldier passing through, no strings attached.

They moved on two days later. It was the custom for billeted troops to give some spare money to their hosts, and as Jack packed up his kit in the cellar Whitfield was counting out coins ostentatiously. He looked towards Jack, jingling the money in his hand.

"Better dig deep. You've got more to pay for than the rest of us, eh?" he said significantly.

Jack refrained from replying. Smith, who was well aware of the conflict between the other two but preferred to stay out of it, continued stuffing his spare shirt and socks into his pack, resolutely turning his back on them. Jack didn't blame him. As soon as he had put all his own things away he picked up his pack and equipment and went up the steps, barging past Whitfield. Marie and her father were waiting by the house door to say goodbye; he pushed some Belgian francs into the man's hand and mumbled his thanks, aware of Marie's reproachful look. He couldn't begin to explain, not with her father standing there, and the language difficulties besides. He felt hopeless, at a loss to know how to remove himself from the situation in any decent sort of way. He shook hands with the father and then with Marie, avoiding her eye. He just wanted to get away. Shouldering his pack, he marched away up the street.

The men were gathering for the day's march. Well-rested, they were now beginning to agitate about de-mobilization; those who thought they had grounds for early release had been approaching the Captain to press their claims. The familiar routine of the war was ended, and no-one was sure what would take its place. There were rumours of troops going on to occupy the Rhineland, and it was unlikely that anyone would be going home before Christmas. It all added to the sense of anti-climax. Like many of the men, Jack had naively supposed that he would be going home as soon as the last shot was fired.

They left the village, many of the inhabitants turning out to wave goodbye. Jack wasn't sorry to leave. His war had ended shabbily.

Part Two

1919

A Return To The Battlefields

Alice stood outside the hospital, her coat collar turned up against the thin rain. London looked festive with the street-lamps lit, rows of them glowing against the twilit sky, like Christmas decorations. She still couldn't quite get used to it, always thinking there must be some special occasion, and having to remind herself that the lamps were lit every night now.

She had been too ill with influenza to take much notice of the Armistice. Afterwards, when she had seen photographs of the crowds thronging hundreds deep in Trafalgar Square and in front of Buckingham Palace, she had looked at the hats thrown high in the air and the jubilant faces with a sense of being distanced from the prevailing mood. She didn't feel at all triumphant; only a sense of overwhelming relief and weariness. Soon after, she had gone back to the 1st London Hospital, where she had worked in 1916. The war certainly wasn't finished there, where men were still dying from their wounds or struggling to adjust to permanent disablement.

Passing motor-cars sprayed rain water over her ankles and skirt as she stood waiting for a tram. It had felt strange to finish her last spell of duty, to change the last dressing and empty the last bed-pan. The hospital was gradually shedding the extra staff who had been recruited to cope with wartime excesses.

179

VADs and other Red Cross helpers were dispersing to their homes, leaving the remaining patients in the care of trained Army nurses and doctors. She felt daunted at leaving the familiar routines behind, heading for a future less governed by restrictions and duty timetables. But for the first time since the Armistice, she had a real sense of one kind of life ending and another beginning. Post-war civilian life waited for her, with its uncertainties and challenges. In the drizzly evening, London breathed out scents of spring; buds were breaking on the plane trees lining the street, and tulips and daffodils made vibrant sweeps of colour against the damp grass behind the park railings. For the first time in years, Alice felt able to greet the spring without gloomily wondering what disasters the rest of the year would bring. Jack was home, and Lorna would be waiting for her, and their new life was about to begin, she thought, her spirits lifting with optimism as she boarded the tram.

Lorna, who had been home from France for six weeks, had already installed herself in the upper floor of the Braithwaites' house, and had made preparations for Alice's arrival. She had installed an old gas cooker and put up shelves in a makeshift kitchen – "there's no running water or sink yet, so we'll have to do a lot of running up and down stairs, but we'll manage" – and there was a small sitting-room, with a gas heater, two armchairs and a dilapidated sofa, shelves, and a desk with the typewriter on it. They had a bedroom each, divided by a partition, and Alice saw to her surprise that the old tea-chest she used for storing her clothes, last seen in Emily's attic, was already on the floor in her room.

"However did that get here?"

"Philip brought it up in his car," Lorna said, "and he's put up a rail for you to hang them on, as well. He's helped me quite a lot. We can probably get ourselves some cheap wardrobes at an auction or something later. And Dorothy and Geoffrey have given us those two old armchairs and the sofa. Isn't it marvellous? We've already got enough to manage with, and when I go home I'll bring back some more of my own things."

"It's wonderful," Alice said. "I can't think how you've managed to get so much done. Lorna, is it really going to work out, the way we planned it?"

"Yes, of course it is! I've already got myself a job teaching History three days a week, and I'm advertising for private pupils to coach, and Dorothy and Geoffrey are letting us have the flat rent free in return for your help in the canteen in the mornings. I hope you don't mind," she added anxiously.

"Mind! It's better than I ever hoped for." Alice sat down on her bed and looked at the vase of carnations on the window-sill. "Flowers too! You've thought of everything. Where did you get those?"

"Philip brought them," Lorna said, a shade guardedly, and then, "Before we settle into our new routines, I think it would be a good idea if we made plans for a break. What would you think of going away for a few days?"

"Going away? What do you mean? I've only just come!"

"Well, it was Philip's idea," Lorna said, with untypical caution. "He suggested that the three of us go to France for a few days – a week, perhaps,

181

hiring a car to travel around in. Not immediately, perhaps at the end of May, when the days are longer. He thought we'd want to visit Edward's grave near Arras, and he'd like to go back and see some of the old places. A sort of tour of remembrance. What do you think?"

"Well, I – " Alice began to unbutton her coat, not sure what she did think. Back so soon to France, with all the memories it held for her? A visit to Edward's grave – yes, she did want to go, to see where he had died and to have a clear picture in her mind of where he lay. But to go there with Philip . . . it would be far pleasanter if she and Lorna went, just the two of them. And then there was the cost, she thought, turning her mind to more practical matters. It seemed a dreadful extravagance . . . but then she had her savings, and surely she could justify spending a little money . . . "I don't know," she said. "I mean, I'd like to go, of course. But wouldn't it be a bit awkward – I mean, I don't know Philip as well as you do. And does he really want to travel about with someone who used to be his servant . . .?"

"Oh, Alice, I wish you'd stop thinking like that," Lorna said rather impatiently, putting Alice's coat on a hanger on the rail. "Class differences seem to matter far more to you than they do to Philip. He's not interested in such outdated nonsense, and why should you be? Hasn't the war proved one thing to you – that you're just as capable and determined as anyone else? Leave all that snobbery in the past where it belongs."

"I . . ." Alice wasn't sure. It was easier to agree with Lorna's views here in London than back in the village, where not much seemed to have changed at all; her niece was a domestic servant in Philip's house and her brother was now his head groom. But she was goaded into acceptance by Lorna's outburst. "Well, yes, let's go. Why shouldn't we? We've worked hard enough to deserve it."

"Good," Lorna said with satisfaction. "I'll tell Philip. He'll be pleased."

Alice seemed to be hearing a lot about Philip, and nothing at all about Captain Aldridge. There must be a romance developing, she felt sure, impossible though she would have thought it two years ago. If Lorna and Philip wanted to go to France together, her own presence would lend propriety to the journey; even someone as unconventional as Lorna might hesitate before setting off on a tour alone with a young man, staying in hotels with him. That must be partly the reason for the suggestion, she decided.

She changed her clothes and unpacked her belongings from her small case while Lorna went downstairs to boil a kettle for tea. Supposing Lorna married Philip? Stupidly, it had never occurred to her that Lorna might marry, and they had made their plans for the future on the supposition that neither of them would. But Lorna, a future Mrs Morland, living at Greenstocks and becoming a country lady, holding dinner parties and opening the village fête? – No, Alice couldn't imagine it, not Lorna, with her campaigning zeal and dislike of parochial life. If Philip wanted to marry her, he would have to live in London, and that would upset his father, who would assume that the son of the family would inherit and run the estate . . . But, she told herself as she brushed out her hair and pinned it up more tidily, she was probably assuming too much, her thoughts running ahead.

They settled into their new routines. On Mondays, Wednesdays and Thursdays Lorna went off to teach at a girls' school in West London, and on the other days she prepared her lessons and marked books, wrote articles and continued with the administrative work of the canteen. Alice helped downstairs in the mornings, and in the afternoons she painted the rooms upstairs, shopped for groceries, and cooked an evening meal for herself and Lorna. She also taught herself to type, and slowly and painstakingly transcribed two articles from Lorna's untidy, much-altered script. One of Lorna's ambitions was to become a freelance journalist, but the first article she produced was returned swiftly by two newspapers in succession.

"Listen to this!" she told Alice angrily, brandishing an editor's letter. " 'Dear Miss Sidgwick, Thank you for sending us your article, *The Forgotten Soldiers*. I am afraid that I do not think the article is suitable for publication, and am returning it herewith. It is now six months after the Armistice and people no longer want to read about the war.' Would you believe it? That's exactly the point I make in the article. The soldiers still in hospitals have no choice but to remember! I suppose the public wants them tidied up out of sight now."

"Is that all he says?"

"No, he does say 'I should like to see more of your work' at the end. But really, it makes me wonder if I wouldn't get further by writing about the latest designer fashions," Lorna said scathingly.

Her second article, on the problems faced by widowed mothers in East London, was accepted, and with the letter of acceptance came a cheque for one pound and ten shillings.

Alice was impressed. "One pound ten! Two of those would be a week's wages! Can you really earn that much by writing articles?"

"Well, it's encouraging. We must have something nice for dinner, to celebrate," Lorna said.

She had already drafted a third article, in which she contrasted the loudly-trumpeted general demands to "Hang the Kaiser" and "Make Germany pay" and "Squeeze Germany till the pips squeak" with the more humane views of many soldiers, who saw the Germans as fellow humans rather than as faceless predators. Lorna blamed the popular newspapers for stirring up hatred. "There's been enough suffering already, to the Germans as much as to us. But some of these narrow-minded patriots won't be happy until Germany starves," she told Alice, hurling a copy of the *Daily Mail* to the floor in disgust.

Alice, sitting at the typewriter and struggling to interpret Lorna's script with its numerous insertions and deletions, remembered the high-minded idealism with which Edward and so many of his contemporaries had enlisted in 1914. What would Edward have thought, she wondered, of this baying for revenge? Would he have thought it worth dying for?

The war was over, but it seemed a shabby sort of peace, with soldiers coming home to find unemployment and inadequate housing and continued food shortages. And there was a new toughness and ruthlessness in the air, Alice thought, an attitude of every man for himself, a marked contrast to the naïvety of the early war years. Where would Edward have fitted in, she wondered?

She, Lorna and Philip left for France at the end of May. Familiar only with the narrow strip of land between Boulogne and Étaples, Alice sat in the back seat of the hired Excelsior Tourer and looked with interest at the scenery beside the quiet road from Boulogne to St Omer. Rural France in late spring: a landscape of high, wide fields, dense forests clustering in valleys, goats and chickens in the orchards, farmhouses with shuttered windows; as picturesque as the Victorian paintings Alice had dusted every day in the Morlands' sitting-room. But the familiar clutter of war was still here; even at this distance from the front, there were hutments and camps, Army lorries, barns taken over for stores, and she remembered that there were thousands of men still waiting to be demobilized. Jack had been lucky; as a married man, and one with a job waiting for him, he had been released in February.

They spent their first night in a small hotel close to St. Omer. Philip had made all the bookings in advance, and Alice was relieved to note that he had chosen a modest hotel, one which she felt her purse could cope with. He had stayed there before, he said over dinner. He spoke fluent French, and he translated the menu for Alice, and recommended dishes he thought she would like. She enjoyed the novelty of eating real French food instead of hospital fare, and lingering over the meal with glasses of cognac instead of rushing off as soon as the last mouthful was downed. She had never had brandy before and was not sure whether she liked the taste, but it made her feel heady and relaxed, and she sat contentedly listening to Philip and Lorna talking about places they had visited in Europe before the war.

"You must go to Paris some day, Alice," Philip told her. "You'd love it – the art galleries, Montmartre, the River Seine – particularly at this time of year . . . it's a pity we haven't got a few days longer, or we could have gone on there."

Normally, Alice would have thought she was as likely to go to Paris as she was to visit the South Pole, but sitting in the candlelit restaurant with her head swimming slightly from the brandy she felt as if anything were possible. After a while Philip got out a map and showed her and Lorna where their next day's route would take them, and where he had booked a hotel for the night. He was enjoying taking charge of the outing, Alice thought – just as well, since she had come away with only the vaguest idea of where they were going apart from the cemetery near Arras, and Lorna had been too busy recently to think about the trip in any detail. It was uncharacteristic of Lorna to let herself be organized, but she seemed quite happy to do whatever Philip suggested, looking on in approval, her face warm in the candle-glow, as he outlined their route on the map. Deciding that it might be tactful to leave them alone to talk in private, Alice turned down the waiter's offer of more coffee and said she was going up to bed.

Next day they drove through the battle-scarred areas. Béthune, Cambrin, Festubert, Noeux-les-Mines

– all the names were familiar to Alice, from Edward or Jack or from the muttered comments of men she had nursed. In many places, the roads were too shell-pocked for the car to progress any further, and they got out and looked at the piles of rubble and the scarred ground in shocked silence.

Heaps of wood and rubble could only be identified as the remains of villages by bullet-spattered signboards propped up against walls. Everywhere the trenches sprawled in irregular patterns, blocked with splintered planks from collapsed dugouts, littered with sandbags and bits of duckboard and sometimes an odd boot or helmet, stagnant water lying in hollows. The trench system was like a huge raw gash across the land, Alice thought, an open sore . . . Skylarks burbling overhead and bright poppies and charlock springing from the churned soil could not mask the desolation. She gazed in fascination, knowing that Jack and Edward – and Philip – had spent days on end living in trenches like these, with only the sky above to look at apart from the shored-up mud of the walls, and shells raining down, and men dying in the squalor . . . How had they stood it?

Lorna was busily taking photographs, muttering to herself and writing notes in a pocket-book. Alice noticed a peeling wooden signboard which cautioned: "*Do not linger here in daylight. If you don't get hit, someone else will*"; the board was riddled with bullet-holes, as if it had been used as a target – ample reason for the warning, Alice thought. She turned to point it out to Philip, who had been standing near her, but stopped abruptly on seeing his expression. He had moved away to stand on a low rise, and was looking down at the straggling trenches, his mouth compressed in a hard line, his face bleak with misery. What was he seeing, Alice wondered? Not the skylarks and the poppies and the blue sky streaked with cirrus cloud, she was sure. Why had he been so eager to come back, if it hurt him so much?

Not wanting to intrude, she went to find Lorna, and after a long while Philip came to join them and they made their way back to the car. Everywhere, they passed cemeteries – sometimes a small hedged garden with a few carefully-tended graves, sometimes vast rows of crosses. Lorna, thinking of a new article, wanted to cross to the areas which had been German-occupied for most of the war. In a German cemetery near the La Bassée canal, they came across graves marked "Here rests in God an unknown British soldier"; these, like the others, had little gardens in front of them planted with small shrubs. The Germans had honoured the British dead just as they had their own, Alice thought, comforted by this. But the number of crosses defied counting. The birdsong in a nearby wood and the wild flowers growing in profusion at the edges of the mown grass heightened her awareness of the wastage; how could it have been allowed to happen, two civilized nations sending thousands on thousands of men to destruction? Now, Gunther Schmidt, Feldwebel, lay alongside an unknown British soldier under the peaceful sky; two men who would probably have had more in common than they had differences. The war to end wars, they had called it; Alice thought there could be no more poignant reminder of the

189

tragedy of war than the two graves side by side, life for life.

Next day they drove southwards towards Vimy Ridge. The name, familiar from triumphant newspaper headlines when the Canadians had finally captured the ridge, became reality in the shape of a long, narrow spur overlooking the coalmining areas around Loos and Lens. Edward had not lived to see the capture of the ridge, nor to read the headlines. Alice had never told Lorna of the conflicting versions of his death; they would never know the truth, but they would at least know where he lay. Alice had the letter from the Commonwealth War Graves Commission in her pocket.

The cemetery was close to a small village, overlooking water meadows by the River Scarpe. The graves were mostly French and Canadian; Edward's was at the back of the cemetery, in a whole row from the same regiment, his cross as stark as the rest. Captain E. R. Sidgwick, Epping Forest Regiment. Alice realized that she did not even know what the R was for. Lorna and Philip stood looking at the grave in silence, and Alice, unable to bear it, walked away from them to look over the thorn hedge towards the river. She was glad that Edward's resting place was in a tranquil setting not unlike the village at home; she would be able to remember the house martins diving under the eaves of a stone barn, the hedgerow thick with elder and dog-rose, the white butterflies, the cattle moving about slowly in the long grass by the river. Edward might have approved.

She looked back. Lorna was crying, and Philip, with his arm round her shoulders, was leading her away. Alice went back to stand alone by the grave. A chiff-chaff was calling joyfully from a poplar tree by the road, its repetitive notes intruding on the edges of her consciousness. She was too numb for tears, only aware that Edward's ghost was not here. She had felt closer to him at home in the village; now, she could not picture his face clearly, nor hear his voice. So many times he had appeared to her unbidden, yet now remained obstinately distant . . . Edward had been twenty-two when he died; she was the same age now, and she would grow older, while he would always be twenty-two, a young man with all the possibilities of his life abruptly snuffed out. It was as if her own youth had died with him. She would never love anyone else as intensely . . . She closed her eyes, and an unexpected vision of him sprang into her mind: his face on the pillow next to hers when he had awoken after the one illicit night they had spent together, his hair black against the white linen, his eyes slowly focusing on her face. The memory wrenched at her; why, of all painful recollections, did she have to recall that moment of intimacy, when the body that had loved hers lay under the smooth turf in front of her?

Lorna and Philip came back, and they fetched the small white rose-bush they had bought in St. Omer and planted it by Edward's grave, and walked slowly back to the car, without speaking. There was nothing to say. They left the graveyard to the chiff-chaff and the butterflies.

Philip had arranged for them to spend their last few days at Hardelot. After so much sorrow, the

191

relaxation came as a relief; the weather was warm and sunny, and they picnicked in the dunes and wandered along the shore and explored the ruins and grounds of the Chateau d'Hardelot. Philip had decided that Alice ought to learn to drive, and he found a quiet area of track through woodlands for her first lessons while Lorna stayed in the sunlit garden of the auberge, writing her new piece.

Alice had been reluctant at first. "I don't know that there's much point in having lessons. I'm not really likely to do much driving in the future."

"It's a handy skill to have. You never know when it might be useful," Philip said. "You might want to get a job where you're required to drive."

"Well – if you're sure you don't mind teaching me," Alice said doubtfully. "I'm sure I won't be very good at it. I don't know a single thing about machines."

Philip was a patient teacher, explaining the procedures to her in understandable terms, and not complaining or visibly wincing when she made the car lurch forward or crashed the gears with a horrible grinding sound. By the end of her first lesson she was driving very slowly and cautiously along the sandy forest track.

"You don't have to hang on to the wheel quite so desperately!" Philip remarked, amused. "You look as if you're riding a horse that's likely to bolt off at any moment."

"That's exactly what I feel like – not that I've ever ridden anything but a seaside donkey," Alice agreed. "Are you going to take over, now that we're back at the road?"

"I will today. Tomorrow you can drive all the way back to the hotel. You've done very well for the first time," Philip said, walking round the car to get back in the driver's seat. "And talking of horses . . . I shall be going over to Ireland soon to see a friend of mine, with a view to buying some brood mares and perhaps some young stock. I want Jack to come with me. He's got a good eye for a horse, and I'd like him to be involved in the buying."

"Oh! I should think he'd love to do that," Alice said. "Irish horses are supposed to be the best in the world, aren't they?"

She felt pleased that Philip clearly intended to treat Jack with respect and consideration. Jack was lucky, she thought, to come back not only to a job but to one he would find thoroughly satisfying.

Next morning Philip took her out driving again, and they stopped at a small village shop and bought red wine and crusty bread and goat's cheese for their picnic. Alice drove back afterwards.

"You ought to keep it up, now that you've made a start, or you'll forget what you've learned," he told her as she pulled up fairly smoothly outside the hotel to collect Lorna.

"Well – thank you for teaching me. It's been fun, but I expect this will be my last chance to drive."

"There's no reason why it need be," he said quietly.

She looked at him, but he said no more, and Lorna came out of the auberge to meet them, very impressed to see Alice sitting confidently at the wheel. They packed the food into Philip's hamper and went down to the beach, where a fresh wind off the sea sent them scurrying to a hollow in the dunes for shelter. It was their last day, and Alice looked down towards the Canche estuary with a sense of regret. The scudding clouds made shifting patterns on the sand, and waders bobbed and dashed at the tide's edge; no-one else was in sight. After the picnic, when Lorna and Philip were finishing off the wine, she excused herself and set off along the deserted shore. Having taken up so much of Philip's attention, she thought he would probably appreciate some time to talk to Lorna.

The waders flew off with shrill cries of alarm, their markings flickering black and white as they wheeled against a background of marram grass and heather. She walked so close to the incoming tide that her footprints filled up with water, and occasionally she had to skip briskly aside to avoid getting her feet and ankles wet; the breeze tugged at her hair and blew grains of sand into her face. She loved the wildness and remoteness of this stretch of coast, the feeling of being alone with just the waders and the gulls for company . . . She turned and looked back towards the car, and was surprised to see Philip coming towards her, walking briskly, his limp only slightly in evidence. Lorna was nowhere in sight; her first thought was that they must have argued. She waited for him to catch up.

"Why did you rush off like that?" he said when he drew level.

She looked at him in surprise. "I just wanted to go for a walk. I thought – "

"Yes?" he prompted.

"Well, it's so lovely here, away from everyone," she hedged. "I used to go for walks like this when I was at the hospital. When you think of all that happened here, you'd think we'd hate it, but we don't – at least I don't."

"No." He looked away from her, narrowing his eyes against the glare from the sea. "The war brought unhappiness to all of us, but there were compensations . . . For some people, at any rate . . ."

He seemed to be talking more to himself than to her; she wasn't sure what he meant. Then he turned to her and said, "The war has brought changes to your life, hasn't it – more than you could ever have guessed?"

"Well, yes." It was the sort of remark she could only agree with, not sure which particular changes he was referring to. Feeling that the conversation was getting rather difficult, she said, "I've really enjoyed the last few days, Philip, in spite of the sadness of it all, coming back. I do appreciate your kindness . . . all you've done."

"No. It was for my own benefit, really, to face up to a few things . . ." He broke off and looked away from her again, holding up a hand to shade his eyes. "I meant what I said earlier, Alice, about the driving lessons. I'd be happy to go on teaching you, if you want to go on learning."

"You mean when you come to see Lorna?"

"I hope I'll continue to call, yes."

"But why shouldn't you? You haven't argued, have you?"

It was his turn to look surprised. "Argued with Lorna? Of course not. Why should you think that?"

195

"Because . . ." she faltered.

He was gazing at her in puzzled frustration, and she had the sense that all along they had been at cross purposes. He tried again.

"Look, I'm not putting this very well. What I want to say is . . . I know how much you cared for Edward, and I know that I could never begin to replace him, and I don't suppose you can imagine ever caring for someone else, but if you ever did, then I . . ."

She could only dimly take in what he was saying, staring at him in astonishment. He broke off and said wryly: "Alice, you should see your face! Is it such a dreadful suggestion?"

"No, but I – I thought you and Lorna cared for each other."

The startled expression on his face told her for once and for all that her assumptions had been completely wrong.

"Lorna! You thought she and I – Good Lord, the thought had never entered my head! Brainy women terrify me – no, Lorna's been very kind to me, helping me through a difficult time, and we've obviously become good friends, but not in that way – did you really think – ?"

She nodded, and his face relaxed into a smile. He smiled so rarely that his features were transformed by it; Alice realized that his habitual expression nowadays was one of sadness. It was this more than anything that made her aware of a sudden warmth of feeling towards him. But what he had just said still jarred her so completely that she was at a loss for a coherent reply.

"Have I surprised you so much?" he said regretfully. "I thought you realized that I was becoming fond of you . . . and I hoped you might be fond of me, just a bit. But you will let me call on you when you're back in London, won't you?"

She hesitated, touched by his thoughtfulness. "I don't know. I've enjoyed your company, of course, and you've been so kind and considerate. But it's too soon . . . for what you say. I can't stop remembering Edward . . . and I don't want to stop."

"I know," he said gently. "As I said, I don't want to replace him – no-one could. And I'm not asking you to promise anything. All I want is to go on seeing you . . . there's no need for any hasty decisions."

She hesitated, unsure what to say to be fair. She was fond of him; the realization surprised her. And after all, he was not asking for any major commitment.

"You mean, we can go on as we are, being friends?"

"Yes, if you like. But with the difference that now I've told you."

"Then – as long as you understand how I feel about Edward – there's no reason why not, is there?"

He agreed to that, and they walked slowly back along the sand to join Lorna. Alice, conscious of the readjustment of all their relationships in her own mind since she had started her walk no more than half an hour ago, wondered if Lorna knew what had passed between Philip and herself. Lorna was very perceptive.

Lorna hinted that she did know while she and Alice were preparing for bed later that night in the hotel room they shared. "I think this trip has brought a few things out into the open, don't you?"

Alice stopped brushing her hair and looked at Lorna's reflection in the dressing-table mirror. "What do you mean?"

"I mean Philip," Lorna said, folding garments. "He did say something to you this afternoon, didn't he?"

"Do you mean you already knew? Before today, I mean?"

"Yes . . . he was concerned about how you'd react. I think he wanted to visit France to put painful memories to rest, but for you and me it was different . . . we don't want to forget."

Alice picked up her brush again. She wasn't sure she liked the idea of Philip and Lorna discussing her, even if they had her own interests in mind. If she were honest with herself, she couldn't help being flattered by Philip's attentions. But did such an admission constitute a breaking of faith with Edward? She frowned at her reflection as she brushed out a stubborn tangle.

"Edward died more than two years ago. You can't spend the rest of your life in love with a ghost," Lorna said.

Harriet and Sarah

The stables and fields at Greenstocks had been neglected during the war. With only the two in-foal mares and the old hunter to look after, and those turned out to grass for the summer, Jack spent most of his time making ready for the new stock. The fields had new post-and-rail fencing, and some of the larger paddocks had been divided into smaller areas where a mare could be put out safely with her foal. Jack had cleaned out all the old stables and whitewashed the walls; the doors and window-frames had been freshly painted, there was a big tub of geraniums by the water-trough in the yard and even the old clock over the archway had been repaired.

"All we want now is the horses," Philip said, looking around with satisfaction. "And I expect you're looking forward to having something to ride with a bit more spark than my father's old cob."

"Yes, sir. It'll be good to see the old place come to life again."

Smoke curled up from a big bonfire Jack had made of the ragwort and thistles and docks he had pulled up from the fields. He and Philip walked around the yard looking at all the improvements, while Philip's golden Labrador lay down to wait on the sun-warmed cobbles. Jack was pleased with the results of his efforts. The yard had looked like this before the war when he had been a humble stable-boy; now he was employed as Horseman, and with the impressive title went the cottage, and three pounds a week.

"I'm lucky to have this job to come back to," he told Harriet. "There's many men out of work now with the munitions factories closing down and all the troops coming back. But at least Philip won't have any trouble when he wants to take on more staff."

He and Harriet and the little boy, Stevie, had moved into the cottage adjoining the stable-yard as soon as he had been demobilized. It was bigger than the cottage Harriet's parents lived in, with a garden at the back already laid out in flower borders and a vegetable plot. Jack imagined that Harriet would be perfectly happy there, with the child and the house to occupy her. He could hardly believe their good fortune – his work was enjoyable, and they had a cottage all to themselves, with electric light, a proper kitchen, and the garden, and a view from the upstairs windows over the meadows towards the woods.

Moving into the cottage and getting straight down to work had helped him to get over the awkwardness of returning to Harriet. She seemed pleased with the independence from her parents, and busied herself about the cottage, arranging things to her satisfaction. The child played out in the garden in a white bonnet to shield his face from the sun, inventing complicated games with sticks and stones and leaves. Jack had been amazed to find that his son was no longer a baby but a small child who could walk and run and name objects and even begin to form sentences; having last seen him as a tiny infant, Jack found it hard to realize that the child had any connection with himself. Sometimes, in the evenings, he went to see Emily and his mother, taking Stevie with him, or if it was fine he took the little boy on walks around the farm, carrying him on his shoulders and teaching him the names of various objects and birds and animals.

When he didn't have Stevie with him, Jack liked to walk up to the ridge overlooking Greenstocks, his old haunt. It was more peaceful than anywhere else he knew, with the sun setting slowly in a red haze behind the woods, the hares sitting up in the long grass of the meadow, and the rooks slowly drifting back to the tallest trees. A barn owl flew round the edges of the wood every evening, gliding low on wings as soft and silent as a moth's. In the twilight, pheasants ventured out to the fields, sometimes flying up in their clumsy way with a rattling cry which echoed through the trees. Jack supposed that as usual the pheasants had been carefully reared and nurtured for the Morlands' winter shoots. He wondered whether Philip would want to take part this year, having been in a few shooting parties too many; shooting had lost any appeal it may once have had for Jack. And much as he liked walking in the woods, he could never venture out on to the open ground of the ridge without looking around edgily for concealed snipers or machine-gun posts, or worrying that his flanks and rear weren't secure. Once, when the gamekeeper had been out after pigeons and had unexpectedly fired his shotgun close at hand, Jack instinctively threw himself to the ground and had to make a supreme effort of will to get up and continue walking normally.

201

When Jack looked after Stevie for the evening, Harriet often took the opportunity to go into the village to visit Rosie Taplin or her other friends. In her own way, she seemed pleased to have Jack at home, as if his presence gave her a new status as a wife and mother with a home of her own. She was never affectionate towards him, but when he made love to her – in their *own* bed, in their *own* house – she responded as eagerly as he could have wished.

Before he had been home more than a few days, troubled by his conscience, he decided that he ought to tell Harriet about his encounter with the young Belgian widow. He expected her to be angry or tearful, but to his amazement she only smiled cynically, as if it were precisely the sort of behaviour she expected.

"I don't suppose you were the only one," was all she said.

"Aren't you angry?" he asked, baffled by her lack of concern.

She shrugged. "It's not going to make much difference to me, is it?"

He felt slighted, and would almost have preferred rage or tears. He would never understand women, he told himself.

Harriet was more resentful over a letter Jack had received from Sarah Cartwright and had left in its envelope on the kitchen table. "Who's this Sarah then?" she demanded when Jack went in at midday.

"Sarah Cartwright – didn't I tell you? She's Stephen's sister. I've been to their house twice, in the East End."

"Is that the one whose mother's always writing to you?"

"Yes. In an odd way I think she looks on Stevie as if he was her own grandson, because he's named after Stephen."

"That's daft," Harriet said scornfully. "He's nothing to do with her. Anyway, this Sarah wants you to go to their house again."

Jack felt annoyed that she had read his letter, but was not really surprised. "In that case, you know why. She says so in the letter. To choose one of Stephen's horse pictures, to keep for myself."

"I should have thought there were enough horses around here, without needing to have pictures of them to look at. Rosie Taplin says it's the same with Jimmy. Horses, horses all the time."

Jimmy, who had worked as a groom at the Hunt kennels before the war, would be whipper-in for the coming season. Jack often came across him exercising the hounds along the lanes, and occasionally they met in the pub in the evening. Jimmy was very envious of Jack's forthcoming trip to Ireland to buy horses.

"Get one for me, will you? All the horses around here that weren't already drawing their old-age pensions went to the Army. All I've got to ride is that big old grey that's as old as I am. Still, with your new set-up, we might be able to get some decent nags from His Royal Highness in a year or two."

His Royal Highness had been Philip's army nickname, used out of his hearing by the members of his platoon. "He's not like that any more," Jack said. "Quite human in fact. The war seems to have knocked all that out of him. And he didn't have to offer to take me to Ireland, did he? He could just as easily have gone by himself."

"Yes, you've got a right cushy number there, you lucky blighter," Jimmy said.

After work next evening Philip asked Jack to come up to the house to talk about the Irish trip. Mary, Jack's niece, opened the door to him – he didn't go up to the house much, and was surprised to remember that she worked there now – and Philip took him into the study and offered him a glass of whisky. To Jack, not used to spirits, it conjured up disturbing memories of tots gulped down hastily just before going over the top on trench raids . . . He banished these uncomfortable thoughts and listened to Philip. They were going to stay with an Army acquaintance near Dublin, he said. "We should be able to buy ourselves some breeding stock, and perhaps get a riding horse or two," Philip told him. "This friend of mine lost his right arm in the war, poor chap. He used to ride like the devil, but now he can only hack about quietly. He's got a couple of good bold hunters and he can't bear to see them about the place doing nothing."

Jack thought about this as he walked slowly back down the track towards the stables. To lose your right arm – in the worst of the fighting, some men would have welcomed it, a definite Blighty ticket. But afterwards . . . all the things you couldn't do, for the rest of your life. He couldn't shake off the feeling that he had somehow escaped unfairly, without a blemish apart from the two small scars on his arm from minor bullet wounds. In London on his way back to be demobilized he had seen a man without arms begging in the streets – begging, in Lloyd George's land fit for heroes to live in. And he couldn't forget his shock when he had first seen a man without legs in one of the hospitals – a young man, about his own age, with both legs amputated at the hip, sitting propped up in a wheelchair in the grounds waiting for the nurse to take him in, childishly helpless. It was too cruel, crueller even than death . . .

In the field beside the track, a horse lay flat on its side, not moving. Jolted out of his thoughts, Jack slipped through the rails and ran over to it. If it wasn't dead already, he'd have to get an officer's revolver and put a bullet through its head . . . he dreaded what he would see, smashed limbs, guts spilled all over the ground, eyes wild with fear and agony . . . a shell must have got it, but where was the rest of the team . . .?

The mare lifted her head as he ran closer and looked at him in mild curiosity, twitching her smooth flanks to shake off an annoying fly. She was a brood mare in the peak of her condition, her bay coat shining with health as she lay in the evening sunshine. Jack stopped dead in astonishment and sat down heavily on the ground, closing his eyes. What was the matter with him? He was going off his head, he thought, completely forgetting where he was, not knowing what he was doing. He was as shocked by his own irrational behaviour as by the vision of the mutilated horse. He got to his feet again, and stroked the mare's ears and inhaled the warm comforting animal smell of her coat. He hoped no-one had seen him rushing about like a madman.

That night his old nightmare came back, as vivid as ever. He was struggling through the deep mud, floundering in his efforts to get to Stephen, but it was already too late . . . He woke up sweating and shouting in terror, fighting the bedclothes.

"Jack! Stop it!" Harriet was shouting at him, gripping his shoulder and shaking him into consciousness.

He looked around the room as it swam slowly into focus. His heart was crashing against his ribs, and his nightmare was still with him; the sweet, rotten trench smell of decay and death was thick in his nostrils . . .

"What on earth's the matter?" Harriet asked.

"Sorry. I was dreaming."

A rising wail came from the other bedroom, followed by a series of sobs.

"Oh, now the baby's awake," Harriet said crossly. She lay back and waited for a few minutes, while Jack tried to get his breathing back to normal, and then she said, "I suppose I'll have to get up. You're obviously not going to."

Jack felt too shaken to attempt to comfort the child. His nightmare was like gas fumes swirling around in the room, waiting to claim him again; as soon as he let himself sleep again he would sink down into them, drowning, helpless. He lay determinedly awake until Harriet eventually came back to bed, turning her back on him firmly as she pulled the blankets up to her ears.

When the nightmare recurred on subsequent nights, she became more and more impatient, especially when on one occasion he grabbed hold of her and almost threw her out of bed, convinced that they were in a trench with a shell about to scream down on them.

"For God's sake – you nearly gave me a heart attack!" Harriet cried. "Can't you get a grip on yourself?"

"You don't think I do it for fun, do you?" Jack retorted, stung by her lack of sympathy. It seemed that the more he worried, the more the nightmares came back, after untroubled months following the Armistice while he had been waiting in France. It was as if the return to normal life pointed up the abnormality of the horrors he had lived through, and made him experience them over again in his mind.

"The war was over months ago. Perhaps you'd better see the doctor."

"There's nothing he can do," Jack said miserably. "I'll get over it in time."

"Well, I damn well hope you do. Otherwise you'll have to sleep in Stevie's room and I'll have him in here with me. I'm sick of having to get him back to sleep in the middle of the night," Harriet said, yawning. "At least I'll get some decent rest next week when you go to Ireland."

Philip had resigned from his staff job in London, and would soon be spending all his time at Greenstocks again. Jack, who understood from Alice that Philip had been seeing a lot of Lorna Sidgwick, wondered whether he would marry. It would go with the country gentleman's life he seemed set on leading, Jack thought: a wife, a son and heir to carry the family name to the next generation. Philip was already in his mid-twenties, old enough to think of settling down. Well, it wouldn't make much difference to Jack, unless he married a horsy woman who would expect to have her own hunters. Lorna Sidgwick certainly wasn't that, from what Jack knew of her.

"Philip and Lorna Sidgwick took Alice to France with them," he remarked to Harriet over breakfast, reading a letter Alice had sent him on her return to London.

"Yes. She's gone up in the world, hasn't she?" Harriet said, evidently not approving. "Odd to think she and I used to be kitchen-maids together. And now your Mary's working there. Must be a bit awkward for Alice to have a kitchen-maid for a niece."

"Why should that bother her? She's not snobbish."

Harriet raised her eyebrows. "Oh, isn't she?"

"You know she isn't."

Harriet didn't answer, turning to Stevie and telling him sharply to eat his toast instead of banging the table with it. Jack, not liking the implied criticism of Alice, put on his jacket and went out.

He and Philip left for Ireland early next morning. Jack was looking forward to the trip – he had always rather wanted to see Ireland, and he was pleased that Philip valued his opinion enough to want him to go. They travelled by train and ship, arriving at Kingstown late that evening. Philip's friend, Captain Michael O'Halloran, met them at the docks in a car driven by his groom, an elderly man with a very tanned and wrinkled face, introduced as Paddy.

"They've yet to invent the car you can drive with one arm," O'Halloran said cheerfully. He was a small, very animated man of about thirty, dressed in tweeds, with the right arm of his jacket pinned at the elbow. His farm was in County Wicklow, not far from Dublin, on the edge of the Wicklow Mountains. It was too dark to get any impression of the scenery, but Jack liked the house, a rambling, rather shabby place full of faded sofas, racing trophies, portraits of horses and hunting scenes. A huge wolfhound followed Captain O'Halloran around devotedly from the moment he entered the house with his guests. A single man, he lived there with an elderly housekeeper, Jack gathered. He had expected to be shown to a room above the stables or in servants' quarters, but to his surprise he was given a room of his own next to Philip's, and told that dinner would be in about half an hour. There was no standing on ceremony here. When he addressed his host as Sir, he was quickly reproved.

"Didn't we all have enough of that *yes, sir, no, sir* in the war? Michael will do. And will I call you Jack?"

Jack agreed, liking the other man's lack of formality but still not sure how he was expected to behave in the awkward no-man's-land between master and servant. He was relieved that the dinner wasn't the smart well-mannered occasion it would have been in the Morlands' house; Michael wore the same clothes he had had on earlier, and the meal was served by the housekeeper who stumped in and out with dishes and tureens, pausing to exchange bantering remarks with her employer. Jack, wary at first, gradually found himself drawn into the conversation, which was mainly about horses and hunting. When the

209

long-drawn-out meal was over, he excused himself and went up to his room, leaving the other two to their whiskey and talk.

Much later, in the early dawn, he awoke abruptly from his familiar dream in the unfamiliar room. He lay for a while staring at the pattern of the grey first light on the curtains before getting up and making his way carefully along the corridor to the bathroom at the end. On his way back, he noticed a glimmer of candlelight under the door of the adjoining room, and heard the faint creak of the floorboards as the occupant moved about. Philip was awake, too. Jack wondered about this as he closed the latch of his own door and got back into bed. Was Philip, too, kept awake by recurring dreams? It was odd to think of them both lying there in the darkness, no more than a few yards apart, each isolated in his own nightmare yet reliving, probably, similar terrors.

He slept again, dreamlessly this time, until the housekeeper knocked on his door with hot water for washing, and tea. He felt refreshed in spite of his broken night. He drew the curtains to see a smooth sweep of green hillside, misty purple hills beyond, and a shallow river with a stony bed. He opened the window wider and leaned out, breathing the clean air. Horses were grazing in the meadows between the house and the river – youngstock, leggy and immature, and mares with foals in an adjoining field. Jack washed and shaved and dressed quickly, eager to get on with the day.

After breakfast, they all went down to the stables – which, in contrast to the house, were smart and

210

up-to-date – and the groom led out a selection of mares and youngstock. They were all of a type Jack liked, quality horses, but with substance to them, and full of condition from the lush grass.

"Now this is my stallion, Erinmore. Thoroughbred crossed with Irish Draught – you can't beat it," Michael O'Halloran said, running his left hand down the horse's shapely foreleg. "The speed and stamina of the thoroughbred, the toughness of the Irish Draught . . . Look at this fellow now. Isn't he grand? This one you can't buy – I worship the ground he treads on. He stands here at stud. I'll show you some top-class foals of his in a while."

The groom, Paddy, brought out horse after horse, and O'Halloran beamed with pride in his animals, urging Jack and Philip to admire the length of shoulder, the short muscular backs, the depth of bone. He pulled the horses' ears fondly as they were led away and gave them pieces of carrot from his capacious pocket. Finally, when it seemed that every horse, mare and foal on the premises had been paraded before them, he said, "Now let's see my big lad," and the groom led out a tall hunter.

Jack looked at it appreciatively. It was a big rangy bay, very dark in its summer coat, with large intelligent eyes. Something about it reminded Jack of Philip Morland's Galliard, the horse he had bought just before the war.

"Now, isn't he a beauty? The grandest horse I ever owned, but he's too much for me these days – with just the one arm, I can hardly ride the half of him. Would one of you like to put a leg across him?"

"Jack?" Philip offered.

"Yes, I would," Jack said promptly.

Paddy led the horse back into its box and fetched a hunting saddle and double bridle. Jack, listening to the familiar clink of the bits and the fidget of hooves in straw, felt a stirring of excitement. It was years since he had ridden a proper horse – Mr Morland's old cob didn't come into the same category as this lovely animal. He hoped his riding would be up to it after so long.

The groom led the horse out and gave Jack a leg up. He adjusted the stirrups and picked up the reins, and the groom opened a gate into a paddock with two jumps set up in the middle.

"Just let him settle a bit first," O'Halloran called out. "He can be a bit of a handful."

Jack rode out into the open meadow. He had forgotten what it was like – the length of neck and shoulder in front of him, the long ears pricked in anticipation, the smooth stride beneath him. The bay was skittish, shying at a pole lying in the grass and almost unseating Jack. He sat tighter. He wasn't going to fall off, not in front of O'Halloran and Philip Morland . . . he made the horse concentrate, walking on a short rein, and then when it was settled pushed on into a trot. The horse ran on at first, gradually coming back to Jack's hand and leg, obedient, arching its neck to the feel on the reins. He pushed on into a canter, working the horse in circles, and finally releasing it into a gallop down the long side of the paddock. He didn't want to stop. He could have gone on over the green hills and mountains, the long stride covering the ground.

"Try him over the fences," O'Halloran called out.

There were two rustic fences in the paddock, about three feet six in height. Jack got the horse back to a steady canter, and turned towards the first; the ears pricked in front of him and the horse dived forward and threw itself over the jump as if in a race. Jack, admiring the horse's boldness, could understand that O'Halloran would have difficulty controlling him. He took the jump again, steadying the pace this time and taking the obstacle in a more controlled fashion, and repeated the performance three more times.

"Will I put the pole up for you?" O'Halloran shouted.

"Yes," Jack called back. Philip and O'Halloran between them raised both jumps to about four feet, and Jack jumped them both, the horse paying attention to him now, waiting for him to release its energy three strides before the fence, and pouring itself over in an easy fluid movement. It was so exhilarating that he jumped both obstacles a second and a third time, then pulled up reluctantly and rode slowly back to the gateway, patting the horse and grinning with pleasure. He tried to wipe the grin off his face as he thought what it must be like to stand where O'Halloran stood, owning a horse like this and having to part with it.

But there was open admiration in the older man's glance. "I've never seen anyone get such a good tune out of him. Isn't he a grand fellow? But I tell you it breaks my heart to see you ride him like that. You're a natural horseman, Jack," he said generously.

213

They took an overnight boat from Kingstown two days later. Philip seemed well satisfied with the expedition; he had bought the bay hunter, as well as two unbacked four-year-olds, a brood mare, and a yearling filly sired by O'Halloran's own stallion. The horses would be sent on by boat and train a week or two later, when shipping arrangements had been made.

"It's a good investment," he told Jack. "You'll have plenty to get to work on. I'm especially pleased about the bay. You can go out hunting on him and perhaps even go to one or two jumping shows next year. It will be a good advertisement, letting people see what quality horses we've got. What we need now is to look out for a stallion of our own. And we must take on a stable-boy, perhaps two, before the winter."

Jack felt pleased too, looking forward to the future with real optimism. He was eager for the new horses to arrive at Greenstocks, feeling that his new job would really begin when they were installed.

Philip had timed their return journey so that they arrived in London in the early afternoon. He wanted to go and see someone, he said as they walked through the crowded railway terminus; he suggested that Jack might as well go on ahead by train to Essex.

Jack thought for a moment. It was Sunday afternoon; there was no particular reason to hurry back. "I could call round and see Alice first," he said.

"Ah yes," Philip said rather awkwardly. "I was going in that direction myself."

214

Jack, about to suggest that they went together, realized that Philip probably didn't want him around if he was courting Lorna Sidgwick. He said, "Well, perhaps on second thoughts I won't go. I can see Alice some other time."

They parted, and Jack bought a cup of tea at the refreshment bar and wondered whether to go straight home. He was aware that he didn't really want to. His parting with Harriet had been cool, and he didn't delude himself that she would be delighted to see him again. He would have liked to have a chat with Alice; he didn't see her much these days. It was a damn nuisance, Philip being involved with Lorna Sidgwick. He and Philip had got on well throughout the trip, Philip going out of his way to ask for his opinions, but that was business – obviously he wouldn't want Jack tagging along while he conducted his love affairs. Then Jack remembered the letter from Sarah Cartwright. This would be as good a time as any to go down to Mile End – on a Sunday afternoon, she and her mother were likely to be at home.

He caught a bus and walked the rest of the way, stopping to buy a bunch of roses at a street stall. As on his previous visit, he felt shut in by the narrow streets, particularly after the quiet beauty of the Wicklow Mountains. How could Alice bear to live in London, particularly in summer? Jack felt he would be stifled if he couldn't walk into woods and fields in the evenings and be completely alone when he wanted to be. Here, you could only be alone by shutting yourself in a room, if you were lucky enough to have one to yourself. He could never, never live in

215

a city. Perhaps Alice would come to her senses soon and return to the country.

Sarah opened the door to him and her face lit up with pleasure. "Jack! What a lovely surprise! What are you doing in London?" She led him inside and called, "Mum! Jack's come to see us!"

Mrs Cartwright came through from the kitchen and he told them about his trip to Ireland, and she asked after Harriet and the baby. They both thanked him for the roses, and Sarah fetched a vase and arranged them at once. As on his previous two visits, Jack could hardly take his eyes off her; she was so like Stephen, with exactly the same colouring and some of the same gestures and expressions. How could she look so healthy, living in this filthy city? Stephen had been the same, with a golden-skinned, almost glowing aura of well-being amidst the worst squalor of the trenches. He had seemed uncontaminated by the filth. Jack sometimes thought that he had been too innocent to survive; he could never imagine him growing hard and embittered, or small-minded, as so many of the soldiers had inevitably become.

Mrs Cartwright made tea, and Sarah fetched the sketch-book, and she and Jack sat together at the table looking at each picture in turn. "You can have which ever one you like," she said. "Mum and I thought it would be nice for you to take one, and I'm sure Stephen would be pleased if he knew."

At last Jack made his choice, one of the close-up portraits, and Sarah put it between two pieces of card so that he could carry it home safely. He would frame it and put it on his bedroom wall, he decided, whatever Harriet said. They had tea, and then Jack said that he ought to be on his way.

"I'll walk with you to the tram," Sarah offered.

Mrs Cartwright said, "Give our best regards to your wife and little Stephen. I do hope we'll see you again."

"I hope so too."

Sarah walked along the street beside Jack with quick light steps. She was a good few inches shorter than he was, and whenever she spoke to him she looked intently up at him for his answer. She was working in a clothing factory now, she told him; she didn't like the work, but there was no alternative, and she was lucky to have a job at all. He hated to think of her still toiling in some dreary workshop for a low wage, after her munitions work in the war. She ought to have a better life. But she was the main breadwinner now; she and her mother couldn't live on Stephen's army pension.

"Mum loves it when you come," she told him while they waited at the tram stop, "and so do I. It makes us remember Stephen, but in a happy way. And you're like him."

He looked at her in surprise. "I'm like Stephen?"

"Yes."

"Oh, I don't think so. He was a much better person."

"But you are like him," she insisted, looking at him gravely. Her eyes were just like her brother's, somewhere between green and brown, with very clear whites. "You're honest. Straightforward."

He felt ashamed that she held such a high opinion of him. "You don't know me very well then, if you

217

think that. I'm not straight – the messes I get myself into – "

She had a way of looking at him that he found faintly disturbing. There was nothing provocative or flirtatious about her, but she studied him with a direct, serious gaze. It was as if she wanted to understand him, a wish so noticeably absent in Harriet that he felt rather stunned by it.

"Oh, look, here's your tram. We will see you again, won't we?" she said above the clatter.

"Yes," he said. On an impulse, he bent quickly and kissed her cheek, and she whispered, "Goodbye, Jack."

"Are you getting on or not, mate?" the conductor called out.

Jack got on to the tram and climbed to the upper deck, where he sat gazing at the roofs and chimneys. He wondered whether Sarah had a young man of her own, and was surprised to find how much he disliked the idea.

Persuasion

"Two articles accepted in a fortnight, *and* an invitation to speak at that debate; you're getting quite famous!" Alice teased, passing the morning's letters back to Lorna.

"Well, hardly. But it is a start," Lorna said. "It's only because another speaker dropped out of the debate at the last minute, and my old tutor happened to have read one of my articles on the same subject. I'm going to have to do a lot of research beforehand – I think I'd better spend a couple of days at the University Library. With an audience of undergraduates I'll need to be sure of my facts. Will you type up that article on birth control for me this afternoon while I'm out?"

"Yes. And you won't forget Philip's coming for supper this evening, will you?"

"Oh – " Lorna clapped a hand to her mouth. "I *had* forgotten. How silly of me. I've arranged to go to a meeting."

"*Lorna*!" Alice said reproachfully. This show of absent-mindedness did not deceive her. "You're impossible! That's the second time you've backed out of an arrangement with Philip."

Lorna grinned. "All right, I admit it. I'm a romantic at heart. It's obviously you he wants to see."

Alice drank her coffee thoughtfully. Lorna seemed

almost to be conspiring with Philip to bring about a closer relationship than she felt she wanted.

"Don't look so solemn!" Lorna reproved. "Most people would be flattered."

"I am, but – well . . ."

"I know. He isn't Edward. But do you really think Edward would have wanted you to go on mourning him for the rest of your life? Don't you think he would have wanted you to be happy? You're still young, and Philip is serious about you – you do realize that? – and you ought to think of your future, not keep dwelling on the past."

"But what about *our* future? We've got it all worked out, living here, your campaigning – "

"It suits me, but it won't always suit you," Lorna said. "You want a family life, children . . . I don't. Here, have another piece of toast. And don't look at me like that. I haven't told you anything you didn't already know."

"We've never talked about it . . . what makes you say that?"

"I'm right though, aren't I? And that's what Philip wants too."

Alice made no reply, and Lorna continued, "You know, he told me once that he rather envies Edward."

"He envies Edward?" Alice repeated. "How can he?"

"It's not really surprising, is it? Edward was in-telligent and good-looking and kind, he was a brave officer and most of all he died young. Philip feels himself to be second-rate on most of those counts. Nothing can tarnish your view of Edward, because he died before you really knew him intimately – he's become an ideal in your mind that no-one else can possibly live up to. Quite possibly he couldn't even have lived up to it himself. And that makes Philip feel inadequate."

Alice was taken aback by this brisk analysis of the situation.

"That's not quite fair," she retorted. "I didn't encourage Philip. It was his own choosing. If anyone does any encouraging, it's you. Do you think I'm being unfair to him, then?"

"It's as well for you to know his point of view. And if you really can't entertain thoughts of him as any more than a friend, it's only fair to let him know." Lorna finished her coffee and stood up. "And now, after all that soul-searching, I really must go. I'll be late for my classes."

She collected her things together and hurried off, leaving Alice to go about her morning tasks of clearing away the breakfast things and tidying the flat before going down to start work in the canteen. She thought over all that Lorna had said. Most of it was true, she acknowledged; the idea of having a family did appeal to her, but her vision of dark-haired, blue-eyed children had died with Edward, never, she thought, to be resurrected. The possibility of marrying Philip was something she had preferred not to think about; he had kept to his word, not pressing her for any commitment, merely treating her with kindness and consideration. She liked him, she enjoyed his company . . . but how could it be more than that, with Edward always in her thoughts? And yet, if Lorna was right, she was in love with a falsified version of Edward, not a real person.

221

This suggestion jarred her more than anything else.

She went to her room and looked at her photograph of Edward in his second-lieutenant's uniform, taken shortly after he had joined up. He looked back at her, his eyes shadowed by his officer's cap, his expression solemn. A remote, idealized vision? She closed her eyes. No . . . she could remember his shifts of mood, through cheerfulness and stoicism to taciturnity and depression. He had been everything Lorna had said, but he had been human, with human weaknesses, and she had loved him the more for that.

She went to Gower Street as Lorna's guest to hear her speak in the University debate. The subject was "This house believes that the terms of the Peace Treaty will bring about further threats to the stability of Europe"; Lorna, seconding the motion, was the only female speaker. Alice sat in the back of the crowded hall, impressed by Lorna's air of authority and the skill with which she picked up her opponents' weaker points and turned them round, using them to her own advantage. She knew how nervous Lorna had been beforehand, but there was no sign of it now.

"She's very articulate – persuasive and well-informed," a donnish-looking character near Alice remarked to his companion. Alice stored this compliment in her memory to pass on to Lorna later.

The motion was defeated by a narrow margin. After the vote, waiting at the back of the hall for Lorna, who was being interviewed by a local newspaper reporter, Alice caught sight of a young man who looked vaguely familiar: thick brown hair, dark eyebrows, broad shoulders. A snatch of what he was saying drifted over to her above the general conversation, and from the deep voice and Irish accent she recognized Patrick Leary. He was with a group of other young men, but she saw him glance in her direction once or twice as if trying to place her, and after a while he detached himself and came over.

"It's Miss Smallwood, isn't it?"

"Yes. Alice. How nice to see you!"

"And you too. Are you living in London?"

"Yes, Lorna and I share a flat together in Mile End and I'm a sort of secretary for her. And you?"

"I'm finishing my Economics degree – I've one year left to do. Did you enjoy the debate? I must congratulate Lorna on her speech. It was very convincing."

Alice remembered that she had last seen him in the cemetery at Étaples, a lonely, desperate figure. "I was so sorry to hear about your fiancée," she said quietly.

His smile faded. "Yes. Thank you. It's a bit of an ironic reversal, really . . . in wartime it's usually the girl who's left mourning her dead sweetheart . . ." He pulled himself up abruptly. "Mother of God. I'm as tactless as ever. I'm so sorry."

"No, please. We're both in the same position, aren't we?"

"Yes. Everyone says time will heal," he said seriously, "but I don't know whether it will. Do you think so?"

"Well, I . . ." Alice didn't get the chance to tell him what she thought, as at that moment Lorna came over to them, pleased to see Patrick. By the time he and Alice had congratulated her on her performance, and they had exchanged news, and he had introduced them both to his friends, the subject of coping with grief had been forgotten.

"Here's our address." Lorna scribbled quickly on a piece of paper and handed it to him. "Now that we've bumped into you, we must keep in contact."

"I'd like that very much," Patrick said, in his courteous, rather old-fashioned manner.

Leaving the hall, Alice remembered the outing at Étaples, nearly two years ago. "Do you ever hear anything of Charles Aldridge?" she asked Lorna casually.

"Oh, Charles? Didn't I tell you?" Lorna said vaguely. "I thought I had. He went back to his wife at the end of the war."

On a misty autumnal evening Philip took Alice out to dinner to his favourite restaurant near Kew. The waiter led them to a table in a candlelit alcove overlooking the gardens and the river, illuminated in the October dusk by globes of light in the restaurant garden. Philip, who seemed to be in a very good mood, ordered champagne. He looked handsome in a black dinner jacket, reminding Alice of evenings at Greenstocks when she had waited at table. She remembered that Harriet used to make eyes at Philip whenever she got the chance, and would gaze out of the windows at him when Mrs Sedley wasn't around. Alice supposed that Philip must have known; Harriet had been far from discreet. Alice had always been rather scornful of her, not sharing her admiration for Philip. Now, she realized again how much her opinion of him had changed.

"Are you celebrating something?" she asked him when the waiter had brought the champagne.

"Not really. But things are going well at home. I've just bought a stallion," he told her, "so we can be in business as a proper stud next spring. Jack's in his element, out in the yard from dawn to dusk, exercising and schooling and grooming and building jumps. He really is very good with the young horses."

"I'm glad Jack's happy," Alice said. "I do appreciate all you've done for him, and I'm sure he does, too. And what about Harriet and Stevie? Do you see much of them?"

"Oh . . . not really. Alfie has come back to work for us, did I tell you? We'll need an extra pair of hands for the hunting season. Cubbing's already started."

Alice hated fox-hunting. She could clearly remember the day Madeleine had come home in triumph with fox's blood smeared over her face by the Master, having been present at the kill. Alice had been appalled, but Madeleine had assured her that it was a great honour. Edward, never having been much of a rider, had hated it too, and she remembered a quotation he had once shown her from Cowper: . . . *detested sport, that owes its pleasure to another's pain* . . . It was a reminder of the difference between Edward and Philip. But now Jack would be going hunting . . . She remembered that once a year the hounds had met at Greenstocks, a tradition which would, she supposed, continue.

The waiter brought their meal, and when he had gone Philip said, rather hesitantly, "Does Jack know that we've been seeing each other?"

"Well . . . He knows that you come to the flat quite often, and that you're friends with Lorna and me . . ." She stopped, knowing that this wasn't quite what Philip meant.

"He ought to know," Philip said. "It makes things rather awkward sometimes. You don't think he'll mind, do you?"

"Well . . . I don't know," Alice said honestly. Her instincts told her that Jack would not like it, and that was why she had avoided mentioning Philip when she had been home for weekends. Jack seemed to be getting on remarkably well with Philip these days, after all their animosity in the past; she didn't want to risk spoiling their working relationship.

Philip looked at her rather sadly. "I wish there wasn't any need for secrecy."

She thought that his parents and Madeleine were even more likely to frown on the friendship than Jack was, but didn't like to ask him directly whether they knew. She felt rather wearied by the prospect of his family's disapproval. It would be like Edward's mother all over again; the Morlands were just as rigid in their outlook. "It's easy here in London, isn't it?" she said. "It doesn't matter who we are or where we came from. But as soon as we go back to the village all sorts of complications start arising."

Philip was silent for a while, and Alice felt sure she had offended him. They exchanged a few desultory remarks on other topics until they had finished their meal and the waiter took their plates away. Then he looked at her very directly and said, "We could circumvent all this quite easily, Alice. I don't want any complications. I want to marry you. I want you to live at Greenstocks as my wife."

She gazed back at him, stunned into silence, for all that Lorna had led her to expect this sooner or later. She saw that it was hopeless to carry on pretending that they were just friends. It simply wasn't fair to take him for granted – to make him feel inadequate, as Lorna had said.

"Don't say anything," he said. "Please don't say anything at all. Just promise me that you'll think about it. I'm not very good at this sort of thing. I didn't mean to come out with it in the middle of a meal."

He smiled at her ruefully, and she wondered how she could ever have thought him cold and haughty. She couldn't think clearly, dazed by the champagne and the candlelight, and the tenderness of his expression. It was a potent combination.

"Thank you," she said rather haltingly. "I shall regard it as a compliment – a very great compliment. And I won't say anything else now. Hasty decisions are often not the right ones."

She thought it sounded a horribly cold and formal speech, but Philip looked relieved. He made no romantic declarations, and she was glad.

"Now we really have something to celebrate – that I've got up the nerve to ask you. It would be a pity to let that champagne go to waste," he said, refilling her glass. "In any case, why don't you come to Greenstocks next weekend as my guest?"

227

"Well . . . it's kind of you, but not without telling Jack first, and my family. And my own niece works there as a maid," she reminded him. "It would really be very awkward. I'd prefer to stay with my own family."

"Maybe we'd better leave it until you've thought about what I said. If you do . . . decide to accept, then we may as well let everyone know."

Later, when he had driven her home, she asked if he would like to come upstairs and have coffee with Lorna.

"No, I don't think so, thank you." He looked at her gravely. "Alice, I know I've gone back on my word. I told you in France that I wouldn't push you into anything. I still won't, but I want you to know how I feel. I know you can't feel about me as you did for Edward, but I can offer you love, and security, and a comfortable home. Please think about it. I'm sorry if it's only second-best."

"Oh, Philip." She was touched by his reasonableness. "You shouldn't think of yourself as second-best. You're far more patient with me than I deserve."

He took hold of her chin and turned her face to his, and kissed her very gently. A few minutes later, much surprised to find herself so moved, and still rather light-headed, she went indoors.

Wounds

"If you really get to work on him, he'll be ready to hunt when the season starts," Philip said, looking on as Jack saddled the grey four-year-old.

Jack frowned, tightening the girths. "It's a bit soon. He needs more quiet work at home first."

"Oh, surely not," Philip said lightly. "You've been doing so well with him. I should think he'd be likely to attract a buyer quite quickly. He's certainly a nice-looking animal."

Jack said nothing, leading the grey out into the yard. Philip followed him to the paddock and said, "By the way, don't ride my horse today, will you? I'd like to take him out myself this afternoon."

"All right. I'll tell Alfie to get him ready for you." Jack mounted and rode out into the paddock, rather hoping that Philip would go away. He preferred to work on the horses at his own pace, not pushing them too far, satisfied with a slight improvement in each training session. Philip always wanted to do a bit more, to carry on when Jack thought the horse had had enough, or to put the jump a bit higher.

The grey four-year-old had only been backed a matter of weeks. It was coming on well, but it was still gawky and adolescent, spooking at imagined monsters in the hedgerow. If he took it out hunting, Jack knew he would have to nurse it carefully, keeping it well to the back of the field. He had been looking forward to riding the bay hunter. He knew that the real reason for Philip's suggestion was that he wanted to take the bay himself.

Philip had started riding again in the summer, beginning with his father's old cob and then, finding that his stiff leg did not impede him too much, progressing to the more exciting Irish horse. He had taken to calling it "my horse". Jack, who had been led to believe that the exercising and training of the horse for jumping shows would be his own responsibility, was disappointed. Still, it was Philip's horse, bought with Philip's money, and he had the other two to ride every day. Philip showed no interest in riding the youngsters, especially since he had been present when one of them, the chestnut, had thrown Jack heavily against the fence, winding him. Jack had got straight back on again, in spite of his bruised ribs. Philip had wanted to take him up to the house and call Dr. Sidgwick, but Jack was more anxious to get the horse going smoothly again before he put it back in its stable.

Philip gave the new thoroughbred stallion a wide berth too, leaving Jack to handle him. The stallion was a very dark bay, almost black, smaller than the other horses but full of masculine arrogance. He wasn't ridden, but was turned out each morning in his double-fenced paddock, where he spent all day pacing up and down, neighing loudly and staring at the mares in the adjoining fields, his nostrils flared. He was a handful, given to snaking out his head or rearing and striking with his forelegs, and Jack had quickly learned that he could give a painful bite. To lead him in and out of the paddock, Jack had to put him in a bridle and make sure he always carried a stick. Alfie was rather frightened of him.

Next spring they would have foals from the four brood mares, and the year after that the stallion would have produced foals of his own. Stevie would love that, Jack thought, imagining summer evenings strolling around to look at the foals with his son beside him. Stevie loved the horses. Sometimes Jack would sit him on the back of Mr Morland's placid cob and lead him slowly around the paddock, while the little boy beamed with delight. And Jack hoped that even Harriet might take some interest when the foals were born. In spite of his enthusiasm, she rarely came out to the yard. "Horses are all the same to me," she said when he brought her out to show her the stallion.

Jack was anxious about Harriet. He couldn't hide from himself the fact that she was getting increasingly bored with her situation – with him too, he thought. Rosie Taplin had moved away to Colchester, and Harriet sometimes caught the train to meet her there, leaving Stevie with her parents. She no longer took much pride in keeping the cottage tidy, and was often not in to get Jack's meal when he came in tired after work. She was restless, but he didn't know what could be done about it. There was no possibility of her finding a job locally, apart from domestic work, which she scorned. There was so much unemployment. Every week young men came to the farm or stables to ask for work, and Philip turned them away.

"If I wasn't married I'd go to Colchester with Rosie," Harriet had said bitterly, more than once.

Jack tried to understand. He had thought she would be happy, with the cottage and the child and the garden. But it wasn't enough. She did the bare minimum of housework and gardening, and had no other interests to fill her time. What did women want, he wondered? Perhaps if she had another baby . . . she had seemed content enough with Stevie at first. Jack, having missed most of Stevie's babyhood, rather liked the idea of having another child, and he could take immediate practical steps to bring it about, rather than worrying himself uselessly. But Harriet rejected his advances more often than not, complaining that she was tired, or had a headache, or didn't feel like it. She told him that he was obsessed with his work. "Horses, horses. You talk about nothing but horses, you smell of horses most of the time. I don't know why you didn't marry a horse."

Jack was stung by her remarks, and equally upset by her growing resentment of Alice. On her infrequent visits, Alice would call at the cottage to visit, often bringing toys for Stevie. But Harriet was grudging.

"She went to tea at the house," Harriet told him disapprovingly when Alice had gone back to London. "They don't invite us up for tea, do they? We're not good enough."

"I wouldn't want to go. Can you see me drinking out of the best china and chatting to Mrs Morland about the latest summer fashions?"

"Philip's sweet on her," Harriet said accusingly.

"On *Alice*. Don't be daft. Of course he isn't. He's courting Lorna Sidgwick – you know, Edward's sister. He's just got a bit friendly with Alice because of Lorna. Anyway, she wouldn't be interested in Philip."

"No? With all his money? I bet she likes it, coming down here lording over the rest of us."

Jack was annoyed. "I'm not going to listen to you talking like that about my sister," he said stiffly. "You've got it all wrong."

"Well, you don't have to listen, but you can't stop me thinking it."

The next time Jack went to visit his mother, he hinted in the course of conversation that Harriet was unhappy.

"She's flighty," Mrs Smallwood said. "She always has been. But she's of an age now to settle down and think of her responsibilities."

But she didn't have any solutions to offer. Jack walked home disconsolately, carrying Stevie on his shoulders. He thought he would go up to London and see Alice again on his next afternoon off. She had little in common with Harriet, but she was female, and she might be able to offer some insight which had eluded him. Meanwhile, thinking that Harriet might well have a point when she complained of his obsession with his work, he made a resolve to wash himself and change every item of clothing as soon as he came in from work in the evenings, and to refrain from mentioning horses of any description. But Harriet appeared not to notice his efforts, and he became increasingly aware that there was very little to talk about. Harriet's only topic of conversation was village gossip, which didn't interest Jack. Giving up, he would go out for a final check round the stables before going to bed.

It was a routine he liked, finding the warm orderliness of the stables more comforting than the atmosphere indoors. He stopped to refill a water-bucket here and adjust a rug there, while around him the horses pulled hay from the racks and chewed with rhythmic jaws, or lay in the straw blinking up at him as he switched on the electric light. He unbolted the door of the grey's stable and went in to examine a fetlock which was slightly swollen from a cut. The inflammation was subsiding now, but Jack stayed to adjust the horse's rug and pull its ears affectionately, aware that he did not want to go back indoors to Harriet. He stood by the horse, gloomily thinking about his marriage. He realized now that he and Harriet had never had much in common apart from the initial physical attraction, and that had already faded. She did not love him, and he didn't love her – he didn't even like her very much, if he were completely honest. If it were not for Stevie, he would have considered his marriage a complete failure; and if it hadn't been for the child he would probably never have married Harriet at all. He found himself regretting the few days' leave and the lustful couplings in the apple orchard. But he remembered the young Belgian widow, and knew that he had been just as foolish again, just as easily led. And he couldn't wish Stevie out of existence. He would have to make the best of it.

Before he had the chance to talk to Alice, Harriet took matters into her own hands.

234

A few days later, having torn his forearm on a loose strand of wire, Jack went indoors to wash the cut and find something to bind it with. He washed the wound at the kitchen sink and then went upstairs to look for a piece of bandage. Harriet was upstairs, banging about in the bedroom. He looked in at the door.

"D'you know where I can find a bit of bandage?"

She turned from the chest-of-drawers and looked at him rather nervously. His gaze fell to the half-packed bag which lay open on the bed.

"What are you doing?"

She said, "I'm going."

"What do you mean, you're going? Going where?"

"I'm going away. I've had enough of living here. I'm going to stay with Rosie in Colchester. She says she can get me a job there." Her voice rose defiantly. "You won't notice. You'll prefer it without me here."

"What do you mean?" he repeated, dim-witted with surprise. "You're leaving me?"

"Yes, Jack. I'm leaving you," she said, her voice sarcastic. She threw another garment into the case and turned to face him.

He sat down heavily on the bed, his cut arm oozing blood slowly and dripping on to the bedspread. "But – you can't just walk out like this. Didn't you even have the guts to tell me? Were you going to sneak out while I wasn't around?"

"I would have told you. You wouldn't have stopped me."

"But what about Stevie? I can't look after him all day, you know that – "

"You won't have to. I'm taking him round to Mum's. She'll have him. She won't mind. She likes having children to look after. I'll come back for the rest of my things some other time."

He stared at her, and she backed off a little, less sure of herself.

"You think you can just give him to your mother – our child?" he said in amazed indignation. "How can you think of it? He's not a parcel, to give away to someone else just because you're bored! I won't let you – he's my son too!"

There was a pause during which he heard the steady ticking of the clock on the mantelpiece.

"No, he isn't," Harriet said quietly.

"What did you say?"

She looked at him steadily, her eyes frightened in her pale face. "I said no, he isn't. He's not your son."

Jack felt dizzy, unable to believe what he had heard. "Not my son – what do you mean?"

"What I said. You're not his father." She flung the words at him this time, almost proudly. He realized what she was saying and before he could control himself he had moved across to her and struck her across the face. She winced from the blow with a small cry, and his outburst of anger subsided immediately as he stepped back, appalled at what he had done.

She recovered quickly and darted forward, her hand flashing out in a stinging blow across his cheek.

"Don't you dare hit me again, Jack," she told him through clenched teeth.

He didn't retaliate. Bewildered and ashamed, he sat down on the bed and looked up at her. There was

236

a patch of flaming red on her cheek. She continued packing as if nothing had happened.

"I'm not his father – who the hell is, then?" he demanded miserably.

"Can't you guess?"

"How would I know?"

She gave him a look almost of triumph. "Think about it. You'll work it out."

"That George Franks bloke you were seeing while I was at the front, I suppose," he said in disgust.

"No, not him."

"Well, it doesn't make much difference to me who it was, does it?" He felt suddenly overcome with weariness. He had heard all he needed to know. He needed to get away from her and think.

"Doesn't it?"

Again he had the sense that she was goading him, that she wanted him to probe further until he found out. Why would it matter? Whoever it was, it couldn't be worse than the dawning realization that she had used him, lied to him, manipulated him . . . the answer clicked into his brain and he stared at her in disbelief.

"You mean . . ."

She smiled, scoring her final point over him.

He couldn't bear to stay in the same room with her for a moment longer. He got up and ran downstairs and out of the house. Stevie was playing in the garden, but Jack couldn't look at him. He didn't know what he was going to do until he got to the stables and then on an impulse he went into the harness room, barging past the astonished Alfie who was eating a biscuit and brewing up some tea.

He grabbed a saddle and bridle and went to the bay hunter's stable.

Alfie followed him. "You taking him out now? Mr Philip said – "

"I don't care what he said." Jack stuffed the bits into the surprised horse's mouth along with some hay it had been eating, and put the saddle in place with shaking hands.

"What you done to your arm?"

Jack glanced down at the blood soaking through his sleeve. He had forgotten all about it. He would hit someone in a minute – Alfie, if he happened to be standing around. "Go away, Alfie, for God's sake," he said harshly, pulling the girths up. Alfie was Harriet's brother. He would know soon enough what was the matter. Or did he know already?

He mounted and rode out along the track towards the ridge, urging the bay into a fast canter. He had to get away. The wind was cool against his burning cheeks and the horse's stride lengthened beneath him, his hooves biting into the sand of the track and throwing up stones. Jack jumped him over a low stile into the field alongside and galloped across the stubble, hardly pausing for the big hedge at the far end. The horse flung himself over it and hurtled on, not needing much encouragement; Jack didn't think he could stop if he tried. The exhilaration of the wild gallop soothed him, gradually bringing him back to sanity. He'd break the horse's legs at this crazy pace, or his own neck . . . at last the horse tired, his pace slowing with the uphill gradient towards the woods, and Jack pulled him up and walked him on a long rein.

The trees were in full autumn colour, the path strewn with shiny black ash leaves and golden beech; the green furry mats of sweet chestnut lay split open like starfish, spilling their glossy fruits on the ground. A faint mist rose, ghostly among the tree trunks, and the only sound was the gentle clop of the bay horse's hooves on the path. Jack felt choked by the beauty of it. The mad gallop had been a release, but he couldn't gallop for ever. And now he was bitterly angry, because he was riding Philip's horse, and the woods and fields he rode in would one day be Philip's, and the cottage he lived in belonged to Philip, and Stevie was not his son but Philip's. Everything he had – or thought he had – was Philip's. How could he have been so dense?

His first instinct was to ride down to the house and demand to see Philip and punch him on the nose, but he remembered that Philip had gone up to London for the day. Well, he would have to give up his job – he couldn't stay here a day longer. But then, more rationally, he thought of what the decision would mean. Jobs like this were not easy to come by, and as a final irony he would need a good reference from Philip. And he would need to live somewhere. And it would mean leaving the horses, after his months of dedicated work with them. But how could he stay, knowing what he knew now?

As his temper cooled, he saw that if he had a grudge against Philip, he had a far bigger one against Harriet. She had used him, and he had been a willing accomplice; he saw it so clearly that it was amazing he hadn't realized at the time. That autumn leave, three years ago, was still vivid in his memory.

Harriet had always been soft on Philip, when she had worked in the Greenstocks kitchen; Jack had known that. That autumn . . . Philip had been at home on leave two weeks or so before Jack – he remembered now. He could imagine how it had been, only too clearly. And then he himself had turned up, a willing victim. Harriet's eagerness to entice him into the apple orchard had not been inspired by passion, as he had so naïvely thought; it was a calculated strategy to get herself out of a predicament – she must have known, or suspected, by then. He knew he hadn't been the first . . . but God, he had been stupid! No wonder she despised him. He despised himself.

He rode back slowly, and spent a long time rubbing the horse down and settling him. He didn't speak to Alfie again. By the time he went indoors Harriet had gone, and Stevie with her. He was relieved not to have to confront Harriet again, but the cottage was coldly empty without the child's incessant questions or his playthings scattered around.

Jack walked slowly upstairs and sat down on the bed with his head in his hands, the ugly scene earlier replaying itself in his mind. He didn't know what he was going to do.

Jack and Alice

The following morning, Jack got up early and went out to feed the horses, and then changed from his working clothes into his suit. When he heard buckets clattering outside he went to find Alfie in the yard.

"I'm going up to London," he told him. "You'll have to manage by yourself today. You can tell Philip Morland."

"Yes."

"Harriet's gone."

"I know." Alfie looked away, lining up his buckets by the water tap.

Of course Alfie knew; she would have gone to his parents' cottage with Stevie first. Perhaps she was still there. He wondered how much she had told her family. Quite possibly she had gone to them and said that Jack had struck her, leaving out the rest; she was a practised enough liar to embroider the story in all sorts of ways. He wished he hadn't hit her, putting himself in the wrong.

He walked to the station to catch the train to London, and arrived at the Braithwaites' house shortly before midday. People were queuing outside to go into the restaurant, and he remembered that Alice would be working in the kitchen or serving food. He didn't know how to get round to the back of the house, so he joined the line and queued at the servery, and

241

finally got to the front. A middle-aged woman told him kindly, "Get a tray from the pile, dear."

"I don't want any food. I want to see my sister, Alice."

He realized that he had spoken rudely. The woman looked taken aback, as if wondering how Alice could have such an uncouth brother. She called "Alice!" and Alice appeared, dressed in an apron and cap and with her hands all floury.

"*Jack!* What are you doing here?" She leaned across the counter to kiss him, leaving a floury handmark on the shoulder of his jacket. She looked at him more closely. "Is there something wrong?"

"I want to talk to you," he said hoarsely.

She said, "Wait a minute. We'll go up to the flat."

A few moments later she appeared without the cap and apron, looked at him anxiously and led the way up the two flights of stairs to her rooms. Lorna wasn't in, he noted with relief. She took him to the sitting-room, and they sat down together on the sofa.

"What is it? It's not Ma, is it?"

"No. It's Harriet. She's gone. Left me."

"Oh, *Jack*. Gone, you mean really gone, for good?"

He nodded dumbly.

"But why? Have you had a quarrel? I thought you were so happy at Greenstocks . . . with the cottage and everything . . . Perhaps she'll come back."

"No, I don't want her to come back."

"But Stevie – has she taken him with her?"

"Yes."

"Oh Jack – how awful for you."

242

The sympathy in her voice made him want to cry. "But what did you quarrel about? Is it something that can be put right?"

He told her what Harriet had said. He could still hardly believe that it wasn't something he had dreamed, but his own sense of delayed shock was nothing compared to Alice's reaction. Her face paled and for a moment he thought she was actually going to faint. He took hold of her arm to steady her.

"You can't mean it!" she cried, pulling away and staring at him.

"It is true. I've thought about it all last night. I know it's true."

"But it can't be – "

Her agitation had the effect of making him calmer. "Harriet used me so that she could get me to marry her when she was pregnant," he continued. "That's all."

"That's *all*!" Alice cried. "How could she be so callous? And what about Philip? How could he? Do nothing and let you take the responsibility for his own misdemeanours?"

Jack had to smile at her ladylike choice of word. "If you think about it, it probably wasn't so much his fault," he said slowly. "He and Harriet . . . well, you know . . . but it was probably her idea, if she was like she was with me. Then he went back to the front and got himself badly injured, and was in hospital for a long time, and by the time he came back it was all sorted out that she was going to marry me. He might not even know the baby was his. And as soon as he found out about Harriet and me, he offered me the job and the cottage."

"But he must have *suspected* . . . And you're making *excuses* for him?"

He said, "Well, in a way, yes. You know what it was like, from Edward, the strain of being at the front . . . when you get away, you'd do anything to stop thinking about it. You can't talk about it, you can't explain, but you've got to get away from it in your mind, as best you can. Some blokes get drunk, some go after women. And if you get a chance for a . . ." – he couldn't think of a polite term, so he continued, "well, it's tempting. I know how it happens."

"You mean you – ?"

It seemed to be the time for honesty, so he said, "Once, in Belgium. It was wrong and I felt bad after, but I'd still done it. Without even thinking."

He saw that he had shocked Alice. She was silent for a moment, looking down at the floor and biting her lip, and then she said, "Do you mean you think everyone, even Edward . . ."

"Oh God no," he said hastily. "I didn't mean that. But I can see how it happened. And I can't really blame Philip, can I, when I've done the same myself? For all I know, I could have caused the same sort of problems. I just didn't think. And I'll never know, will I?"

There was a pause while Alice took this in. Then she asked, "Have you said anything to him?"

"No. I haven't seen him."

"Well, don't. Not yet." She seemed to pull herself together. "Don't do anything hasty. But he ought to know."

He guessed that she was thinking of Lorna Sidgwick. If Lorna was thinking of marrying Philip Morland, she would certainly be interested to know that he already had an illegitimate child. But then Lorna was one of those modern women who might not even mind that much . . . Philip would get out of it all right. His sort always did.

He said, "It's knowing about Stevie that really got me. Harriet . . . well, she and I hadn't got on for a long while, if we ever did. It wasn't going to work. But Stevie . . . well, now I keep telling myself that he's not my son, nothing to do with me really, but it doesn't make any difference . . ."

"I know. You love him. Oh Jack, it's awful for you. I wish I could do something to help . . ."

"You have helped."

Alice got him some food and made him eat it, and then she said, "Jack, I'm sorry, but I've got to go back to the canteen for another couple of hours this afternoon. One of our regular helpers is ill. Do you want to stay here, or will you go out somewhere and come back later?"

"I suppose I ought to go back to Greenstocks. I just cleared off without telling Philip. But I'm not going to, not yet. I'll go out for a walk round and come back in a couple of hours, shall I?"

He went out into the streets and walked in the direction of Victoria Park. Realizing that he was only a quarter of a mile or so away from the road where the Cartwrights lived, he decided that he might as well break the news. It would be a good time, with Sarah out at work; he didn't think he could face Sarah, much as he would have liked to see her

245

at any other time. And he would have to tell Mrs Cartwright sooner or later, even though it would be difficult. She would have to stop sending knitted garments and toys for Stevie, something which he guessed gave her enormous pleasure.

But it was Sarah who opened the door to him.

"Jack! What – "

He stepped back, unable to stop his dismay from showing in his face. Her smile faded.

"Sarah. I didn't think you'd be in."

"Oh – it's mother. She's been taken ill. I've stayed at home today to look after her. Will you come in?"

He followed her inside and said, "I hope it's not serious."

"I don't know. The doctor's coming later."

"I won't stay then. I just thought I ought to let you and your mother know – "

He told her briefly that Harriet had left and taken Stevie with her, not going into the rest of the details. Sarah was upset, and he wished he hadn't come. Why was he worrying her with his own problems? She had enough of her own to cope with. He could hardly look at her. The conversation was stilted, and he left after only a few minutes.

"I hope your mother gets better soon. And I'm sorry for bothering you like this."

"It's all right."

He walked away from the house quickly, cursing himself for a fool. He wished he hadn't seen her; he had only succeeded in upsetting her, and himself too. He was acutely aware of how different his circumstances could have been, if he hadn't got involved with Harriet, if he'd been unmarried when he met Sarah . . . *if* . . . But it was too late now. He tried to dismiss the feelings she stirred in him. He was a married man, embroiled in this awful mess, and Sarah was a young single girl. It was stupid to think about what might have been.

After Jack had gone, Alice went downstairs to the canteen and went about her work mechanically, preparing meat pies for the evening meal. Her hands kneaded and rolled and cut pastry as if they belonged to someone else, her mind elsewhere. She was amazed at her self-control. When Dorothy or Mathilda spoke to her she answered quite rationally, giving no sign of the mental turmoil she had been thrown into.

The night before, she and Lorna had talked long into the small hours about whether or not she should marry Philip. If she did, it would be a compromise or sorts; both she and Philip knew that. She didn't love him, not as she had loved Edward, but she was fond of him . . . very much so.

"And that can be as good a basis for marriage as any," Lorna had said. "The question is whether you think you can be happy with Philip, and he with you. A relationship based on friendship can be longer-lasting than one based on romantic infatuation."

Alice wondered whether she spoke from experience. Lorna, for all her readiness to discuss Alice's emotional entanglements, was very reticent about her own relationships.

"Think of everything you're being offered – a kind and considerate husband; a secure future for your mother and Jack as well as for yourself; children of your own and a comfortable upbringing for them," Lorna continued. "Are you going to dismiss all that because you can't marry Edward?"

"I don't know." Alice wasn't sure she could dismiss her romantic ideal so easily in favour of these practical considerations. Were practical considerations a good enough basis for marriage? Lorna obviously thought so. And when Philip had kissed and embraced her she had known that she was not indifferent to him, not at all. Was it possible that affection could turn into love?

Well, she wouldn't find out now. She shoved a trayload of meat and vegetable pies into the oven and tucked a loose strand of hair under her cap. All these questions, discussed and mulled over at length just a few hours ago, were irrelevant now. She could never forgive Philip for the mess he had made of Jack's life.

The Opening Meet

Horses and riders thronged the forecourt of Broadlands Hall. The tall ivy-clad building with its imposing entrance had been a Red Cross Hospital during the war; now, it had been restored to its peace-time function as the elegant country home of Lord and Lady Calderdale. Jimmy Taplin, immaculately scarlet-coated as whipper-in, waited aside from the rest on his old Roman-nosed grey, the hound pack milling around his horse's feet. Occasionally, he cracked his whip and harshly reproved a hound which was wandering away or showing too much interest in the trays of food carried by the Broadlands Hall maids.

Jack stayed away from the main crowd too. The young grey he rode, unused to being with so many other horses, was quivering with trepidation, ears alert to every new sound. Aware that it might lash out in fear if he took it too close to strange horses, Jack walked it in small circles, trying to calm it. It was a blustery day with occasional showers of rain, the sort of day when the wind got under horses' tails and made them excited.

It was a new experience for Jack to be here at the meet waiting to move off with the rest, and being offered a glass of sherry – which he refused, having his hands full already – by a pretty girl in a maid's uniform. Before the war, his task on hunting days had

249

been to keep in touch with the hounds' whereabouts and to be ready with Philip's second horse when he wanted it. Trailing about the lanes and tracks, always within earshot of the hunt but never participating, Jack had always envied the mounted followers, who came back at the end of the day spattered in mud and full of tales of how well their horses had gone or how big the last hedge-and-ditch had been. Today, smartly dressed in the riding clothes Philip had paid for back in the summer, Jack would have his chance to ride with them, even though he would rather have been mounted on the bay Philip was riding.

He glanced across the forecourt to where Philip sat talking to the Master's son. Perhaps he was drumming up business, Jack thought; Philip had told him that hunting days would be useful times for making and renewing social acquaintances as well as for showing how well the horses could go. Philip didn't look as if his heart was in it today, though; he looked stony-faced and miserable, as he had looked for the last few days. Jack felt the same himself. Poor Alfie must have had a dreary week, with the two of them going about looking as if they were at their own funerals, hardly speaking.

Jack had exchanged only a few words with Philip since Harriet's revelation, not trusting himself to say more. Philip knew that Harriet had gone, but no more; he had seemed concerned when Jack told him, but hadn't referred to it again. And it wasn't Harriet's departure that had brought on Philip's current mood of gloom, Jack knew. Philip had gone up to London the day after Jack and had stayed at home since, appearing at the stables at intervals with his golden

Labrador at his heels and sometimes riding out alone.
Jack wondered whether Lorna Sidgwick had turned
him down after all. If she had, he had played his own
part in the rejection by speaking to Alice; it was odd
how his life and Philip's seemed inextricably linked,
before the war, through it and now after it as well.
And Jack still didn't see how the situation was going
to change. He was dependent on Philip for a job until
he could find something else, and that wasn't going to
be easy.

The servant-girl crossed the driveway to offer drinks
to a group of newcomers, something in the turn of
her head reminding him of Sarah. He looked again
and saw that there was no real resemblance in build,
colouring or feature; his frequent thoughts of Sarah
had made him see a likeness where none existed. He
stared after the girl all the same, taking no notice of
his horse pawing the gravel. He wanted to see Sarah
again, and yet he knew it was unfair to involve her in
the tangled mess of his personal life. A couple of nights
ago he had got as far as taking out writing-paper and
beginning *Dear Sarah* before throwing his pen aside
in frustration. He wasn't much good at writing, and
besides, what was there to say that could make any
difference?

The sound of the huntsman's horn cut into his
thoughts; it was time to move off.

People from the village who had come to the meet
on foot stood aside as the riders jostled together,
following the pack down the gravel drive which led
to Broadlands Farm and the fir plantation beyond.
The Master kept the mounted followers up on a
ridge above the plantation while the huntsman took

the hounds in among the young trees. For a long while nothing happened, apart from the sounds of the horn, shouts and whipcracks from Jimmy and the other whipper-in, and hounds crashing through the undergrowth.

"Hike back . . . Hike . . . Get forrard . . ." The shouted commands echoed around the woods and fields. The older horses stood with ears pricked, looking down at the plantation, knowing what to expect; nothing would happen until the assorted yelps merged into a more purposeful chorus. Jack's grey, having sweated up at the meet, was getting cold and impatient. He kept it moving, walking it steadily up and down behind the lines of riders. He was glad he didn't have to stand still and make conversation; he felt out of place amidst the elegant ladies in side-saddle habits and veils, the vicar in his clerical collar riding a dock-tailed cob, and the male acquaintances of Philip's who came to the Morlands' in winter to shoot pheasants and eat paté and smoked salmon. Jack wasn't interested in the social side of hunting, although from what he had seen in the past he thought that some people went for that alone – a chance to parade themselves in their newest attire or show off a flashy horse. He just wanted to ride, although he wouldn't have much chance for galloping and jumping fences today on this youngster – he'd have to go through the gaps and gates with the children and the nervous ladies and the vicar.

At last the hounds gave voice, moving off on the far side of the wood. The Master led the field off in the same direction, keeping them to a narrow fenced track at first. Then the riders filtered through a muddy gateway which gave on to open meadow; the thrusters at the front of the field surged ahead in full gallop, spreading out across the grass like a sporting print, the horses' hooves throwing up clods of mud. Jack's mount plunged and snatched at its bits, so that his breeches were flecked with foam from its mouth, but he kept it on a tight rein until at last he was through the gate with a splatter of mud over his face from the hooves of the horse in front, and cantering up the hillside. Most of the riders were jumping the hedge at the top, flowing over like a wave. Jack saw Philip Morland among them, but the jump was too high for his own inexperienced horse and he had to go a long way round to find a gate. Cantering along the edge of a field of kale, he began to relax; his horse, away from the others, was less likely to leap unexpectedly into the air and unseat him, or to barge into someone else's mount. He jumped a low stile into deep-shadowed woodland and cantered along the leaf-strewn track, bending over his horse's neck to avoid the low branches that lashed at his neck and shoulders. There were voices and hoofbeats behind, and he realized that other riders had followed him.

"That's a nice-looking animal you've got," a woman in a top hat and veil said to him as he dismounted to open a gate at the end of the track. "I haven't seen him out before, have I?"

"No. He's a youngster, belongs to Philip Morland."

The woman made her horse stand while Jack waited for the other riders to come through before hauling the gate shut. "Oh yes. I heard he was setting up as a breeder and trainer. That bay he's riding looks a useful sort, too. Are they for sale? My son's looking out for a quality horse for himself."

"This one is. And there's another nice chestnut, a four-year-old, with the same sire."

"Really? Tell Mr Morland I'd like to come and see them some time, would you? It's Mrs Hopcroft, from Alders End. He'll know the name."

"Yes, I'll tell him." Jack remounted his wheeling horse with difficulty, and rode on. Well, he'd earned his outing today, he thought, doing a bit of advertising for Philip. He crossed another few fields behind the riders who had overtaken him, keeping in touch with the hunt but not too close. He didn't think he'd stay out a lot longer. The young grey had had its first taste of hunting, and he didn't want to tire it. There would be plenty of other opportunities.

Before long he pulled up by a hedge at the top of a rise to take stock of his whereabouts. A fine rain, little more than a mist in the air, dampened his face and eyelashes, but the sky looked heavy with rain. He could see Epping's church in the distance and the buildings of its main street strung out along the farther ridge; he estimated that he was about six miles from Greenstocks. He looked across the wintering landscape. The horse-chestnuts along the lane were already bare, the trees showing their skeleton shape against the sky. Soon the first frosts would come, and the dark evenings. Left to think his own thoughts, away from everyone else, Jack found himself contemplating the approaching winter with a sense of despair. He would work, and look after Philip's horses, and each night he would go indoors to the cold deserted cottage. Stevie's small room would be

254

bare, his toys all gone, only the remembered echo of his childish voice remaining. His own life seemed empty, leading nowhere. What was the point of going on?

He thought the pack had gone down towards Cobbin's brook in the valley, but as he listened he heard hounds coming back his way. His horse stiffened and pricked its ears, and looking in the same direction Jack saw a tired fox running out from the hedgerow, its red fur bedraggled with mud and its tongue lolling; it loped across the plough to a clump of trees and was gone. Jack should have hallooed loudly and waved his arms to attract the attention of the huntsman, but he did nothing. He didn't want to see an exhausted fox torn to pieces in front of him. He had seen enough killing.

The grey horse, looking down into the valley again towards the distant cries, let out its breath in a big sigh. The pack had checked in the middle of a grass meadow poached by cattle; they had lost the scent, but after a few moments a single hound spoke, and the huntsman brought the rest round to the same line. In a moment there was an excited babble of hound voices, heading up to the ridge. Jack, who had just made up his mind to go home, now found himself not only in front of the field but in front of the pack as well. He rode along to the edge of the plough, not wanting to find himself in the middle of the field in full cry.

He heard hooves drumming up the ridge and in a moment they were into the kale alongside, first the hounds, struggling through the hedgerow, and then the riders, exploding over it with a thwack of hooves on hawthorn twigs, and shouts and curses, giving Jack a searing vision of going over the top in the first wave of an attack . . . but there were no screams, no bodies littering the ground. Philip Morland was still among the riders, his horse going well. The hounds had gone into the undergrowth of the wood, but the Master was leading the field round to the right towards Jack, over a high thick hedge with a rail behind it. The less bold riders veered away to the other side of the wood, shouting to each other to point out a gateway, but the point-to-point riders and the thrusters were already galloping for the hedge, looking for the best places. Philip's horse looked barely under control, its neck and flanks soaked with sweat; Philip wouldn't be able to stop him if he wanted to, Jack thought, knowing how strong the bay could be – you might as well try to stop a five-nine shell in flight. His own horse curvetted and pranced underneath him, wanting to take off with the others, and Jack watched with a sense of sickening inevitability as the bay, leaping forward with a plunge which almost jerked Philip out of the saddle, approached the hedge fast – too fast. Unable to get its hooves out of the clinging mud in time, the bay struck the rail with its front feet and somersaulted, crashing heavily to the ground and throwing Philip clear. The other riders galloped straight on, only one glancing back to see what had happened. Philip's horse, winded for a moment, heaved itself up on braced forelegs, staggered up and careered after the rest, reins and stirrups flapping. Philip lay on the ground, not moving.

"God Almighty – " Jack cursed. His own horse half-reared, upset by the commotion, but he slithered off and dragged it over to where Philip lay sprawled on his back. The drumming of hooves faded; everyone had gone on except the one rider who had seen what happened and was pulling her horse up, turning back.

Jack crouched down beside Philip. He lay still, breathing fast, his face contorted in pain. Relieved to see that he was conscious, Jack loosened his stock, not easy while he was still hanging on to the reins of his agitated horse. He saw that Philip's right leg was bent awkwardly. The other rider approached, a young woman on a raking chestnut thoroughbred with heaving sides and reddened nostrils. She must be a goer, Jack thought, to have taken that hedge riding sidesaddle.

"My goodness, that really was a purler," the young woman said. "Is he all right?"

"I don't know," Jack said, and then Philip opened his eyes and looked at him.

"It's my leg . . . The same place . . ." He winced with pain. "No, don't move it . . . I'm sure it's . . . broken again."

"Can I do something?" the young woman asked.

"You can't move, can you?" Jack said to Philip, who shook his head vehemently.

"I'll go for a doctor," the woman said. "I can telephone from the nearest village. It's not too far. Will you stay with him?"

"Say we'll need a stretcher," Jack said, and the woman nodded and galloped off towards the Epping Upland road.

Left alone with Philip, Jack felt helpless. He hoped someone would catch Philip's horse before it hurt itself. He tied his own horse's reins to the rail in the hedge and then went back to Philip and said, "What should I do?"

"Nothing . . . It's all right," Philip said. He raised himself slightly and reached into his coat pocket for a small brandy flask and a cigarette case. Jack took the flask and unscrewed the stopper and handed it back to him. Philip propped himself up on one elbow to drink, pale and shivering. Shock, Jack thought. He took off his jacket and laid it over Philip for extra warmth. Of all the bloody ironies, he thought. Here he was looking after Philip yet again, like the night of the trench raid when Philip had broken his leg in the first place.

The same thought struck Philip, for he handed Jack the flask and looked at him with a faint grin, and said, "At least you haven't got to carry me in under shell-fire this time, Jack."

"No." Jack lit up a cigarette for Philip, and another one for himself. "But there are no stretcher-bearers handy either, and the Aid Post's a long way off."

Philip smiled again and closed his eyes, lying back on the damp grass. "We seem to make a habit of this sort of thing, don't we?"

Jack breathed out cigarette smoke. "Yes. It's always one or other of us on the floor," he said evenly.

He saw that Philip knew what he meant. His eyelids flickered open; his eyes were the same blue-grey as Stevie's. Jack wondered how he could have failed to notice before. But then he had failed to notice a lot of things . . .

"I expect you wish you'd left me out in No-Man's-Land," Philip said quietly.

"It had crossed my mind. Perhaps it would have been better if a shell had finished off both of us."

They both smoked in silence for a few moments, and then Philip said, "You must think – that I arranged everything very nicely."

"It doesn't matter," Jack said. It was hardly the time or the place for a confession, for God's sake, with Philip shivering in the grass and biting his lip with the pain. Jack was getting cold too, without his jacket. He wondered how long they would have to wait. It would be bad for Philip, he knew – the leg had set awkwardly the first time, and he had had to have another operation since. Jack wondered whether this day's hunting would be Philip's last.

"It does matter," Philip went on. "I don't want you to think . . . I didn't know, you see. Not until I heard you were going to marry Harriet. And by then it was too late to interfere. You seemed content. I never thought Harriet would tell you. And of course I didn't know, not for sure, whose the baby was."

Jack said bitterly, "Harriet did."

"Yes."

A thought struck Jack. "What are you going to do, now that you know? What are you going to do about your son?"

Philip looked at him in alarm, and Jack realized that in spite of his noble sentiments he was too much of a coward to face up to that.

"I don't know. But if it's any consolation to you, I've lost the chance to marry the woman I love because of all this."

"Well, I'm sorry," Jack said. He thought Philip sounded rather melodramatic, like someone in a play. "That's nothing to do with me. I'm only worried about Stevie."

"I'll – do what I can for him," Philip said.

Yes, Jack thought. Philip would do what he could. What would that mean? Giving Harriet's parents a few pounds on the quiet, to bring up Stevie. He'd end up marrying whoever he wanted in the end. He had money and position. He could get away with it. He would carry on with his comfortable life while his son was taken in by Harriet's parents like a stray dog. He didn't want Stevie, and neither did Harriet. But Jack did. It didn't even matter much any more that Stevie was not his own son. He wanted him back.

"But I have done something on your account," Philip said.

"Oh." Jack looked at him warily, not sure that he wanted any more interference from Philip.

"You want to leave – of course – I understand that. And I know how difficult it is at present. But I can help you – you can have another place immediately, if you want it."

"Oh?"

"With Michael O'Halloran – in Ireland. He'd take you on at a day's notice – he told me that when we were there. And I've written to him to say that you want to leave my employment – for personal reasons."

Jack stared at him. "Ireland? You want to get rid of me to Ireland?"

Philip closed his eyes wearily. "Not to get rid of you. I was trying to help. You're welcome to stay, but . . . I understand if you don't want to. You

260

must hate the sight of me, Jack, and with good reason."

"I don't," Jack said. Did Philip really think that? At this moment, looking at his pale drained face, Jack felt more sorry for him than anything else. "It was the war," he said. "It did for us both."

A Letter from Harriet

"Four, all for you." Alice threw the morning's letters down on the desk, and Lorna picked them up and looked at the writing on the envelopes.

"One from my father . . . this one's probably a cheque . . . I wonder what this one is?"

"Is it good news?" Alice said, noticing Lorna's surprised expression as she unfolded the letter and read it.

"Yes. It's an offer to run a course for the Workers' Education Association on current affairs," Lorna said. "Weekly classes and debates. That must have been my tutor's doing – he said he could put me in touch with some useful contacts."

"Good! I'm pleased for you," Alice said. "I should think you'll enjoy it."

"I will," Lorna said, already opening another letter. "But it would be even better if I could find a publisher for my book. Here's one rejection already." She crumpled up the sheet of paper and tossed it into the waste-paper basket.

"But won't you have to write it first?"

"Well, yes. But it won't do any harm to find out first whether a publisher might be likely to take it on. That one wasn't."

Lorna wanted to write a book about the war from the point of view of the people engaged in it. "A colloquial history," she called it. "A look at as many different aspects of the war as possible, told in the words of the people involved. I want it to be as vivid as Barbusse's book, but with a number of different viewpoints."

She had already started writing to various regimental headquarters and hospitals and depots to make enquiries about names and addresses, and there was no shortage of interviewees among her own acquaintances. She wrote down her findings in the form of scrawled notes, which Alice later deciphered and typed up in a more easily understandable form, filing them all carefully afterwards.

"I think it's a marvellous idea for a book," she told Lorna. "A sort of living history of a generation."

"Yes. If I can play some small part in reminding people of the tragedy of war, I shall feel I've done something useful with my life," Lorna said.

Patrick Leary came round to the flat and spent a great deal of time talking to Lorna about his experiences in Gallipoli, where he had been severely wounded. Alice, typing up the notes later, was shocked to realize that Patrick's good-natured exterior concealed such bitter memories. Having gone through the catastrophic Gallipoli landing, and his later posting to the Western Front, and the loss of his fiancée, he had had his share of suffering – too much for a young man of twenty-six. But there was a whole generation like him, Alice thought: people who had suffered as much and far more, people who had seen too much and grown up too quickly.

But life was going on, as it had to. Lorna worked purposefully at her book and her articles, and Alice was gradually taking on more and more work for her. Lorna was hoping that soon she would be able to pay her a proper wage instead of simply sharing the proceeds of her teaching and writing. Their life together was shaping up much as they had planned it, and yet Alice was aware of a sense of regret, of wanting more.

She had told Lorna that she wasn't going to marry Philip after all, without going into the details. Lorna had seemed surprised and disappointed, but hadn't pursued the matter any further. Now that she didn't see Philip any more, Alice told herself that their relationship would not have worked anyway; she had never seen herself taking Mrs Morland's place as mistress of Greenstocks, hosting dinners and shoots. And it was the life Philip wanted, carrying on the traditions set by his father and his grandfather. He wouldn't have given up Greenstocks for Alice. He would find someone else to marry, she thought, someone of his own class, who would fit into the role more easily. Probably, in years to come, he would be glad she had refused. She couldn't have married him with the knowledge that her good fortune was built on Jack's misery.

She could make herself think of the drawbacks, but she couldn't ignore her renewed sense of loss.

"We don't need men," Lorna said briskly during Alice's period of readjustment. "Thousands of women of our generation have got to learn to make their own way. And we can. That was one thing the war fitted us for."

Lorna was right, Alice knew; women could lead fulfilling lives without men. She would never marry now. Her vision of one day having her own family – her own children – flickered and died. She had her memories of Edward, and that would have to be enough. At least she had him to remember.

In the mornings she looked out of her small bedroom window at the untidy yard behind the house and at the grey November sky cut into angular shapes by roofs and chimneys. She thought of the village at home in November: smoke uncurling from the cottage chimneys against the sombre green of the yew trees in the churchyard, the sweep of ploughed fields behind Greenstocks, the tangle of untidy rooks' nests in the tops of the elms. She was never satisfied, she thought, impatient with herself. When she had been in the village she had been eager to get away to London. Now that she was in London she wanted to be back in the country. She would have to stop dreaming and be content with what she had.

One Friday afternoon, when she was in the middle of typing Lorna's latest article, Jack arrived unexpectedly.

"Did you come especially to see me?" she asked, taking him upstairs. "I mean, it's lovely to see you of course, but I'm coming home to the village on Tuesday for the Armistice Day service."

"Oh – I didn't know," Jack said. "But I came to see someone else as well, anyway."

He looked considerably more cheerful than he had the last time she had seen him.

"Has something happened?" she asked.

"Well, yes. I've got a chance to work in Ireland."

"Ireland?" she echoed. Jack was obviously so pleased about it that she tried to look cheerful too, but her only thought was that she was going to lose Jack on top of everything else.

"Yes, near Dublin, in the Wicklow Mountains, where I went before. Oh Alice, I know it's a long way, but perhaps you can come and visit me there. And I can come home sometimes. You'd love it – the mountains, the river, the wild scenery – "

She listened, trying to be pleased that he had something positive to look forward to, while he told her about Michael O'Halloran, and about the horses, and about Philip Morland's accident.

"He arranged for me to have the job. And Mr O'Halloran – Michael, I mean – wrote back to say he wants me to be his *partner* – not just a groom or a trainer."

"It does sound like a marvellous chance for you. Will you go, then?"

"I think so. I shall write back tomorrow. It was good of Philip to fix it up, wasn't it?"

"Yes, I suppose it was," Alice said. It would be good for Jack to have a complete break with the village, she thought; Greenstocks and the Morlands had dominated both their lives for too long. But she would miss him . . . it would be another part of her life disappearing, she thought sadly, and a part which was very dear to her.

"Harriet wants a divorce," Jack said. "I got a letter this morning. But I've no idea how you go about it."

"Oh. Well, I suppose it's up to Harriet to sort it out," Alice said, "if she's the one who wants it."

"I think it's best."

"Yes. I suppose it would be better if you could make a completely new start."

She hated to think of Jack going through the ugliness of a divorce. Would Harriet have to stand up in court and make all sorts of dreadful claims about him? Or would it – rightly – be Jack making the complaints? Alice had no more idea than he did of how it worked.

"And now Philip's laid up again," Jack continued. "It was a nasty break, and they say it'll be difficult to set again, like before. Perhaps you might go in and see him at the house, if you're coming back next week? He's a bit down, you can imagine."

"Well . . . perhaps," Alice said cautiously. She was never going to let Jack know how nearly she had accepted Philip Morland's proposal of marriage.

After saying goodbye to Alice, Jack walked the short distance to Ladysmith Road along the darkening streets, and hesitated before knocking on the door of the Cartwrights' house. He was not at all sure he ought to have come. But at the very least, he had the excuse of wanting to apologize to Sarah for his last visit.

There was a long silence, and then he heard feet running down the stairs. Sarah opened the door, looking tired and anxious.

She stared for a moment as if she had never seen him before, and then said, "Oh. Jack. Come in," and went back inside. He followed her, closing the door behind him.

Perturbed by her aloofness, he couldn't think what to say. She was standing with her back to him,

267

facing the fireplace. She didn't want to see him, he realized with numbing disappointment. Well, it wasn't surprising, he told himself – why should she? He was nothing but a nuisance to her, coming round uninvited to bother her with the sordid complications of his private life. Then he saw that she was in tears, and trying not to let him see. His first thought was that her mother must be seriously ill.

"What's the matter?"

She didn't answer, but he heard a stifled sob. Her tears gave him the excuse to do what he wanted to do anyway. He went up to her and put his hand on her shoulder, and then he turned her round to face him and took her in his arms. She didn't resist, but carried on weeping quietly while he held her and stroked her soft hair. He said again, "What's the matter? Is it your mother?"

"No, she's getting much better. The doctor says she needs country air," she mumbled, her face turned away from him against his shoulder.

"What, then?"

"I thought I'd never see you again," she said indistinctly.

"Oh, *Sarah*." He kissed the top of her head and held her close, and her arms crept round him. He felt as if he had stopped breathing. He said, into her hair, "I love you."

She pulled away and looked up at him. Her eyes were red with crying, and instead of answering she said, "Have you got a handkerchief?"

He groped in his pockets and found a clean one, and somehow fumbled and dropped it in handing it to her. They both bent down, bumping heads, and then Sarah picked up the handkerchief and stood up, blowing her nose. He thought she hadn't heard what he had said, but then she looked at him and said, "Did you mean that?"

"Yes."

"Really?"

"Yes."

He had meant to explain everything first. He had intended to tell her about Ireland, and Harriet's letter, and that he understood that Sarah – even if, by some miracle, she thought of him that way at all – probably wouldn't want to be involved with someone whose life was in such a mess.

But Sarah came close to him and he put his hands on her shoulders and looked into her tearful face without speaking, hardly able to convince himself that his feelings for her were returned. There was no need to explain anything, not yet. He gently brushed the tears from her cheeks and then he bent to kiss her, hesitantly at first, then with more conviction as her arms came up around his neck. And after a while he said, "I want you to marry me when all this is over."

"Yes," she said quietly. "It's right."

Right. Yes, that was how it seemed to him. It would be as right as his marriage to Harriet had been wrong.

"Yes," he murmured. "At first I thought it was because of Stephen, and it is, but not just that. It's because of you as well."

She said, "I think Stephen would be pleased."

Remembrance

It was unusual for Alice to be travelling home to
the village by car. Unlike the railway line, which
skirted Epping Forest, the road went straight through,
passing between banks of tall beech trees and thickets
of holly, and alongside open grassy areas where
cattle grazed. Patrick Leary was at the wheel of
the Crossley, borrowed for the day from a friend,
and Lorna sat beside him in the passenger seat.
Alice, in the back of the car, gazed at the forest
with a sense of nostalgia, recalling outings to the
forest retreats and fairs on Bank Holidays. The trees
were almost bare, but she knew that the forest kept
its beauty throughout the year; even in winter, the
golden leaves strewn in thick drifts on the ground
were fired into glowing colour by pale sunlight.
The quiet depths of the forest appealed to her,
making her wish she could get out of the car and
walk among the stately trees in solitude. It was a
day for remembering, and she wanted to be alone
to remember.

They reached Bell Common on the edge of Epping,
fringed by a row of timbered cottages, and closer to the
town Patrick pointed out his father's house behind a
tall hedge. He would be returning there to go to the
remembrance service in the Epping church as soon as
he had taken Lorna and Alice on to Littlehays, and

would be coming back for them in the afternoon to visit the Sidgwicks. He had told them that he intended to go back to Dublin next summer as soon as he had taken his degree: he didn't know what he was going to do, but he felt that Ireland held happier memories for him than England. Another friend who would be vanishing from their lives, Alice thought. Everything was changing.

But later that morning, when she sat beside Jack and Emily in the small village church, she had the familiar sense of returning to her past. The Morlands were in their front pew: Mr and Mrs Morland, and Madeleine with her husband Geoffrey. Philip was absent, somewhat to Alice's relief; she was sorry he had been injured, but felt grateful for being spared a difficult public meeting with him so soon. Behind the Morlands were Dr and Mrs Sidgwick with Lorna beside them. If Alice closed her eyes she could see Edward there too; she had sat here every Sunday as a girl, looking at the back of his neck as he bent over his hymn-book, and hoping he would spend a few minutes talking to her after the service. But if Edward really were here now, she knew he would feel the same as she did, finding meaning only in private recollection during the two minutes' silence ordained by the King. She made no more than a token effort to sing the hymns and kneel for the prayers she no longer believed in; it was an ordeal to be got through. There was a new memorial tablet on the wall concealed by short red curtains, waiting to be uncovered; she could believe in that. She believed in death.

There were other ghosts in the dim shadows of the church, too, among them Jack's old friend – boys who had been at school with him, and had joined up with him and gone out to France at the same time. He had seen some of them die, in the Somme fighting. He sat beside Alice with compressed lips and a distant expression, and she wondered whether he was remembering the church service two days before the outbreak of war, when all the young men of the village had been on fire with excitement, wanting to outdo each other in joining up at once.

There were few of them left now.

At the conclusion of the service, the curtains were drawn over the stone tablet. One by one the members of the congregation filed past to leave flowers or little crosses in front of it. Alice had brought a spray of evergreen foliage for Edward: spruce, and spreading fans of cypress, and glossy laurel and holly. She looked at the inscription cut into the tablet in sharply-defined letters. *In glorious memory of the men of Littlehays who died for their country in the Great War, 1914–1918*. And underneath, towards the end of the list of fifteen names: *E.R. Sidgwick*.

Fifteen lives. Names on a wall.

By next November a War Memorial column would have been erected on the village green, and there would be another dedication service. She would come back again, she supposed, to revive old sorrows. She went out into the chilly November air, where people stood talking quietly in groups before dispersing to their homes. Alice didn't want to talk to anyone, except Edward. She glanced along the church wall at the bench where she had sat with him on a calm autumn evening four years ago. It had been just after he returned from the fighting at Loos, his first involvement in a major battle. He had been withdrawn, hardly speaking to her, and she remembered how hopeless and let-down she had felt after longing to see him for so many months. She could see him as clearly as if he sat there now, flicking ash from his cigarette, his troubled blue eyes staring at nothing. He was beyond her reach now, eluding her attempts to know and understand him. How would he have been changed, if he had survived? It was one of the many things she would never know.

People were gradually leaving the churchyard. By the lych-gate, Mary stood with her young man, a boy of eighteen who worked with Jimmy Taplin at the Hunt kennels. Alice could hear the murmur of their voices and their soft laughter. They were the young generation now, one which would grow up never having experienced the war except at second-hand. For them, the war would fade into history, something their parents and older brothers and sisters talked about; they had their own lives to think of. Watching them, Alice felt that a huge gulf existed between her generation and theirs. The young men and women of her own age had had four vital years taken from them and squandered. They were left – if they had survived – old for their years and lonely. The war had stolen her youth, Alice thought.

But had it all been loss? She knew that she was a different person from the girl who had worked at Greenstocks and dressed Miss Madeleine's hair and

273

listened to her accounts of the latest Fancy Dress Ball or débutante's coming-out party. Would she still be there now, older but not significantly changed, if there had been no war? Would she and Edward have loved each other with such intensity if the tensions of war had not brought them together and kept them in perpetual fear of being separated? And would she have become so close to Lorna – now one of the most important people in her life – who had helped her to break away from the narrowness of village conventions and build a life of her own? No; she had to acknowledge that alongside the terrible losses there had been gains, however hard-won.

She heard muffled giggles as the pair by the lych-gate broke furtively apart, and then Jack's voice saying something that made them laugh again, and the creak of the gate opening. Jack walked down the cinder path, looking for her.

"There you are. Ma and Emily were wondering where you'd got to," he said. "Aren't you coming back?"

"Yes, I'm coming."

They left the churchyard together, and he linked his arm through hers and said, "Will you come round to the stables this afternoon? It's Alfie's half-day, so I'll have to go straight back. I've got something to tell you about, but I don't want to tell everyone, not yet."

Wondering, she looked up at his face as they walked towards Tom and Emily's cottage. She knew that he, too, was changed from his pre-war self; less impulsive perhaps, more thoughtful, more quietly sure of himself. She had the feeling that the split with Harriet had resolved a lot of things in his mind. She wished he wasn't going away.

"Is it something nice?" she asked.

He smiled secretively. "Yes."

After having lunch with her mother and Emily and Tom, Alice went up to Greenstocks, preferring to get this difficult visit out of the way before going to see Jack. Mary, who had gone back to her duties after eventually leaving the church, opened the door to Alice without surprise.

"You've come to see Mr Philip, I suppose," she said. "He could do with cheering-up."

Alice, not at all sure that her arrival would have that effect, followed Mary along the panelled hall towards Philip's study. Mary was neatly attired in a black dress with a white frilled apron over the top, the straps crossing at the back, and a white cap – exactly the uniform Alice had worn, except that the skirt was shorter. Not much had altered at Greenstocks, Alice thought: not so many servants, perhaps, fewer elaborate dinner-parties, but the Morlands' wealth and position as landowners buffeted them against change. Alice wondered how long Mary would be content to go on working there. From what Emily had said, it was likely that she would leave soon to get married.

For all her feelings of being pushed aside by the young adults of the village, Alice knew that she would not have changed places with Mary.

Philip was sitting on a couch with his right leg stretched out in a plaster-cast in front of him. He looked up as she entered, and she saw the wariness of his expression.

"Hello, Alice," he said. "It's good of you to come. Won't you sit down?"

He was smoking a cigar and reading *Horse and Hound*. He put the paper down on a low table beside the couch and laid the cigar in a glass ash-tray, and said, "Will you have something to drink?"

"No, thank you," Alice said, sitting down in a studded leather armchair. She looked at him. "I'm so sorry to hear about your accident. It's awful for you, after all the trouble you had before."

"I'll get over it. Today of all days. I'm aware that there are worse things."

She felt awkward in his presence, and he seemed equally ill-at-ease. It was partly Greenstocks' fault, she knew. She looked round at the study she had swept and dusted so often in the past. It was exactly the same as it had always been, with the predominantly masculine air created by the cigar smoke, the gilt-edged writing table, a pair of muskets mounted on the wall, and leather-bound books on a shelf.

"Jack told me about his job in Ireland," she said. "That you'd arranged it for him."

"Yes."

"It was kind of you."

He looked at her. "It was the least I could do, Alice. I wanted to do something positive for Jack, after everything else. And it's a very good opportunity for him, better than he could hope for anywhere else."

"Yes, he appreciates it."

"I think, at first, he thought I was doing it to get rid of him. I wouldn't like him to misunderstand."

"He doesn't," Alice said. "It was Jack who made me see – after my first reaction – that you'd really

276

done as much as you could all along. He doesn't blame you."

Philip smiled ruefully. "No. He is remarkable. I don't know how I shall replace him – there are plenty of people looking for work, but it'll be hard to find someone else as good with the horses. I think it's best – for his sake – that he goes, but I shall miss him. I shall miss both of you. I'm sorry."

He didn't say what he was sorry for, but she thought she understood. She said, "I think one day you might be glad that things didn't work out between us. I think, now, I was deluding myself that they might, perhaps you were too. But our lives are too different. I can see that more clearly here at Greenstocks."

He looked away from her and gazed at the fire-screen. After a few moments he said, "I thought things like that didn't matter any more. Perhaps they do, after all. But I'd like to think you didn't have any hard feelings towards me."

She said, "I don't. And I hope, when you're over this, things will work out for you too. I wish you well."

"Thank you, Alice. As I do you. I hope we'll keep in touch."

There seemed to be no point in her staying any longer. They shook hands, and Alice left with the sense that a lot of things had been left unsaid. It was probably for the best.

Jack was in the stallion box adjusting the horse's bridle when Alice arrived in the stableyard.

"Don't stand too close," he warned her, opening the door.

The stallion, irate at having been shut in all morning, erupted from his box in a fury of energy, almost pulling Jack off his feet. He tugged and pranced all the way across the yard in high-stepping excitement, and then snorted impatiently inside the paddock gate while Jack unfastened the bridle. As soon as the bit was out of his mouth he took off in a flurry of hooves, splattering divots of mud over Jack, bucking and leaping and snaking his neck in a display of virile egotism.

"I'm glad I don't have to go anywhere near him!" Alice exclaimed, venturing closer now that the gate was firmly bolted.

Jack grinned, brushing the clods of earth from his jacket. "He's a character, isn't he? He wants everyone to stop what they're doing and look at him."

"I should think everyone has to," Alice said, laughing at the stallion's acrobatics. At last he came to a halt and stood neighing shrilly at the mares, his head pushed over the fence as far as he could reach.

Jack showed Alice all the horses, the clipped hunters in their smart day rugs, and Mr Morland's cob, and the brood mares, who grazed placidly two paddocks away from the stallion, ignoring his antics. They were sleek and full-bodied, their eyes full of peaceful contentment. The first foals would be due in the early spring. Jack was sorry that he wouldn't be around to see them.

"Their lives are so much more straightforward than ours, aren't they?" Alice said, watching the mares. "All they have to do is eat and wait."

He looked at her, amused. "You want to change places?"

"Not really. But what about your good news? You haven't said any more about it."

He told her. Talking about it made it seem more real to him; since coming back from London he had found it hard to make himself believe that his meeting with Sarah had really taken place outside his imagination. He had finally left the Cartwrights' house on Friday evening feeling slightly dazed, and had somehow managed to get on the right train home, although he had hardly been conscious of the rest of the journey. He could think of nothing but Sarah.

Alice, quickly recovering from her surprise, was as pleased as he had hoped she would be. He showed her the photograph of Stephen and Sarah together, which Mrs Cartwright had given him, and she looked at it for a long time, and then said, "She does look nice. And very like her brother. And she wants to go to Ireland with you?"

"Yes. I shall go on my own first to sort things out and to wait for the divorce. And then I shall come back for Sarah. You must meet her – she doesn't live far from you. I know you'll get on well with her."

"I'm sure I will. I must go and see her as soon as I get back to London."

"She'd like that." He leaned back on the fence, smiling at her. "And, to make things perfect, we're going to try to have Stevie to live with us. We talked about it. Harriet doesn't want him, but I do, and so does Sarah. It seems right."

"Oh Jack, it would be wonderful for you if it all works out. You deserve some good luck for a change. And you named him for Stephen, didn't you?"

"Yes. He already seems like part of Sarah's family. It doesn't seem to matter that much, after all, who his real father is. He'll be our son."

"What about Sarah's mother, though? What will happen to her? Sarah won't want to leave her alone, will she?"

"I don't know yet. We talked about it. She might go to live with her sister in Norfolk, or perhaps she could even come out to Ireland as well. The way I feel at the moment, anything's possible."

He was aware of the slight wistfulness underlying Alice's pleasure in his change of fortune. He knew how much she would have liked to have a family of her own, for all her purposeful determination to make something of her life. He wished she could meet someone to share her future with; surely someone as sympathetic as Alice couldn't be destined to spend the rest of her life alone? It had been a difficult day for her, he knew, with her sorrow for Edward unabated, and soon she would be going round to the Sidgwicks' to see his parents, stirring up more memories. It would be better for her when this painful anniversary day was over and she could get back to normal life. But he hoped she would eventually have more to look forward to than she seemed to have at present. You could never tell: the war had messed up his own life, just as surely as it had messed up hers, yet now, when he had thought nothing good would ever happen to him again, his future was brighter than he could have imagined. He wished Alice could be as lucky.

It was getting cold out in the fields, the chilly wind making them turn up their coat collars. They returned to the yard, and Alice went into the cottage to heat some water so that Jack could bathe a wound on the bay horse's hock. Jack went into the harness-room to fetch a piece of lint and a bandage, and came out to see a stranger standing in the yard, a young man perhaps a little older than himself, with thick brown hair and a broad, attractive face. Some acquaintance of Philip's, probably, coming to see a horse, although Philip hadn't mentioned any visitors.

"Excuse me," the stranger said in a southern Irish accent, seeing Jack. "I was looking for Miss Smallwood. Dr Sidgwick told me I'd find her here."

"Yes," Jack said, surprised. "She's in the cottage."

"You must be her twin brother?"

"Yes. Jack Smallwood."

"Hello. I can see the likeness," the young man said, smiling. "I'm Patrick Leary, a friend of Alice's."

He held out a hand and Jack shook it, intrigued. He'd never heard of Patrick Leary.

"From what Alice tells me, our paths have nearly crossed on a number of occasions," Patrick said.

"Have they? You mean at the front?" Jack noticed Patrick's way of turning his head slightly and frowning in concentration while listening, as if he found it difficult to hear clearly.

At that moment Alice came round the corner of the stable-block carrying a bowl of hot water, and said, "Patrick, hello! I wasn't expecting to see you here."

"I've been to the church to see the memorial stone," Patrick said, "as a sort of proper farewell to Edward. And then I felt like a walk, so I thought I'd come and meet you and see if you were ready to walk back."

"Oh! Patrick's an old friend of Edward's," Alice explained to Jack. "You might bump into him again some day – he's going back to live in Ireland. But we were just going to bathe a horse's cut leg," she added, turning to Patrick.

"I can wait while you do that," Patrick said. "I didn't know your nursing skills extended to quadrupeds."

"They don't," Alice said, laughing. "I'm terrified of horses. I was just going to act as stable orderly."

Jack took the bowl from her and said, "Don't worry. I can do it just as easily by myself. You won't want to be late for the Sidgwicks."

Alice hesitated, glancing up at the stable clock. "Well, if you're sure . . ."

"Yes. Go on! I'll see you again before you go, won't I?"

"All right then. Yes – I'll see you this evening at Emily's, and again tomorrow before I go back." Alice took her gloves out of her coat pocket and pulled them on, and then kissed Jack's cheek. "I'm sorry to rush away, but the time is getting on. I hadn't noticed."

"I'm very glad to have met you," Patrick Leary said to Jack, with polite formality.

"Yes. Goodbye, then. Perhaps we'll meet again."

They walked away across the yard, while Jack stood by the harness-room door holding the bowl of steaming water and the lint and the bandage, slightly bemused by Alice's departure with this pleasant-looking young man who had so suddenly materialized. A friend of Edward's? He remembered what he had been thinking earlier. Could it be that Edward's ghost was as well-intentioned as Stephen's? Or was he making too much of it – was Patrick just the casual friend Alice had implied?

He watched as the two figures passed beneath the stable archway and out into the lane, and he wondered.

Run With the Hare

LINDA NEWBERY

A sensitive and authentic novel exploring the workings of an animal rights group, through the eyes of Elaine, a sixth-form pupil. Elaine becomes involved with the group through her more forceful friend Kate, and soon becomes involved with Mark, an Adult Education student and one of the more sophisticated members of the group. Elaine finds herself painting slogans and sabotaging a fox hunt. Then she and her friends uncover a dog fighting ring – and things turn very nasty.

£2.50 ☐

Hairline Cracks

JOHN ROBERT TAYLOR

A gritty, tense and fast-paced story of kidnapping, fraud and cover ups. Sam Lydney's mother knows too much. She's realized that a public inquiry into the safety of a nuclear power station has been rigged. Now she's disappeared and Sam's sure she has been kidnapped, he can trust no one except his resourceful friend Mo, and together they are determined to uncover the crooks' operation and, more importantly, find Sam's mother.

£2.50 ☐

ARMADA

Stevie Day
Series
JACQUELINE WILSON

Supersleuth	£2.25	☐
Lonely Hearts	£2.25	☐
Rat Race	£2.25	☐
Vampire	£2.25	☐

An original new series featuring an unlikely but irresistible heroine – fourteen-year-old Stevie Day, a small skinny feminist who has a good eye for detail which, combined with a wild imagination, helps her solve mysteries.

"Jacqueline Wilson is a skilful writer, readers of ten and over will find the (Stevie Day) books good, light-hearted entertainment."

Children's Books December 1987

"Sparky Stevie" *T.E.S. January 1988*

ARMADA

RUN

WITH
THE
HARE

LINDA NEWBERY

Elaine has to decide whether to run with the hare or hunt with the hounds – is she really committed to Animal Rights or is she more interested in Mark?

"It is a genuine novel, setting its interests within a satisfying context of teenage relationships and activities. The book is a good story, an intelligent argument . . ." *The Times Literary Supplement*

"Elaine is an intelligent and sensible heroine and by setting the romance in the world of Animal Rights, the author focuses attention on the adult world which appears confusing and often unfeelingly harsh to young people." *The School Librarian*

The Pit

ANN CHEETHAM

The summer has hardly begun when Oliver Wright is plunged into a terrifying darkness. Gripped by fear when workman Ted Hoskins is reduced to a quivering child at a demolition site, Oliver believes something of immense power has been disturbed. But what?

Caught between two worlds – the confused present and the tragic past – Oliver is forced to let events take over.

£2.50　☐

Nightmare Park

LINDA HOY

A highly original and atmospheric thriller set around a huge modern theme park, a theme park where teenagers suddenly start to disappear . . .

£2.50　☐

ARMADA

All these books are available at your local bookshop or newsagent, or can be ordered from the publisher. To order direct from the publishers just tick the title you want and fill in the form below:

Name _____

Address _____

_____

Send to: Collins Childrens Cash Sales
PO Box 11
Falmouth
Cornwall
TR10 9EN

Please enclose a cheque or postal order or debit my Visa/Access –

Credit card no:

Expiry date:

Signature:

– to the value of the cover price plus:

UK: 80p for the first book and 20p per copy for each additional book ordered to a maximum charge of £2.00.

BFPO: 80p for the first book and 20p per copy for each additional book.

Overseas and Eire: £1.50 for the first book, £1.00 for the second book. Thereafter 30p per book.

ARMADA